D0357040

PEARLS
AND
PERIL

A Novel

Lynn Gardner

Covenant Communications, Inc.

Dedication

To Jeanne and Emily, who were there through the conception and birthing of both *Emeralds* and *Pearls;* and to Glenn, who patiently puts up with the erratic lifestyle of a struggling writer—encourages it, and even finances it.

Published by Covenant Communications, Inc.
American Fork, Utah

Copyright © 1996 by Lynn Gardner
All rights reserved

Printed in the United States of America
First Printing: July 1996

01 00 99 98 97 96   10 9 8 7 6 5 4 3 2 1
ISBN 1-55503-932-4

Library of Congress Catalog-in-Publication Data

Gardner, Lynn, 1938-
    Pearls and peril: a novel/Lynn Gardner.
        p. cm.
    ISBN 1-55503-932-4
        I. Title.
PS3557.A7133P43 1996
813' .54--dc20   96-28361
                                                  CIP

Bart and Allison had barely escaped their wedding with their lives . . . an old enemy had tried to blow them to kingdom come. But now, safe on their Hawaiian honeymoon, the newlyweds would have time to relax and get to know each other. Then, a little later, perhaps they would look into Mormonism—the intriguing new religion to which Bart had been introduced by his cellmate in a Tibetan prison camp. There would be time for everything, now that they were together and out of harm's way . . .

Chapter One

I stood frozen in the doorway, trade winds billowing the curtains in our sixth-floor Oahu hotel room.

"Someone's ransacked our room!"

Bart peered over my shoulder into the honeymoon suite of the Turtle Bay Hilton.

The contents of my makeup case were strewn all over the bathroom counter, my clothes had been torn off their hangers and thrown on the floor, and my suitcase had been dumped upside down.

"Allison, I should have known someone as beautiful as you couldn't possibly be perfect, but this?" Bart's teasing sounded light-hearted, but he immediately retrieved his gun from the false bottom of his suitcase and checked out the closets, balcony, and under the bed to make sure the intruders were actually gone.

"Why did they only tear *my* things apart? Why not yours? What were they looking for? I don't have anything valuable that anyone would want to steal—besides this."

I flashed my five-carat emerald engagement ring—worth a small fortune to a thief but priceless to me. I wasn't about to leave that or my wedding band in any hotel room, so if that's what they were after, they'd have to take it from my finger. With Bart at my side, I was confident they wouldn't succeed.

"Check to see what's missing."

We searched our belongings. Everything was accounted for.

There was even something I'd not seen before.

"Look at the surprise Mom slipped into my suitcase. It was tucked inside this shoe."

Bart looked puzzled. "A tennis ball?"

"No." I tossed the exotic bottle of lotion across the room.

"On closer examination, it looks like a giant pearl." He tossed it back. "How thoughtful of her."

Unscrewing the top fourth of the bottle, I poured some vanilla musk-scented lotion on my hands, rubbing its satiny smoothness over my arms, then dropped the lotion into my beach bag to enjoy after a swim. I'd have to remember to thank Mom for her thoughtfulness.

"Bart, who would do this and why?" I hesitated as I picked up my clothes. "And am I getting paranoid, seeing bad guys everywhere?"

"I don't know, Princess. What are you seeing?"

"Promise you won't laugh?"

"No, but tell me anyway." His face crinkled in a smile.

"As we came into the lobby of the hotel, I thought I saw Nate, Tony's right-hand man."

"Where?" Bart was suddenly serious.

"At the entrance to the patio room. When I did a double take, he turned his head, but I'm sure it was Nate. What would he be doing here? Maybe I'm suffering post-traumatic shock. After all, how many brides have their wedding vows punctuated by explosions meant to wipe out the whole wedding party? Was it Nate? Or am I . . ."

Bart put his fingers to his lips, signaling an end to my questions. Retrieving a "bug catcher" from a hidden compartment in his can of shaving cream, he swept the room and found three listening devices, one in the phone and one each in the bathroom and bedroom. He quickly removed them.

"The balcony?" I mouthed.

Bart looked dubious, but there was one hidden under the crossbar on the patio table. He did away with that one, too.

"How about a walk on the beach?"

I had just time to grab my beach bag before Bart dragged me out the door and down the hall toward the elevators.

"What's the surviving member of the cartel doing here instead of Southeast Asia? Why didn't he keep running?" Bart pondered aloud as soon as we were out the door.

"I'm still working on that. Maybe just to spoil my honeymoon! Who'd bug our room? Nate? What for? Oh, Bart!" I wailed, stricken with a sudden horrible realization.

He stopped in mid-stride.

"What's the matter?"

"They've heard all our conversations!"

"Probably just the last few minutes—you didn't embarrass yourself." Bart laughed with relief. "Allison, I thought something was wrong. Don't scare me like that."

"Something *is* wrong! My honeymoon is becoming a voyeur experience for someone and I don't like it one bit! What if our room was bugged at the Marriott?"

"On our wedding night?" Bart grinned, pushing the elevator button. The doors opened immediately. I was grateful to find the elevator empty.

He put his arms around me and held me close.

"It's okay, Princess. I guarantee it wasn't bugged. We didn't make reservations ahead. No one, including us, knew where we were staying until we checked in, and we didn't leave the room after we arrived. We left for the airport immediately after breakfast in our room. Does that make you feel better?"

He tipped my chin up to look into my eyes. "Okay?"

"Okay."

We strolled silently along the gentle curve of deserted beach, attempting to deal with our ordeal of invasion. I felt both vulnerable and violated.

"Penny for your thoughts." Bart's quiet voice penetrated my musings as we walked, holding hands, through the fine white sand.

"My thoughts are racing as fast as my heart. First I'm wondering if they really wanted something I have. Then I wondered how Nate escaped the trap you and Dad set for Antonio Scaddono and crew. How was Nate the only one to get away?"

"He may have seen the FBI move into place, or he got suspicious when the ship's crew disappeared after we put them out of commission. Maybe he just didn't like the idea of wiping out a whole wedding party to get control of Margo's estate. There's no doubt he was the real brains behind Tony's drug cartel. The fact that he high-tailed it before the net was closed tells you he was a lot smarter than Tony Scaddono."

We sat in silence on the rocks, each absorbed in our own thoughts. Bart broke into mine once more.

"Wishing you were somewhere else?"

"Of course not! Where on earth would I rather be than with you?"

"Maybe with your former fiancé, or one of those dunderheads from the U.N. who didn't have sense enough to grab you while you were unattached," he teased. I knew he was trying to direct my thoughts away from the break-in. "By the way, what did Milton have to say when you called him?"

"He'd already seen the news broadcast showing our 'explosive' wedding, the house burning, the capture of Scaddono's crew, and Scaddono's death. He wished me happiness, said I'd need all the good wishes he had for me, and he was glad you came back into my life now instead of after we were married. I'm sure his mother was morti-fied to see me on TV. She probably thanked her lucky stars she escaped having me as a daughter-in-law." I paused and glanced in the direction of our hotel. "Bart, look! Someone's in our room!"

He searched the building for our balcony, but whoever was watching had seen me point and quickly disappeared back inside.

I nearly dropped my beach bag as we sprinted for the lobby, bypassing the elevators packed with vacationers and kids. We headed up the stairs two at a time, Bart slightly ahead of me.

Bart had his card key ready for the slot and his gun drawn. "Stay here and out of the way—in case there's shooting," he hastened to add.

That stopped me. I didn't like being shot at. I'd had enough of that in the past few days to last a lifetime. I paused briefly, then followed on his heels as he burst into our room. Our empty room.

It hadn't been empty for long. The smell of stale tobacco lingered heavily.

"What now?" I was a novice at this sort of thing. Bart was a professional agent with Anastasia, a branch of Interpol specializing in anti-terrorism.

"I think a call to your dad might be in order."

"More than simple robbery?"

"If you're right—and I don't doubt your powers of observation or your intuition," he added with a grin as he brushed a kiss across my nose, "this is the third attempt someone has made on your luggage: the bellboy at the Marriott in Los Angeles on our wedding night who insisted he thought the luggage belonged next door, the man at the airport in Honolulu who swore it was his wife's luggage, and now here at Turtle Bay. Somehow, that doesn't strike me as just coincidence. Assuming it's the same party, what are they after?"

"What have I got?"

"What you've got, they can't have!" He teased and rolled with me onto the bed.

"Agent Allan, aren't you in the middle of an investigation? Can you afford to be sidetracked while the culprits vanish into the night? They're making a clean getaway," I protested, all the while snuggling in his arms. How good they felt around me.

We got back to the investigation, eventually, my mind generating enough questions to generate a headache.

Was that Nate I'd seen? Why would he chance being recognized? What was he doing hanging around Hawaii when safety lay in Southeast Asia?

Bart's thoughts must have been running parallel to mine. He swept the room again with his bug-catching gadget, found two new bugs, and disposed of them. But nothing was missing as far as we could determine. What was the reason for the buggings? And what did they want in our room?

"Let's grab a snack and catch some rays for a while," Bart suggested. That translated into "Let's go where we can talk."

As I reached for a brush and some lipstick to make myself presentable, Bart slid his arms around my waist from behind and bent to kiss my neck. I studied our reflections in the mirror. Bart's six-foot-four, blond, blue-eyed good looks were a direct contrast to my five-foot-four frame, green eyes, and long dark hair. I was so glad he'd come back into my life before I actually married Milton. It was

Bart I'd always loved, from the time I first laid eyes on him when I was five years old and Mom became manager of Margo's estate. Though he was four years older, he'd been my friend, my big brother, my first love.

"What else should I stash in my beach bag? We shouldn't leave anything valuable lying around if our room is going to be a major thoroughfare."

"Whatever you like, Princess," Bart said in a distracted tone, holding the door open for me. I tossed my camera in my purse and locked a small box of costume jewelry in my suitcase. It was nothing valuable, but a pain to replace.

"Time to run this by your dad," Bart said as soon as we were in the hall. "Jack may have some ideas."

Dad was Bart's boss and head of Anastasia. Mom, I'd discovered the week of our unusual wedding, was also a member of this elite group. All my life I'd known her as a teacher and lecturer at the university, an author and recognized authority on native folklore and music. To discover she was connected with Interpol, and I'd never suspected a thing, had caused me to question my powers of observation.

I thought about Mom as we walked to the phones in the lobby. For twenty years I'd puzzled over who the glamorous Margo was and why she'd mysteriously vanished, abandoning her multi-million-dollar estate on the California coast. I'd been astounded to learn on my wedding day that my own mother was Margo. She'd been hiding from Antonio Scaddono after witnessing him execute an important political family in Vietnam twenty years earlier.

I shuddered, remembering the terror of the chase through the smoke-filled garden, the horror of Antonio's sadistic attempt to murder Bart, and the feel of the two-by-four in my hands as it crushed Antonio's skull.

"Cold?" Bart put his arm around my shoulder. "You're not talking."

"Thinking. Remembering. I don't understand why Nate didn't hightail it back to wherever he came from. The North Shore is too out of the way to be coincidence."

"Your conclusion?"

"I haven't reached any conclusions yet. I still just have questions. . . ."

"Questions!" Bart interrupted with a smile. "Your trademark."

We had the public phone area to ourselves and Bart reached Dad on the estate in California immediately. We held the phone between us so I could listen in on their conversation.

"What are you doing calling me on your honeymoon? Decided you want to give her back already?"

"Dad!"

"Hi, Bunny. How's the old married woman?"

"Great, except I'm getting paranoid. I'm sure I saw Nate here at Turtle Bay."

"That's only half the story." Bart took over the narrative. "Someone tried to switch Allison's luggage at the Marriott, and very nearly succeeded, then again at the airport in Honolulu. Someone's bugged our room twice in the couple of hours we've been here and searched it. Do we report this to the authorities or be more vigilant until we figure out what's going on?"

"Dad, what's Nate doing here? Who'd want my luggage? Why would they bug our room?"

"Whoa. Hold on, Allison. Let me talk to Bart. Three of us on the phone, if you're one, will result in all questions but no answers."

"Dad!"

"Please."

Reluctantly I relinquished the phone to Bart. I paced back and forth two feet from him, listening to his end of the conversation, using a deadly glare to discourage all comers hoping to use one of the five other public phones in the room.

"So what did he say?" I demanded when Bart hung up.

"He suggested we could give up the honeymoon suite and change to another room, or we could go to another hotel, come home, or sit tight and see if we can figure out what their game is. He's alerting Interpol that Nate may be here."

"And?"

"What do you want to do? It's your honeymoon."

"It's yours, too."

"You know what I mean, Princess. If you're uncomfortable or

afraid, or even worried, we'll change plans immediately."

Leaving the hotel by the back entrance, we ambled across the undulating green lawns toward Kahuku Point, the shelf of black lava that forms the northernmost point of Oahu. A refreshing breeze softly rustled through green palms waving overhead, bearing the scent of fresh sea air.

We had the point to ourselves—there wasn't another soul in sight in any direction. Secluded near the wind-shaped shrubs, a bench with a peaceful, idyllic view of the ocean invited potential wave-watchers.

"Now, this is my idea of a honeymoon. All alone on an island paradise with a handsome hunk of a man, no bad guys, no mysteries, no guns, no bugs, nobody but us. I've felt like the object of a peep show."

"Mine or somebody else's?" Bart teased.

Ignoring his question, I closed my eyes and snuggled into the protective curve of his arm, soothed by the steady pounding of surf on rocks and the cheerful song of birds calling to one another.

I had been raised on the coast above Santa Barbara, spending weeks on the islands of Greece while Mom gathered folk songs and stories from there and other countries in the world, so I was no stranger to oceans and beaches. But the Hawaiian Islands were something else entirely. *Eden* and *paradise* were two words that came instantly to mind.

"Decision time. Shall we stay and see if we can figure out who, why, and what, or shall we change our plans?" Bart asked.

After some discussion, but no conclusion, we opted for a nap before making a decision. Had I known what was ahead, I'd have fled paradise immediately.

Chapter Two

I climbed slowly out of a deep sleep and stretched lazily, bringing life back to my exhausted body. I reached for Bart. He wasn't there. Nor anywhere else in the room. Raising up on one elbow, I checked the clock. Good grief! Evening already.

I rolled off the bed and hit the floor running.

"Bart?" He wasn't in the bathroom or on the balcony. I scanned the tropical paradise below. Turquoise water now glimmered silver, and the palest of blue skies was streaked with pink and lavender clouds. Palm trees were black silhouettes still waving *aloha* on the gentle breeze. Normally, it would be a soothing scene. But not now. My skin was prickly, my stomach a tight knot.

Calm down, Allison. He got hungry and went to the snack bar. Or got restless and took a walk. His hair grew out and he's getting a haircut. His muscles got flabby and he's in the exercise room. The sound of the surf hypnotized him back into the water.

Nothing worked. Bart wouldn't leave his bride of two days without at least a note telling me where he'd gone. I checked everywhere. No note.

I ran back to the balcony, my eyes scanning every path in the dusk below me, every clump of bushes, looking for that white-blond head of hair. No one was on the well-lit paths.

Leaning far out over the railing, I glimpsed three men running from the point back toward the hotel. As they passed under one of the path lights, I thought I recognized Nate! I scanned the far path between the well-manicured lawn and the jagged black lava. Bushes shaped by the wind hid most of it, but here and there bare crooked limbs allowed a glimpse of the sandy footpath. I traced the route of bushes and path with fearful eyes. Where Nate was, trouble was not far behind.

Then I saw him. One white trouser leg, a blue sleeve—and white-blond hair.

No! An invisible fist hit me in the stomach, knocking the wind from me. *Not Bart! Please don't let anything happen to Bart,* I prayed as I flew out of the room and raced down the long carpeted hall to the elevators. I jabbed the button, then ran to the stairwell instead and stumbled down the stairs.

A gaggle of people waiting for the elevator parted in astonishment as I burst through the service doors into the lobby and out the revolving side door.

My legs wouldn't carry me fast enough. My lungs lacked sufficient air. Wind whipped my skirt, tangling my legs in the long, gauzy folds. Huge lights flashing on to illuminate the late-evening darkness beamed across the now-purple water, blinding me momentarily. I left the path and bright lights and cut across the lawn, stumbling over a small hill I didn't see. I fell to my knees beside the still form stuffed under a bush, face down in the sand.

Gently I rolled him over. Blood oozed from an ugly sand-filled gash above one ear.

"Bart! Bart! Don't you dare die!"

I pressed my fingers to his throat, looking for a pulse. Yes! It was there.

With one corner of my voluminous skirt, I brushed the sand from his mouth and his eyes and pressed another corner against the wound to stop the bleeding.

"Bart, wake up! Don't you dare leave me a widow when I'm barely a wife!"

He stirred, groaned, slowly opened his eyes, and spit sand from his mouth. His attempted grin turned into a grimace.

"What happened? How did you get out here? Was that really Nate?"

"Ohhh, whoa, Allison. One question at a time, please."

He reached for his head and winced as his fingers found the gash above his ear.

"It's time to bring in the police. It was one thing for them to be after my luggage, but quite another for them to be after you."

"They're not after me, Princess. They're after something you've got."

"Bart, we've been all through my luggage. There's nothing there."

I helped him to his feet. A huge silver moon lit our way across the rolling lawn to where the golden circle of artificial light claimed the path. A folded handkerchief replaced my skirt to stop the flow of blood. *Why do head wounds always bleed so much?*

Avoiding the lobby, we used the service tunnel underneath the hotel to get to the parking lot. I remembered a small hospital down the road a couple of miles. It's a good thing Bart had his wallet and car keys in his pocket. I'd left our room without anything.

I tried to be witty and light-hearted, but that wasn't how I felt. I was shaken to the core. Driving as fast as I dared on the narrow two-lane main road, we arrived in a matter of minutes at the bright, anti-septic, and empty emergency room.

"Ah, we have a live one this time," joked the big, broad-shouldered islander who greeted us. "On your toes, people," he called to his colleagues down the hall.

I couldn't believe the profusion of paperwork at a hospital. A friendly young man named Scottie guided me through the maze of forms while Sione, the big islander, took Bart around the corner.

"I hope you don't bleed to death before I get this all filled out," I called to Bart as they cleaned his wound.

"Don't worry, Mrs. Allan. We're taking good care of him. We have a student here who thinks she wants to be a doctor, so we're letting her practice to see if she can stand the blood."

I raced around the corner with Scottie close on my heels to see what was going on, and found four laughing faces awaiting me.

"Allison, meet Skip, Ilsaba, and Sione. Ilsaba isn't really a student, she's an intern. Did she do a good job?" Bart turned his head, displaying the stitches neatly tucked behind his ear.

"I didn't even have to ruin his haircut—well, much." Skip's laughter was contagious. He seemed to be in charge of the interesting and diverse group. Sione was Samoan, a gentle giant with massive hands. I guessed that willowy, blonde Ilsaba was Scandinavian from her accent. Scottie, with his shock of red hair and sprinkling of freckles across his face, had a decidedly New England accent. Skip was older than he appeared at first glance, his sandy crewcut and energetic manner contributing to his youthful appearance.

We talked to the fun foursome for awhile, getting advice on the best beaches for snorkeling, eating spots, where to go kayaking and parasailing, and what to see and do on this side of Oahu. They walked us to the car, advising Bart to come back in a few days to have his stitches out.

"If you run out of things to do and need a little excitement, come on back. We're here every night, all night. Oh, be sure you don't miss the waterfall at McDonald's," Sione shouted as I shut the door.

I rolled down the window. "I thought you said something about a waterfall at McDonald's?"

"Sure did. Go for breakfast, but don't be in a hurry. Islanders don't hurry. We're pretty relaxed. You should be, too." He flashed a gleaming white smile and waved goodbye as I backed out of the parking spot.

"Okay, Bart. As usual, I have a million questions. Do you feel like telling me what happened? Was Nate behind this? If I've got something they want, what on earth is it? Why did they attack you?"

"Slow down, Princess, and give me a chance to tell you." Bart leaned back and closed his eyes. "When I woke up, I went downstairs to get you some coconut-covered macadamia nuts from the snack bar. I saw Nate slip through the revolving door so I took off after him."

"Without my macadamia nuts?"

"Without your macadamia nuts. Two guys joined Nate. I heard him say 'Get it from her room.' Obviously they spotted me—they took off running toward the back of the hotel through the service tunnel. I was right on their heels. I must have gotten careless. When I passed the pillar, something came down hard on the back of my head, and that's all I remember."

"But it was Nate?" I persisted.

"Yes, my sharp-eyed little sleuth." He opened his eyes and turned to me with a smile. "You weren't seeing things. It was Nate."

By this time we were back at the hotel.

"Okay, Special Agent Allan. Do we stay here and risk life and limb, or should we uproot and try to ditch them?"

"I think it was just a fluke I got hurt. They probably attacked me because I was chasing them. I don't think they intended to hurt us. They could have done that anytime before we even knew they were around. I'm convinced they want something you've got. I just haven't the foggiest idea what it could be."

"What if you're wrong?"

"Then we'd better call the police."

"If we have something they want, they'll be watching us too closely to slip out of here without leaving everything behind—which would give them what they want. I wish we could simply fly to another island and get lost there."

"Princess, we can do anything you want."

"Except be left alone at Turtle Bay."

We entered the lobby as a young couple came out of the Liberty House shop. I didn't mean to eavesdrop, but I couldn't help overhearing their conversation.

"But, honey, I want you to have it. You look good in it and it's not that expensive."

"Paul, I couldn't. It would take our last hundred dollars and we'd have no cushion. That money was for emergencies."

"Our room's paid up for the week, and the food money is counted out. We have plane tickets home and enough to rent equipment for snorkeling. I think you should have it, Cathy."

We followed them into the elevator and exchanged pleasantries. When we all got off on the same floor, we discovered they occupied the room next to ours. They introduced themselves as Paul and Cathy Davis.

Suddenly I had a wonderful idea. We bid them goodnight and as soon as their door was shut, I grabbed Bart and headed back down the hall.

"I know that look. What wild idea has possessed you?"

"We can give them a hundred dollars to spirit some of our luggage out of the hotel. We'll keep our room here, maybe even come back to it, but if we check out, Nate will know. We'll help them, and they can help us escape so we can enjoy our honeymoon while we puzzle this out—without fear of bodily harm."

Bart looked bemused. I could see him working through all the ramifications of my idea.

"That might just work. I'd question your financial wisdom if I didn't know your bank account was bottomless."

"Bart! That's not fair. I thought we agreed that would never be an issue."

"It's not an issue. I simply meant, from a poor government agent's point of view, the room is pretty expensive to leave empty and go somewhere else. It's nice that you don't have to worry about that."

"*We* don't have to worry about that. Bart, something's bothering you. What is it?"

"Now?"

"Now."

We walked slowly down the hall. His remark had struck a sensitive nerve. This was the first cloud to descend on our blissful relationship, and I didn't like the feeling.

"Allison, we were brought up the same way. We had all we needed, though not always all we wanted. We were careful with our limited funds and had a great time. When you discovered you were heir to many millions of dollars, I didn't give it a second thought. I didn't think it would change you."

"Have I changed?"

"The old Allison wouldn't have even considered leaving an expensive hotel room empty and getting another one somewhere else."

"The old Allison had never been shot at before or had a gun pressed to her neck so hard it cut off the blood supply to her head. The old Allison had never found her husband stuffed under a bush and left to bleed to death. This is a new ball game and it calls for new strategy. If that means dipping into money that's just been sitting for twenty years to save our lives, I certainly mean to do just that. I seem to recall some dire tactics you and Dad used when you needed bait to get Tony out in the open—me. Drastic circumstances call for drastic measures."

Bart was quiet. I turned and looked up into his face. I needed him to understand how I felt. I was not being extravagant—I was simply utilizing a resource we had the luxury to use.

He opened his arms and I quickly filled them. He tipped my chin up and looked down into my eyes.

"I want you to know it's not the money I was thinking about. I just don't want you to change. You can do whatever you want with the money, whenever you want. I just want you to stay the same sweet, innocent Allison I've always known."

"I'd be glad to—if you'd quit getting me involved with all these low-lifes you collect. Now let's get you to bed before I have to drag you there. You look like you could collapse at any minute."

As I threw open the sliding doors in our room and stepped into the tropical night air, I heard voices on the balcony next to us. Paul and Cathy were leaning on the railing, absorbing the sounds of the surf pounding the shore and the moonlight illuminating the scene below.

I grabbed the notepad and pen provided by the hotel, and scribbled a note.

We need a favor. Can you help us? Don't speak. Just write your answer.

I leaned far out on the railing and caught their attention, signaled silence with a finger to my lips, and passed the note around the pillar.

They exchanged puzzled glances, read the note, then nodded affirmatively.

Quickly I wrote another note.

My mother is having us followed—she's very rich and thinks someone will kidnap me. A honeymoon's no fun with more than two people. Will you deliver a bag of clothes to the hospital for us so we can slip away for a couple of days?

They sent it back. *Yes.*

Bart was through with his de-bugging task for the third time, and we hastily threw some clothes in a duffle bag he'd brought for a beach bag.

I wrote another note. *Thanks loads. Tell* no one *what you've done. Deliver this to Skip at the hospital emergency room and tell him to keep it till Bart comes for it.* I folded two fifty dollar bills inside the note, and passed them and the bag around the pillar to the waiting couple.

When they saw the money, the look on their faces was incredulous. I cataloged their emotions: wonder at their good fortune, dismay when they decided it was too much for such a little favor, disappointment because they'd have to return it.

Hurriedly I scribbled one last note. *Mom is filthy rich and very generous. Please accept it!*

This time they acquiesced, nodding vigorously. Cathy impetuously blew a kiss and they hurried away on their errand. I could really enjoy becoming a philanthropist. It was gratifying to see the joy in their faces when they realized they had the money to get what ever it was they wanted.

I felt smug, thinking we'd outwit Nate by this little contrivance. Only in my dreams!

Chapter Three

After a leisurely breakfast of mangoes, papaya, and muffins, we left the hotel with buoyant spirits, looking forward to a day of tropical sun. I hoped it would be free from people looking over our shoulders.

We headed southwest on Kamehameha Highway toward Sunset Beach. In the winter, waves could peak at thirty and forty feet, but in the spring and summer, the big waves were on the South Shore. Surfers were out already, so we drove on until we came to an expanse of beautiful white sand that stretched to the bluest water I'd seen yet.

"This is it!" I exclaimed. "Look at that water!"

Bart pulled the car off the road and parked on the shoulder. I couldn't believe the beach was empty, but this looked like a swimming beach and only surfers were out this early.

I raced Bart to the water. He won. For the first time in what felt like eons, I pushed fear and worry aside and enjoyed the moment. What a marvelous feeling—to splash and play in incredibly clean, clear, turquoise water in a lush island paradise, knowing I was loved as much as I loved. *It doesn't get any better than this,* I thought to myself.

Breathless from the intensity of our swim, we staggered out of the water and crashed on the beach to soak up some tropical rays before our next exploration.

We were silent for a few minutes, then Bart rolled over on his side to face me. "I've been thinking a bit. I've never known anyone to attract trouble like you do." He grinned widely, but I could tell he was serious behind his teasing. "I'd better teach you a few tricks in case I'm not always there to protect you." While we relaxed in the warm sun, Bart proceeded to teach me some of the finer points of self-defense, tricks he'd used, things to do if I found myself alone and in danger. Then we were off again.

Our friends at the hospital had recommended Shark's Cove for snorkeling. That didn't sound like anywhere I'd want to get in the water, but apparently it was both popular and safe. The cove had been filled with snorkelers when we'd first seen it on our way to the hotel.

Today there were only a few others—a young couple teaching their offspring to snorkel, two tanned teenage girls in little teeny bikinis, and a solo surfer-type flirting with the girls.

After donning fins and masks, we slipped into the clear warm water and entered another world. As we swam through corridors of ochre seaweed waving gently in the current, I marveled at the ocean floor a few feet below, teeming with life, brilliant and beautiful. There were myriads of colors and varieties, but in this world made up of hues and curves, my eye was drawn to what looked like long straight sticks moving through the water. On closer examination, I discovered it was a small school of Mexican needle fish.

Bart signaled he'd found something. The *humahuman-ukanukaowapawa*, national fish of Hawaii! A little bright orange and blue fellow flashed his tail and beckoned me to follow him through a valley of seaweed. I heeded the call, oblivious to where he was taking me or how far out I was getting. I was completely entranced by this strange underwater world of color, movement, and quiet.

Suddenly something big and dark came at me out of the sun, casting a shadow on the fish I'd been watching below me. *Shark! What do I do?* No possibility of outswimming it. Panic and fear swelled inside me making breathing difficult. My throat constricted in terror. *Calm down. What do the experts say—hit the shark on the nose if he hasn't already taken your arm off?* Frantic, I whirled to face the oncoming menace.

But it was only another swimmer. Relief flooded through me

and I could breathe again. Where was Bart? I raised out of the water and lifted my mask, searching the cove for a horizontal shape bobbing in the gentle waves. He was on the far side of the cove. We'd been swimming in opposite directions instead of together.

There was a quick splash behind me—too close, and suddenly a hand clasped my mouth, pinning my mouthpiece firmly in place. A strong arm slipped like an iron band around my waist. I tried to wriggle free, splashing with my hands, reaching behind my head to scratch whoever had hold of me. My fins made any kicking movement against him totally useless.

He towed me backward through the water with a huge, rough hand under my chin, holding my mouthpiece so I couldn't spit it out and yell. I couldn't turn around. I couldn't get to him. Kicking my feet, splashing, thrashing wildly, I tried to attract Bart's attention, anyone's attention! Everyone was under water except one small boy who waved happily at me.

Too quickly, we reached the beach. The man dragged me roughly over the rocks as he hauled me out of the water, scraping my legs mercilessly. I struggled to reach my flippers, to get them off and have some control over my legs. I was finally able to spit out the mouthpiece that cut into my lip.

The big one who'd dragged me out of the water held my arms and legs while a short, pudgy man who'd been waiting at the water's edge tried to tape my mouth. But Pudgy made a mistake, letting me get my mouth open. I clamped my teeth down on one of his fingers, harder and harder, until I could feel the bone.

He cursed and I screamed. "Bart! Help!"

Bart would never have heard me had he not at that moment surfaced looking for me. Immediately he stroked for the beach nearest him, but there was no way he could make it to where I was before my captors could get me to their car.

The pudgy man with the sandy-colored hair and droopy mustache started up the beach in one direction. The other, tall and big—actually huge, dwarfing even Bart—tucked me under one arm and covered my mouth and nose with his other hand. He jogged up the sandy part of the hill toward the car, bouncing me on his hip all the way.

I wasn't sure which would break first, my back or my neck. I scratched and kicked and wiggled and fought. What had Bart said? *Never, never get into a car. If they're going to kill you, make them do it right then and there, because if you get into the car, you're dead anyway.*

The hill became steep and rocky—not an easy climb. I tried to make it more difficult. I clawed at a bush, grabbed hold, and jerked him backwards, but it only delayed him momentarily. Regaining his footing, he gave me a thump to the side of my head with his fist. I fought to stay conscious. I couldn't let him make it to the car. How could I slow him down and give Bart time to get around the cove?

My arms were pinned to my side by his strong grip, with my legs flailing behind. I might as well have been tied with ropes. We were almost to the top of the rocky trail and the parking lot. Only one more boulder stood between us and the car. My last chance. I flung my legs backward as hard as I could, catching him in the kidney with both heels. He staggered but barely broke stride. With a lunge, he made it over the rock.

Bart hadn't been slowed by a rocky climb from the other side of the cove. He was coming—if I could buy a only few more seconds . . . .

This pachycephalosaurus didn't seem concerned about Bart, just about getting me to the car. Where was Pudgy? Coming the other way around, too fat to climb the rocks? Pachy would have to wait for Pudgy to get to the car. Could Bart make it before then?

By kicking and wiggling, I managed to free one hand. I dug my fingernails into the huge, hairy hand that covered my mouth, choking me, smothering me. I clawed at him until he loosened his grip enough for me to get my teeth into the fleshy part of his hand, then I bit into him with fervor. He tasted so foul, I almost gagged. I tasted his blood, felt its warmth in my mouth. It made me nauseous, but I wouldn't let go.

Howling in pain, he dropped me on the gravel. Sharp rocks tore into my bare flesh. It was then that Bart exploded on the scene, tackling Pachy at the knees from behind. They crashed into the side of the car. As the behemoth staggered, Bart was instantly back on his feet, and grabbing both hands full of greasy hair, he smashed Pachy's head against the car with such force that the window shattered in a thousand pieces.

This giant of a man was only stunned. He reached for Bart with a murderous look in his eyes, but Bart darted in with a quick, sharp, well-placed karate chop to the neck. It finished him. Pachy sank slowly to his knees, then fell face first into the gravel.

The squat man with the paunch hanging over his belt watched all of this, then turned to run. Bart quickly overtook the pudgy man, whose short legs wouldn't carry him fast enough through the sand, and brought him back to the car. I was picking the gravel carefully, painfully, out of my bleeding knees and legs.

"Looks like it's your turn for the hospital, Princess." Bart picked me up and hugged me tight. "I guess I can't let you out of my sight. You attract trouble like a magnet. Are you all right?" His tone turned from joshing to gentle.

"My dignity is probably hurt more than anything, although my legs don't feel wonderful. What are we going to do with Pachy and Pudgy?"

"Pachy?"

"A pachycephalosaurus is a thick-headed dinosaur with a minute brain, hence, a large, dim-witted person. Good description of the big one, don't you think?"

"I think you hit it on the head. We'd better get them to the authorities and file kidnaping charges against them."

I groaned. "My honeymoon!"

"Sorry. Can't just turn them loose. We'll call the police from the hospital and have them picked up there." He wrapped a towel around my bleeding legs and lifted me into the car.

Bart dragged the unconscious hulk into the back seat of our rented convertible, tied his hands behind him with the belt he'd pulled off Pachy's pants, and wrapped a beach towel around him straight-jacket fashion before buckling his seat belt. He motioned to the stubby, now docile, little man to get in, and we headed for Laie, leaving their car for the police.

This was certainly not how I intended to spend my honeymoon. What did they want with me? Was this Nate's way of getting back at my family? I wouldn't think so. If anything, Dad and Bart had cleared the way for Nate to take over the cartel by getting his boss, Tony, out of the picture. That should have made Nate happy. I couldn't imagine a revenge thing. It didn't make sense.

Before I'd puzzled it out, we reached the hospital. Bart called the police and two officers arrived while I was being cleaned up. One was a short, wiry Japanese-Hawaiian with dark eyes that bored through me with each question. The other was a brown-haired, brown-eyed mainlander who ate too many candy bars and had the waistline to prove it.

We had no answers to Lt. Nakamura's "why" questions, and could only report what happened, twice, before his companion, Lt. Craig Carrigan, was appeased.

We mentioned the luggage incidents, and Bart identified himself as Interpol. After answering their questions—but clearly not to their satisfaction—I asked if we could please go back to the hotel. I was exhausted.

In a parting shot, Lieutenant Nakamura questioned, "You will stay where we can get hold of you?"

"We're not checking out of Turtle Bay, Lieutenant," Bart said. "We're on our honeymoon and plan to stay for the duration."

I hastened to add, "We'll be all over the island, though, so if you need to talk to us, leave a message at the desk. We'll get back to you as soon as we check in from our excursions."

I lay my head back on the seat as Bart drove us back to our hotel.

"What now, Fearless Leader?" I asked.

"The first thing is to get you off your bruised and battered legs and get a little rest."

"And a little lunch?"

Bart laughed. "You're not hurt as bad as I thought."

"No, actually, I'm not really hurt. My scrapes and scratches will heal quickly. Of course, I won't look fantastic in a swimming suit for a while."

Bart gingerly patted an unscraped portion of my leg. "Then we'll just skip the beach for the next few days, keep your scarred body covered, and find more interesting things to do. I can't think of anything I'd rather do than be locked up in a hotel room with you for a week."

I loved the romantic tone in his voice. "What could you

possibly do to keep from being bored in all that time?" I teased.

"How about lots of this?" Bart suddenly stopped the car right in the middle of the long blossom-lined drive leading to the Turtle Bay Hilton. He leaned across the seat and kissed me.

"Bart! We're impeding traffic! You can't stop in the middle of the road."

"Honeymooners have special privileges."

Honking and laughter from a passing car convinced him I was right. My face blazed with embarrassment, and I pushed a laughing Bart away.

"This sounds like a stupid question, but since we can't figure out what Nate wants, do you suppose it could be ransom money he's after? After all, I am worth a lot of money now, or will be."

"Anything's possible."

"I wouldn't have thought that would be his style—though we can't rule it out. He has so much money already from the cartel."

"Those types never have enough money. You had something else in mind. What?"

"Supposing that's the motive, though I'm not convinced, if they're bugging our room to determine what our plans are, what's to stop them from bugging the car?"

"Nothing. About the only places you're pretty safe in talking without being overheard are near the surf and in the shower."

"The shower?"

"The water makes too much background noise and drowns out the sounds they're trying to pick up. Just like the beach."

"We have no privacy!"

"That's about right, Princess. With today's technology, if somebody really wants to hear what you're saying and has the money, equipment is available to allow them to do it."

"Bart, that's awful."

"It gets worse. There are now telephones you can plant in a room that are imprinted with a signal that allows you to call that number—the phone won't ring, but it activates the microphones. The person listening in another room can hear everything going on in that room."

"Without anyone lifting the receiver?"

"Without anyone doing anything."

"Then even if your bug catcher locates all the listening devices in our room, they're still privy to everything we say just by planting a special telephone there."

"You got it. You've also got a tail. Nate didn't waste any time replacing the two we just eliminated from his employ. Princess, what have you got that's he's so determined to get his hands on? Besides the obvious, of course," he amended with a grin.

He was making light of a situation I knew had him more than a little worried. Already I could recognize the shift from John Q. Citizen to Special Agent, Interpol; from adoring husband to professional investigator and bodyguard.

I was comforted by the protection, but furious that Nate made it necessary. All I wanted was a nice, normal, private honeymoon. Was that too much to ask?

Chapter Four

Refreshed by a late afternoon nap, we awoke to sun-burnished blue water that was streaked with amber as the tropical sun dipped toward the horizon. Donning swim cover-ups and hats, and with beach and duffle bags, we looked for all the world like we were making an evening excursion to the beach. Except we drove to the hospital instead.

"Hi, Skip. Good evening, Ilsaba. You're looking lovely as ever." Bart's greeting was warm and friendly.

"And your alluring wife's emerald eyes are greener than ever tonight," Scottie laughed.

I blushed. I hoped the flash of jealousy I'd experienced when my husband greeted the lovely, long-legged Ilsaba in that cordial manner had gone unnoticed.

"You're one of few adults I've met who have any blushes left. Congratulations." I couldn't tell whether Skip was serious or joking.

I recovered quickly. "I'm curious, Ilsaba. What brings you all the way around the world to the islands? You're a little far from your origins, aren't you?"

"Yes," she replied, tucking her silky blonde hair behind her ear. "Where would you rather be—an island paradise or the land of ice and snow?"

"You have a point," I agreed.

"I'm doing my residency here before returning to Norway to

practice. The cold isn't really that bad, but in comparison . . ." she shrugged off the rest of her answer.

"Slow night tonight?" Bart asked.

"So far," Sione said, flashing his dazzling smile. "We just hope it stays that way."

"We've come to ask a favor. We need to disappear."

"You're not joking," Scottie said, leaning forward on the admitting desk when he heard the seriousness in Bart's voice.

"No. Our honeymoon is being derailed by someone dogging us. We need your help to drop out of sight for a few days so we can enjoy a bit of solitude, then we'll come back and play games with our pursuers."

"Your 'pursuers' play a little hard, don't they?" Skip asked. He didn't wait for an answer. "Sure. We've been craving some excitement around here. A little cloak-and-dagger action should liven things up."

They all agreed. "What can we do?"

"We need someone to change clothes with us, take our car, and lead our trackers on a merry chase while we pull a disappearing act."

Sione pointed at my hat. "I wondered about the beach gear this time of evening,"

"We figured they'd follow the clothes and the car. Do you know somebody who could do that?"

Scottie spoke up. "My sister and her husband are about your size, not your coloring."

"That's what the hats are for—to cover up the obvious. What're they doing for the next couple of days?"

"Right now they're between semesters."

"Could they take a short vacation?"

"Well, they'd have time . . ." Scottie hesitated.

"This would be a working vacation," I interjected. "We'd pay a hundred dollars a day, plus expenses."

"What about me? Can I go?" Sione offered, his mischievous smile lighting his whole countenance.

"Will it be an inconvenience or a hardship for them to do this?" I asked.

"Not for a hundred dollars a day and expenses, if they can get someone to fill in for them at the Polynesian Cultural Center. What would it entail?"

"Simply pretend to be us . . . remain in disguise or out of sight," Bart said.

"They could get a hotel room and watch TV all day, sending out for meals," I suggested.

"You've been roughed up a couple of times. Are they in for the same kind of treatment? I wouldn't want them in any kind of danger."

"I think the rough stuff is over," Bart said. "The two muscles that did the damage are in custody."

"And while they're leading your pursuers on a merry chase, what will you be doing?" Skip asked.

I answered with a low whisper, "If you don't know, you can't tell. They can't torture it out of you."

The quartet laughed. "Okay, we'll play your game," Scottie agreed.

"Where do your sister and brother-in-law live?" Bart asked.

"They have a little apartment right off Brigham Young University-Hawaii campus, about five minutes from here."

"Does anyone live with them?"

"No. They're newlyweds, too."

"Are they home now? Can you get them here?"

"They're both working at the Polynesian Cultural Center. They'll be through when it closes after the big show."

I looked at my watch. "What time will that be?"

"Usually between 10:00 and 10:30, depending on how long it takes the crowd to move out."

"There's no way we can get hold of them sooner?"

"No. They're part of the show."

"What kind of show?" My curiosity was piqued.

"Haven't you seen any of the ads for the PCC?" Sione asked.

"No. We just arrived on the island a couple of days ago . . ."

Skip interrupted. "Come on, Sione. They're newlyweds. The only reading material they've seen lately is their airline tickets."

Again I blushed. It was true, but there simply had been no time to read anything.

The next couple of hours flew by as they explained the purpose of the Cultural Center. Two of the four, Scottie and Sione, were Mormons. They told us about their beautiful white temple and explained the sacred ordinances performed there, including the sealing of families for eternity.

I watched Bart, waiting for him to disclose his interest in The Church of Jesus Christ of Latter-day Saints, but he was strangely silent, leaving the comments and questions to Ilsaba and Skip, who seemed interested.

Bart had been anxious to relate to me all he'd learned about the Mormon church from a Frenchman in a Tibetan prison before our wedding, but there had been neither time nor opportunity. The bishop who married us told me Bart had approached him about being baptized, yet now Bart revealed no knowledge of the church at all. In the end, he did ask some probing questions, keeping the discussion going longer than it probably would have.

Sione bore testimony of the reality of Jesus Christ as Savior and Redeemer of the world, of his sure knowledge that Christ had suffered and died for our sins so that we could return to our Father in Heaven's presence if we sincerely repented of all wrong doing. It gave me chills. It was doctrine not new to me, yet it sounded fresh and exciting as these young people verbalized their beliefs.

Bart's only outward reaction was to pull me closer to him. We needed quiet time to discuss these things that Bart had been so enthusiastic about finding, things we'd both searched for years ago. Quiet time. Something that had become nonexistent.

At 10:15 Scottie called his sister and found her home. He gave a brief explanation of our dilemma, and Megan and Tapata arrived in less than twenty minutes.

"We'd have been here sooner, but we had to make half a dozen phone calls before we could find someone to fill in for us at the performance for the next few days," Megan explained breathlessly.

Scottie was right. Although, they were nearly the same sizes as we were, our coloring was not similar. Where my hair was long, dark, and curly, Megan's was honey-blonde, cut short and very stylish. She had a peaches-and-cream complexion, with large, expressive brown eyes and a warm, gracious smile.

Tapata was Bart's size, maybe a little broader in the shoulder and thicker through the neck . . . definitely athletic looking, with beautiful bronze skin, coal black hair, a dazzling, friendly smile, and a handshake that nearly loosened my teeth.

After quick introductions, we explained our needs—peace and quiet on our honeymoon without people watching us. We warned them there might be some danger and apprised them of what they might expect.

"We suggest you check into a hotel away from this side of the island, which we'll pay for, and have room service deliver your meals. You need to be together at all times. One can't leave to get food or run errands. Remain in disguise so no one sees your faces or the color of your hair. If they do try any rough stuff, call Lt. Nakamura, but I don't expect them to approach you," Bart instructed. He handed Tapata a card with Nakamura's number on it.

Megan produced a shopping bag filled with wigs.

"We're involved with the drama department at the college, and on the off chance they might be needed, I brought some wigs. Here's one for you," Megan said, handing me a blonde wig styled similar to her own hair, "and a dark one for me. It's a little straighter than your hair but if they don't get close, no one can tell."

Digging deeper in her bag, Megan pulled out a man's blond wig.

"This is for Tapata. He's used it several times in plays we've done."

"As long as no one's checking skin color too close, we'll be all right," Tapata laughed.

Delving into the bag once more, Megan brought up a dark wig. "This might do the trick for you," she said, handing the dark wig to my very blond husband.

We were instantly transformed. I slipped into Megan's oversized T-shirt and gave her my swim cover-up and hat, then transferred my belongings from my beach bag into her shopping bag. Bart and Tapata traded jackets and hats, then transferred the contents of Bart's duffle bag into the shopping bag.

When the teasing and joking subsided, we expressed our gratitude to Megan and Tapata, pressed some money into their hands, and promised to pay for any unforeseen expenses they incurred.

"In the dark, they'll never be able to tell it's not us. You'll be checked into a hotel and out of sight before morning. Scottie will be our go-between. Keep in touch and he'll let you know when you can come home. If you even suspect your cover has been blown, call Scottie immediately," Bart directed.

We retrieved the bag of clothes the couple from the hotel had delivered earlier. Bart described our rented red convertible as we exchanged car keys.

"You're getting the short end of the stick on transportation," Tapata apologized. "She's not jazzy, but she's dependable. We'd be happy to have you use our apartment as long as you need it." He pointed out the house key on his key ring.

"Wait, Megan!" Ilsaba cried. "You need some bandages to be authentic." They quickly swathed the appropriate areas on Megan to match me bandage for bandage. That done, Megan and her now-blond husband exited the hospital, got in our car, and drove into the night.

Bart slipped out a side entrance of the hospital and watched a car parked across the road pull onto the highway a discreet distance behind our convertible and follow it. There was no other activity, no other cars in the parking lot except Megan and Tapatas', which we now would use, and those of our four friends at the hospital.

We were fortunate this had been another quiet night in the emergency room. But then, Kahuku was a very small town.

"Looks like the coast is clear," Bart said when he came back in. "Our tail is on their tail, and we may have free sailing for a couple of days."

"I can't tell you how good that makes me feel!"

We got Scottie's phone number and the numbers of the others in case we couldn't reach Scottie.

"Can we know your plans in the event we need to get hold of you?"

"We'll be in touch," Bart said. "At the moment, we don't know ourselves. We'll check in periodically to make sure Megan and Tapata haven't had any trouble and their cover is still valid. If you haven't heard from us in five days, though, call this number." Bart scribbled Dad's number in California. "Jack Alexander is Allison's father. Tell him everything you know."

"But we don't know anything."

"Tell him everything that's happened. That'll be enough. He can go from there. We've been in touch already."

I laughed. "But don't worry. We'll be back."

We bid goodbye to our accomplices and stepped out into the warm, tropical night. Golden parking lot lights couldn't dim the huge silver moon shining high over the dark Koolau mountains.

Bart pulled me into his arms.

"I feel different," I murmured, snuggling close to him.

"In what way?"

"Like I'm free—no longer on the wrong end of the binoculars."

"Okay, Megan," Bart said, holding me at arms length, "whither shall we go?"

"Home, Tapata!"

We climbed into the little Volkswagen beetle and found our way to Megan and Tapata's modest but immaculate one-bedroom apartment. There was a note on the cabinet. *Mi casa es su casa*—the familiar "My house is your house."

The note continued: "Eat anything in the refrigerator. The sheets are clean. Stay and enjoy, or simply use as a base to come and go." It was signed "Meg & Pat."

"Do we crash here, get a good night's sleep, and start our new lives tomorrow, or do we leave for the airport now and make our getaway under cloak of darkness?" I asked.

"You're really getting into this, aren't you?" Bart laughed.

"Do I have any choice? I'm there, whether I want to be or not. When you said you'd have to take me into your world, you weren't kidding."

Bart pulled the blonde wig from my head, tousled my hair, then held me close.

"I had no idea it would be so soon or so intense. If I had known it would bring you this close to danger, I might not have married you."

Leaning my bruised, weary body against Bart's solid, muscular one, I felt safe and secure in those strong arms that held me with such tenderness.

"Had I known it was going to be so painful, I'd have had

second thoughts about marrying you," I countered.

Bart pushed me from him, searching my face to see if I was serious.

I laughed. "Sorry, Charlie. You're stuck with me."

"And you're stuck with me. For better or for worse. I just hope it doesn't get worse, for your sake," he answered seriously.

Little did we know.

Chapter Five

"I feel like a new woman this morning!" I exclaimed as I donned my blonde wig.

"You look like a new woman, too," Bart laughed as he stood behind me, watching me in the mirror.

I turned into his arms. "Do you like me better as a blonde?"

Bart cocked his head to one side and looked at me. "Why not? A little variety never hurt anything."

I jabbed at him. "Know what I'd like to do today?" I asked.

"Nothing would surprise me."

"How about if we play tourist? There's a place called Sacred Falls just down the road. The guide book says it's an hour hike through a rain forest to the falls."

"Sounds good to me."

We raided the refrigerator for breakfast, then Bart made a quick call to Scottie to see if Megan and Tapata had encountered any problems during the night. They'd reported they'd been followed and could see the white sedan from their hotel window and two men watching their room. The burden was gone. I felt a wonderful new freedom knowing we weren't being watched anymore. I only hoped Megan and Tapata would be safe.

We piled into the Volkswagen bug which by morning light turned out to be a bright lime green.

"So much for being inconspicuous!" I laughed.

"Sometimes the best disguise is being the most conspicuous."

"Is that my next lesson in spying and subterfuge? I need a crash course, the way things are happening."

While Bart drove the winding, two-lane highway that served as the main thoroughfare around Oahu, I consulted the tourist brochure, pointing out places of interest.

Giant cottonball clouds drifted lazily in the cornflower blue heavens. In the distance, the sky merged with shimmering shades of water—cerulean, turquoise, aquamarine, cobalt, and teal.

The road paralleled one white sand crescent after another, which were, even at this early hour, becoming populated with sun worshippers, swimmers and wave riders. Campers and picnickers resembled Bedouins in their billowing, colorful tents.

Bart suddenly whipped off the highway into a dirt parking lot. We had arrived. I transferred swimsuits, towels, and my little bottle of lotion to Bart's backpack, and helped him adjust it comfortably on his shoulders.

The bright tropical sun blazed hot and the humidity was heavy. White clouds bumped against velvety mountains, casting a patchwork of shadows on the jungle green ahead. We ascended a trail that wandered beside a working banana plantation and wound slowly higher into the mountains.

The wig was hot. Sweat trickled down my neck and between my shoulder blades.

"Hey, husband, are you as miserable as I am?"

"Probably not. I don't have as much hair stuffed under my wig as you do."

"Can we take them off? There's no one around."

"Sure."

We stuffed the wigs into the backpack and I shook my hair free.

Suddenly our trail opened into a wide clearing. Straight ahead lay a tangle of twisted, gnarled trees and what appeared to be a tunnel through the center.

A sign warned "Danger! Do not advance beyond this point if it is raining! Flash flood area."

"As hot as it is, I'd welcome a little rain," I told Bart.

We checked the clouds, which were still leap-frogging white and glorious over one another, then snuggling against the rugged, green peaks towering high above our heads.

"Guess that doesn't apply today," Bart said as we stepped out of the sunshine into the tunnel of trees.

An eerie canopy of black limbs twisted overhead, shaded by an umbrella of green boughs. The umbrageous path seemed to be no more than the bottom of a creek bed filled with rocks and tangled roots. Footing was treacherous.

A melodious trickle of water over rocks serenaded us where the creek paralleled the path. It was the only sound in the hushed, heavy, almost suffocating atmosphere. A spooky sense of danger prickled up the back of my neck.

"I feel like Audrey Hepburn in *Green Mansions,* or Snow White in the Enchanted Forest. These twisted trees are oppressive. They make my danger antennae tingle."

At that instant, we heard someone coming up the trail behind us. Bart pulled me behind a rock. Crouching out of sight, expecting more of Nate's men, we were astonished to hear a child's laughter.

I whispered to Bart, "We're getting paranoid. I was sure it was Nate again."

"Stay put and let's see who it is."

Two couples advanced single file up the rocky path, each father toting a small child on his shoulders. A young woman with a bouncy brown ponytail carried on a soft monologue with a brand new baby she held in a sling in front of her.

"Comin', Livi?" the slightly-built, pleasant faced young man asked, turning to check on his wife.

"We're coming. Your daughter and I are having a deep conversation."

"Anything I should know about?" He turned again, his big brown eyes bright with amusement.

"I'm just warning her about her father and her older brother," she teased.

The tow-headed youngster on his father's shoulders piped up, "What did she say about me?"

I wanted to hear her reply but their voices faded as they moved up the trail, leaving a good feeling in their wake.

"Onward and upward, m'lady," Bart said. "We don't need to dally all day."

But we didn't hurry. I enjoyed the aura of the happy couples in front of us. It had changed my strange mood. Still, I didn't want to intrude on their privacy, nor let them intrude on ours. I felt foolish, remembering the flush of fear I'd felt just before we heard them behind us. My danger antennae didn't usually malfunction like that. *Could I possibly be overstressed?* I laughed to myself.

Gradually, the scenery changed as we climbed. The canopy became greener and more dense, and gnarled black limbs were replaced by a profusion of lush ferns. The air remained sultry and pungent with the smell of wet vegetation. The path up the mountain became steeper, and the sound of the water was more pronounced.

We'd hiked about forty-five minutes when the path crossed the stream we'd been paralleling. We hopped from one boulder to another as we negotiated the width of the creek.

"I see why the trail is designated dangerous."

Bart agreed. "That babbling brook could become a raging river in no time with these steep canyon walls on both sides."

The green gloom deepened as we climbed higher on the mountain. Then I heard splashing and laughter. Pausing as we traversed a huge tree trunk serving as a bridge, I caught sight of a spectacular ribbon of white spray splicing the shadowy green mountain.

"Oh, Bart! Look!" The narrow canyon ended, widening slightly where the falls cascaded into a dark emerald pool of shining water surrounded by a tumble of boulders.

Laughing and playing in the refreshing spray of the waterfall, two little boys with brightly colored water wings cooled off after their hike, supervised by their fathers. A beautiful young woman with waist-length black hair dried herself, then took the infant so the baby's mother could swim.

One of the little boys waved as we descended the last of the huge rocks that formed the end of the trail. "Come play! It's cold!" he invited us.

"Thanks. We will," Bart responded.

We introduced ourselves to Mark and pony-tailed Olivia, our friendly greeter, three-year-old Michael, and their infant daughter,

Amber. The other family consisted of two-year-old Todd and his parents: Doug, whose blond, blue-eyed Teutonic looks contrasted sharply to his exotic-looking, dark-haired wife, Jill. All four adults were students at BYU-Hawaii.

The water was the best thing that had happened to me all day. Refreshing, reviving, invigorating, bracing—adjectives that aptly applied spilled over one another in my mind, but nothing could describe sufficiently how great it felt to be cool. Diving into the deep pool from a high, rocky ledge was the game of the day. Soon I offered to hold the baby and watch Michael and Todd so Olivia could join the others. Even Bart entered the impromptu contest to see who could make the biggest splash.

I relaxed on a rock with the baby, visually exploring the beauty of the narrow canyon, the hills, then tracing Sacred Falls all the way to the top. For the first time in over an hour, the sky was visible, but it was no longer blue. In fact, those drops weren't splashes from two playful little boys as I'd thought.

"Bart!" I called in alarm. "It's raining!"

Glancing at the dark, threatening clouds, he asked the group casually, "How serious is it when it rains up here?"

"It can get pretty hairy," Doug answered, his sharp blue eyes scanning the clouds overhead. "Depends on how long it rains and how fast it comes down. You can depend on a few sprinkles a day when the clouds try to go over the mountain. That's no problem. We'll watch the clouds. If it gets heavy, we'll head back immediately."

I tried to cover the baby, but Olivia called, "Don't worry about Amber. She loves the water."

An only child, I knew nothing about babies, assuming they had to be warm and dry all the time. Olivia soon came dripping out of the water to take Amber.

"She loves her bath, and a little rain won't hurt her. You go enjoy the water."

"Are you sure? I'd be glad to hold her."

"No. You go." Olivia glanced uneasily at the sky. "I've had enough. I think I'll get dressed."

Jill joined her and they called Michael and Todd from the water. Sprinkles turned to rain.

"Not much point in putting clothes on," Jill laughed as she towel-dried her long, lustrous hair. "They'll just get wet."

"Mark, I think we'd better head back," Olivia called.

Bart, seeing the concern on my face, made one last dive from the rocks and climbed out of the pool. Mark and Doug followed close behind.

"You two are a couple of worrywarts." Though Mark's voice was full of teasing, his warm, brown eyes kept a careful watch on the mountains above us. He turned to Bart. "We'll humor them. It'll probably stop as soon as we get on our way, but there's no sense taking any chances."

While they tucked wet little feet into colorful tennis shoes, Bart and I headed down the trail, calling goodbye as we left.

Light rain soon became a heavy downpour, turning the trail into a slippery, muddy mess. As we crossed the log, I noted with alarm the height of the water below us. Rivulets running down the hillsides everywhere swelled what had been a tiny, babbling brook into a good-sized stream of water.

Even the thick green canopy didn't keep the rain from soaking us. It accumulated on large leaves, then rolled off in giant drops, drenching us as we slipped and slid down the trail.

When we arrived at the intersection of trail and stream, where we'd crossed hopping from rock to rock, the rocks were no longer visible in the rushing water.

"Bart, they'll never make it across here with those little children."

"We may not either, Princess." Bart surveyed the stream, looking up and down for another crossing. This seemed the widest spot, therefore, it should be the most shallow. But at this point it appeared to be waist-deep. While Bart searched for an alternate route, the group caught up with us.

"Is there another crossing point?" Bart shouted over the noise of the cascading water.

"This is the only one I know of," Mark answered, his lips drawn in a thin, grim line.

"Can we sit it out and wait for the water to subside?" I asked.

"It could get worse. If we got a really good downpour, we could end up with trees and boulders washing us away."

Olivia had seated herself on a rock, cradling her baby in one arm, and speaking in soft, quiet tones to Michael, who was snuggled in her other arm.

"Heavenly Father knows where we are, and he'll watch over us, Michael," she reassured him.

I think I'd have been frantic knowing the danger my children were in, yet there was a serenity in her demeanor that surprised me.

Bart returned from his scouting trip.

"There's a wider spot just downstream with trees close to the water. If we tie our towels together I can take one end across, tie it to the other side and make a lifeline we can cross with."

"Sounds good to me," Doug said as he hoisted Todd back up on his shoulders.

Bart led the way through the ferns and heavy undergrowth as we slid single file down the hill, each taking a turn at a tumble or fall. The little boys were loving this adventure. Mark and Doug laughed and joked to keep the mood light, but I knew they were even more concerned than I was. Mark told Olivia to hang on to his belt so she wouldn't slip.

"We're okay," she said.

In the ravine below, dead limbs, leaves, and small plants uprooted by the churning muddy water raced past us. When we reached the wide spot Bart had found, the men tore the towels into strips and knotted them together to form a rope. Bart secured one end to a small tree on our side of the bank and prepared to plunge into the angry, swirling water with the other.

"Be careful," I whispered. "I need you in one piece."

"Don't worry, Princess. I wouldn't do anything to spoil our honeymoon, or did we do that already?" He grinned mischievously as he bent down to give me a quick kiss, then turned to face the turbulent tide.

"Wait, Bart. Tie the towels around your waist."

"Good idea," Doug said. "If you get washed off your feet, we can drag you back for a second try."

With the rope firmly fastened about him, Bart stepped into the wild water, placing each foot carefully, searching for secure footing.

Progress was agonizingly slow as he fought to stay upright in the swiftly flowing current.

He was about midway across the muddy torrent when a loud crack shattered our concentration. A dead tree toppled into the water above us.

"Bart, look out!" No need for warning. Bart grasped the obvious. As the tree uprooted and tumbled into the stream, boulders held in place by its rotting roots came crashing with it, creating a crest of water that surged downstream.

"Hurry!" I shouted. "Hurry!"

Two more carefully placed steps, then Bart lunged for the other side, catching a leafy branch hanging over the water. I watched, horrified. The leaves stripped off in his hand one by one as the water tore at him, pulling him back with its swirling force.

Above us, the tree bumped and buffeted in the roaring water of the narrow channel, a battering ram headed straight for Bart.

He grabbed at another branch whose tender leaves couldn't withstand the tremendous drag of the water and they, too, gave way. Heaving forward with his right hand, he grabbed a higher, stronger branch and hauled himself laboriously out of the muddy maelstrom.

I breathed again, then checked the progress of the dead tree. It had rammed into a boulder and become wedged crosswise between that and a sapling on the other side. The little tree bent with the pressure of the huge trunk and the thrust of the water behind it.

"Quick! Before that log comes loose, get over here!" Bart ordered. "Allison . . . ."

"No, let them take the kids first."

Mark told Michael to hold on to him tight, to not let go for any reason. He took Olivia by the hand and led her to the water.

"Do you want me to take Amber?"

"No, she's fine in the sling." She cinched it higher and wrapped her left arm firmly around baby and sling.

"Go!" Doug shouted. Mark plunged into the angry water, clinging to the towel rope stretched tightly between trees on either side of the bank. Bart waded in and grabbed Michael from Mark's shoulders, depositing him safely on the other side, then they pulled Olivia and Amber up the slippery bank.

The little tree upstream creaked and groaned ominously under the heavy load pressing against it.

"That big tree's going to uproot that sapling any minute now. Allison, come on!" Bart shouted over the roar of the rising water.

I rushed in behind Jill and Doug, with Todd on his shoulders. I was halfway across when the sapling gave way with a resounding snap and the huge dead tree trunk shot forward like an arrow from a taut bow.

Bart leaped into the swirling water.

"Grab my hand!" Bart yelled, reaching for me. Mark grasped Bart's belt and Doug gripped Mark. With a mighty pull, they fell backward into the ferns, tossing me out of the water, as the log plummeted where I had been a second before.

No one moved or spoke, stunned by our narrow escape.

Todd's two-year-old eyes were wide. "Wow!" was his only comment.

Michael expressed everyone's feelings as he quietly said, "That was close, huh, Dad?"

Laughter relieved the tension.

"Yes, Michael. That was close."

"Were you scared?" I asked.

"Oh, no," he said matter-of-factly. "I said a prayer, and I knew Heavenly Father wouldn't let anything bad happen to us."

I realized I had been praying, too, and murmured a fervent thank-you.

"We're not out of the woods, yet," Bart said, pulling me to my feet and reaching to help Olivia.

"You're right. There are another couple of low spots that could be under water by now," Doug agreed. "We'd better get a move on," he urged, hoisting Todd back on his shoulders.

We climbed the slippery, sloping hillside up to the trail—or what had been the trail. Now ankle-deep, it had become a rushing little stream.

Bart relinquished the lead to those who knew the trail better, and as he fell behind, offered to carry Amber.

Olivia smiled. "I'm so used to carrying her, I hardly know she's there, and I know she's happier where she is. But thanks. I appreciate the offer."

Our footpath widened as we left the jade jungle, the lush green rain forest of the higher elevation, and descended the slippery trail to the umbrella of gnarled black branches.

"How's Amber holding up?" I called ahead to Olivia.

"She's taking it all in stride," Olivia laughed. "We've got a real pioneer here."

As we'd climbed to Sacred Falls, the creek had been a pleasant murmur ten or twelve feet below us most of the time. It was now an angry roar only a few feet away. I couldn't believe so much water had been dumped in such a short amount of time and was rushing down the mountain toward the ocean.

Then it happened. As I watched in horror, the bank under Olivia's feet gave way and slid into the water, plunging her and the baby into the raging torrent.

Mark whirled at her cry and ejected Michael from his shoulders in one smooth movement. In a flash he and Bart were tumbling down the muddy bank into the tumultuous water after Olivia and Amber.

Olivia struggled to keep her own head above water, as well as Amber's. My silent prayer was interrupted by Michael's clear small voice.

"Dear Heavenly Father. Please bless my Mom and please bless Amber to know how to swim. I promise I'll be a good boy forever if you'll please bless them. Thank you. In Jesus' name, Amen."

I looked into that sweet, innocent, faith-filled face. Hurrying around the slide area, I went down on my knees and reached for him. He hugged me tight.

"They'll be okay," he whispered, reassuring me, when I should have been reassuring him.

Hand in hand we hurried carefully along the slippery path, trying to catch up with Doug and Jill who were running ahead keeping track of the quartet being swept along by the swiftly running water. Todd clung desperately to his father's shoulders.

"Can you see her? Can you see my Mommy? Is Amber swimming?" Michael asked breathlessly as we raced as fast as we dared down the liquid trail.

"As soon as we get around this corner we should see them.

Watch out."

Michael stumbled over a root stretched across the path. I got him back on his feet and we hurried around the boulder that blocked our view. There, like a lighthouse shining forth its beacon in the darkness, was the entrance to this labyrinth of green and black. The path flattened out, and the creek widened considerably. I could see Bart and Mark struggling to their feet with Olivia between them.

Her attention was on the baby.

"Amber's not breathing! She's not breathing!" Her anguished cry pierced my heart.

"Oh, please," I prayed. *"Please answer Michael's prayer. Don't let anything happen to his baby sister."*

Doug tossed Todd to Jill and raced into the waist-deep water, helping everyone back to higher ground.

Jill ran to Olivia. "Give me Amber. I know CPR." Olivia hesitated. Jill pled softly, "Trust me."

Olivia thrust her still baby into Jill's outstretched arms, and they all knelt around the infant as she cleared its airway and administered mouth-to-mouth resuscitation on the tiny body.

"Daddy, does Amber need a blessing?" Michael piped up.

All eyes but Jill's turned to the three-year-old.

"Yes, son, I think she does," Mark said quietly. He reached for one of the pockets on his dripping backpack and retrieved a tiny vial. He handed it to Doug.

"Please?"

Doug carefully dripped a drop of something from the vial onto the baby's head. Whatever he said was extremely short, then the big hands of Mark and Doug covered the crown of the tiny little head under them. Jill never stopped her efforts.

Michael knelt down, bowed his head, and folded his arms in a very serious manner. Olivia dropped her head and closed her eyes.

I leaned forward, straining to hear the words of the drama occurring in front of me. I caught only snatches: "power of the priest-hood" and "command you to live."

Suddenly the tiny body arched and the baby threw up, her pale little face quickly regaining its color. She cried. So did I.

We breathed an almost unanimous sigh of relief, but it was

Michael who said what we were thinking.

"Thank you, Heavenly Father." Then he added quietly, "I won't forget my promise to be a good boy forever." His family hugged him and each other, laughing and crying at the same time.

Watching them, I felt like we were intruding on something very sacred. Bart reached for my hand, and we quietly departed the tunnel of twisted trees into the open field. The worst of the downpour was over, and blue sky peeked through over the ocean.

We walked arm in arm, neither of us speaking for several minutes.

"I almost felt like God was right there with them."

"I think he must have been," Bart answered softly. "Olivia was under water so long I was afraid she'd drowned. There was no doubt in my mind that Amber was a goner. She was submerged twice as long. I think we've been witness to a miracle."

I threw my arms around Bart.

"Oh, Bart! If anything had happened to you . . ." The thought was too devastating to even finish.

He held me tight. "But it didn't, Princess. You had a pretty close call yourself." He tried to laugh, but the sound that emerged was half laugh, half sob. "Your guardian angels were on duty today. Remind me to thank them properly."

Arms around each other's waists, we headed back to the car.

"Wait! Wait a minute!" Mark called after us.

We turned around.

"We didn't thank you."

"For what?"

"For helping save our lives," Olivia said gratefully.

Bart answered quietly, "We aren't the ones you should thank."

"Oh, we already took care of that." Mark's brown eyes were warm with gratitude. "Now we'd like to thank the guardian angels He sent along to help us." Olivia's arm slipped around my waist, and she gave me a hug.

They all extended a hand, even Michael and his buddy, Todd. When Michael offered his little hand, I shook it solemnly and said, "Thank you, Michael, for a lesson in faith. I won't forget you."

We bid them farewell and walked on ahead while their slower

pace accommodated two little boys who had to explore everything on either side of the road.

But my thoughts were back on a circle of people kneeling over the still and lifeless body of a tiny child, and I felt a pressing need to know more. If this was an example of the faith of the members of this church, it was no wonder Bart was impressed. Would it bear up under an intense investigation?

Chapter Six

Our bright, shiny, lime green VW bug greeted us obnoxiously as we made our way back to a parking lot inhabited by three other cars: two empty ones and one parked in the shade containing two men reading newspapers.

The prickles started on the back of my neck again.

"Remember the sense of impending danger I had as we entered the enchanted forest?"

"Turned out there was plenty of that. Your intuition was right on, as usual."

"No, Bart. That wasn't it. I just experienced it again when I saw that car under the tree." I motioned to the occupied auto. "They couldn't have found us, could they?"

He frowned. "If they did, they're awfully good. Let's see if they follow us."

We threw the soggy backpack into the back seat and peeled out of the parking lot, watching behind us as we wound down the road, but the white sedan didn't follow us. I sank back in my seat, relieved, yet puzzled by the disquiet I felt, the foreboding of unpleasant things approaching. My intuition didn't usually lead me astray.

"How could anyone have tracked us if our decoys have done their job?"

"Someone's always coming out with better technology. We'd like to be the ones who get it first, but that doesn't always happen. It's possible they've got a device my equipment didn't pick up."

Bart kept checking the rearview mirror, but the white sedan didn't show up.

I was suddenly overcome with weariness.

"This may have been the longest morning I've ever spent."

"And one of the wettest!" Bart added.

"I need a shower first of all. Then we'll need a washing machine or these clothes will be good for nothing but the trash. Once the mud dries, it may never come out."

"As you wish, Princess. Keep your eyes out for the first likely prospect and we'll stop."

It wasn't long before we found a nice little motel across from the beach. Bart had no trouble convincing the managers to waive their 2:00 p.m. check-in time. We probably looked and smelled so bad they knew we couldn't wait any longer to get cleaned up.

"I feel I may never be clean again," I said, heading immediately for the shower.

"We wouldn't want that. Let me assist you there." Bart joined me in the shower and scrubbed my back vigorously. This was one part of married life I was thoroughly enjoying. What a luxury!

"Thank you very much, sir," I said, reaching up on my tip toes and bestowing a wet kiss on his soapy face.

"You're very welcome. What for?"

"For becoming my personal back scrubber."

"I assure you, it's my pleasure." His eyes twinkled as he lathered his hands with gusto. "Is there anywhere else you'd like me to scrub, m'lady?"

I ignored his innuendo and turned him around.

"Your turn." I rubbed soap gently over Bart's back, not sure how sensitive the scars still were that crisscrossed him from neck to waist. I hated to think of him being whipped within an inch of his life in that Chinese prison in Tibet, or the agonizing healing process in Nepal.

Wrapping my arms around his chest, I pulled him close to me with soapy hands. I lay my head against the still red, angry-looking lines and let the water stream over us, wishing it could wash away the scars as easily as the mud. Bart turned, took me in his arms and kissed me, long and lingering.

"That's the most liquescent kiss I've ever had," I said breathlessly, turning off the shower.

"Is that good or is that bad?"

I turned my back to Bart so he could dry it for me. "Oh, good, of course."

"Look me in the eye and say that." He whirled me around, but I dodged behind him and toweled his back dry.

"Look it up!" I laughed. I busied myself washing our wigs and drying them while Bart retrieved the smuggled suitcase from the car.

"I'm glad Paul and Cathy sneaked our clothes out for us, but I probably sent all the wrong things. I don't know what to wear." I collapsed on the bed wrapped in my damp towel while I decided.

"I like you just the way you are," Bart said, diving playfully on the bed beside me. "It's nice to be married to somebody who doesn't have to have expensive clothes to make them beautiful. Think of all the money we could save if you dressed like this all the time."

"Not especially. I'd have to have a towel in every decorator color, and, of course, I really prefer dry ones."

"You are pretty damp, aren't you?" Bart said as he tugged at the towel. "You're going to have to sleep in a wet bed."

"No, I'm on your side of the bed. You'll have to sleep in a wet bed," I laughed.

"Oh, no!" He grabbed the towel away from me and threw it across the room.

I squealed and whipped the blanket over me, rolling up like Cleopatra in her rug, right into Bart's arms. He nibbled my earlobe and started down my neck.

"How about something a little more substantial?" I whispered seductively in Bart's ear.

"What do you have in mind?"

"Dinner."

Bart propped himself up on one elbow. "Is that all it takes to make you happy?"

"No, I like hot showers, too."

"And?" he pressed.

"And a certain blond, blue-eyed guy who keeps saving my life."

"It looks like that has become my life's work, Princess," he teased with a sigh. "It's a tough job, but somebody's got to do it." He kissed my reply right out of existence.

* * * * * * *

"Where to for dinner?" Bart asked as we climbed into the lime green bug, trapped once again in the wigs.

I consulted the tourist map. "It says there's a Crouching Lion Inn just down the road."

"Sounds interesting. Lead on, McDuff. Your chauffeur is at the ready."

Bart maneuvered the little car through the parking lot and onto Kamehameha Highway. I caught myself examining every car, parked or moving, and its occupants. Were we still being followed? A nagging feeling persisted that we hadn't really eluded our pursuers.

We wound around breathtaking vistas toward Kahana Bay, high green mountains on one side with a splendid white sand beach and bluest-of-blue water on the other. Suddenly, there it was, nestled under tall, slender palms at the foot of a massive rock formation.

The Crouching Lion Inn was a long, high-roofed building with an English flavor, and an open air lanai filled with diners enjoying the Elysian view.

The huge rock towering behind the inn did, indeed, look like a lion crouching, ready to spring. According to Hawaiian legend, it was Kauhi—the ancient demigod brother of Pele, the goddess of fire—who was chained to the cliff.

The ambience of the large dining room reminded me of an English hunting lodge. Four high square-backed wicker chairs enclosed each table in complete privacy. A huge red brick fireplace with a ten-foot, hand-hewn mantle dominated one wall, above which hung a remarkable painting of the inn. The mantle intrigued me. Was it made especially for the Crouching Lion, and by whom?

Next to our table, Old-English-style colored glass windows stood wide open to admit a delightfully refreshing sea breeze. Above us, large rectangular woven fans swung back and forth, circulating the air as they moved. A unique image of a lion's head stared down from each of the white enameled lamps lining the wall.

Our waiter had a French accent and an attitude, the first person on the island we'd encountered that wasn't falling-down friendly. But he wasn't an islander. He returned quickly with the house specialty, Portuguese bean soup and hot cheese-filled hard rolls. What a delicious way to appease our hunger!

I snuggled into my wicker throne feeling like royalty, the back of my chair towering three feet over my head and on both sides. With our chairs close together, we completely blocked out the rest of the world.

"Remind you of an old spy movie?" I whispered huskily, leaning toward Bart.

"All that's missing are the trench coats. The script usually calls for something like this." He reached across the corner of the table and kissed me.

"Your bean soup tastes pretty good," he said, his blue eyes crinkling in a teasing smile.

"That's not my soup. That's me."

"Even better." He kissed me again. "By the way, can you cook?"

"This is a fine time to be asking a question like that. What will you do if I can't?"

"Eat out a lot," he said ruefully.

"If it makes a difference, that's one of the questions you're supposed to ask before you say 'I do'."

He reached for my hand. "If you couldn't boil water without burning it, I'd still have married you. But knowing your mom, I suspect your culinary skills were not left lacking."

We finished our soup and worked on a plan for the rest of the day, but I couldn't shake the nagging feeling that we weren't through with Nate.

"Will you excuse me, please? I'm going to find the little girl's room before our dinner arrives."

It wasn't an easy task. I wound my way around the waiters' station, through the lanai room, the bar, and into a breezeway where someone was talking on the telephone. The breezeway opened onto an enclosed square of green lawn with a huge ivy-covered tree in the center. I paused just for a moment to admire this delightful spot.

As I reached to open the door to the ladies room, a tingling sensation began on the back of my neck and spread down my arms; the hairs were literally standing on end. Whirling around, I stared directly into the eyes of the man on the telephone, who was stretching the cord around the corner, watching me. When our eyes met, he turned abruptly, the phone still to his ear.

He looked vaguely familiar. But where had I seen him? The shirt! The purple and white shirt! He was one of the men in the car at the Sacred Falls parking lot, when I'd experienced this same sensation.

I hurried back to our table, glancing back at the phone as I did so. The man had vanished.

"Bart! He's here!"

"Who's here?"

I pulled my chair in to close out the world once more, but it didn't work this time. The romantic illusion of privacy had been shattered.

"The guy from the parking lot. I thought we lost them. Am I enduring this miserable wig for nothing? Who are they? What do they want?"

"Whoa! How do you know it's the guy from the parking lot?"

"He looked familiar—then I recognized his purple and white shirt. Terrible shirt."

"You think he's following us?"

"Bart, he was on the telephone and watched me walk around the corner to the ladies room. He had to stretch the phone cord all the way."

"Any man would watch you walk around the corner. You're a beautiful woman."

I ignored the compliment. I knew I wasn't being hysterical, nor unreasonable, nor paranoid. This was real.

"Bart, they're following us."

"I believe you, Princess. I'm just surprised our little deception didn't work. What kind of bug do they have that my catcher didn't find? Where is it? And why is it important that they know where we are?" Bart sat quietly for a few minutes. I didn't disturb his deliberations. My instincts were to run, as hard and fast as I could, away from here, but Bart was the expert. He'd know what to do.

The very polite accent came back with his attitude, bearing our dinner. I thought I'd lost my appetite until its aroma assailed my senses. I decided I could act far better on a full stomach than an empty one.

Bart absently picked up his fork and cut off a piece of steak smothered in marinated mushrooms. A look of surprise crossed his face.

"Hello! This is delicious."

"So's mine." I took another bite. "Bart, what are we going to do? Who are these men? How did they find us? What do they want?"

"These are two we haven't seen, right?"

"Right. The two in our hotel room were the same two that tried to snatch me at the beach—the same two that were with Nate at the hotel the first night we got there."

"Those two should still be in police custody. We can suppose the car that followed Megan and Tapata in our car are Nate's men. When we switched cars, the only way they'd find us is with an electronic device on something we brought with us. Puzzling."

"But what could be bugged? We left our luggage in the hotel. I even left my makeup case. I just brought a few essentials and some clothes."

"Jewelry?"

"Nothing valuable. In fact," I paused to flash my emerald engagement ring at him, "this is the only valuable piece I have. The rest is just costume stuff."

He took my hand and kissed it. "Well, they can't have that, or you, so we'll have to find out what they want and make sure they don't get it."

I finished my coconut chicken and sat back, enjoying the breeze from the open window, but still pondering our enigmatic situation. Suddenly the answer was obvious. "Let's skip out the window."

"What do you mean, skip out? Not pay for our dinner?"

"No, silly. You can leave money on the table for that. The high chair backs block the window so no one could see us go, unless they're waiting under the window."

"That little green Volkswagen is pretty easy to spot."

"We'll leave it."

"Abandon Megan and Tapata's transportation, such as it is?"

"We'll call Scottie and tell him to pick it up."

"Hmmm. It may work. That way, if they have planted a bug on anything we had with us, it would go back in the car."

Our waiter returned at that moment. Bart asked if he could bring a telephone to the table to make a local call.

"There is a phone in the hall."

"Do you have a portable one you could bring to the table, please?"

Bart opened his wallet and looked the young man straight in the eye.

"Yes, sir. I believe I may be able to find one." He did, quickly. Bart rewarded him with a ten-dollar bill. The waiter's attitude changed immediately.

When he was out of earshot, Bart called Scottie.

"Any change in the situation in Honolulu?"

"Not since this morning or they would've called. What's up?"

"Somehow we've picked up another white sedan. We're at the Crouching Lion Inn where we'll leave the Volkswagen. Can you come and get it, as well as our belongings at a motel? Both keys will be at the desk here at the Crouching Lion Inn. We paid in advance at the motel so just take our clothes and leave the key."

"Anything else?"

"I'll include the key to our Turtle Bay room. If you'll leave our stuff in our room, maybe it'll lead them back to the empty room at the hotel. There must be a device we didn't find. We don't want to lead them to any of you. Thanks, Scottie. We owe you!"

The waiter returned for the phone. He seemed to be in a much better mood. Bart opened his wallet again.

"We need a favor."

"*Oui.* I will do whatever I can to help."

"We're going out the back way—someone out front is waiting for us. Please give these car keys and room keys only to a guy named Scottie who'll come for them. If anyone else asks for us, you know nothing. Here's payment for our dinner with a generous tip for you, plus something for your trouble, my friend, and your loyalty." Bart gave him a hundred-dollar bill.

"*Oui!* I shall do everything you asked. *Merci!*"

"Oh, one other thing," I added. "Please bring us two of your most scrumptious desserts. Leave them for us to eat, and don't come back to our table for at least thirty minutes."

"As you wish, Madame. *Merci!*" He left, beaming.

"Didn't take much to change his attitude," I laughed. "We'd better get out of here before he brings dessert or I'll never get through the window. Ready?"

"Ready."

With a slight shift of the table, we slipped to the window which was hidden from every other spot in the room by the high backs of our wicker chairs.

Pausing only to determine that no one outside could see us leave, Bart went through the window, then turned to catch me. I hiked my long, cotton skirt up and threw both legs over the sill, then dropped into Bart's waiting arms.

"Did I ever tell you you have very nice legs?" Bart whispered.

"Did I ever tell you you have a weird sense of humor?"

We raced around to the back of the building, then quickly got lost in the dense green foliage behind the inn.

"Are we going to wait here till Scottie comes for the car or make our getaway before they discover we're gone?" I asked.

"What's ahead on the highway?"

"Let me think." I tried to picture the road as I had seen it on the map. "I don't remember very much, just a lot of green."

"There's a lot of green everywhere in Hawaii."

"No, I mean I don't remember that there were many towns ahead."

"Then we'll have to make our way back to the one behind us and catch a taxi to the airport—or the bus. Unless . . ." Bart grabbed my hand. "Come on. We've got to get to a place where we can see the parking lot and they can't see us. Didn't I see a couple of boats across from the inn when we came in?"

"If we could get to the beach, maybe we could convince someone to take us to the airport."

"Splendid, Sherlock. Let's go."

Threading our way through dense tropical undergrowth and down the hill, we crossed the highway beyond the curve from the Crouching Lion Inn. We dropped the six feet to the sand and were hidden once again from the highway.

Two boats were docked across the street from the Inn, both cabin cruisers, one slightly larger than the other.

We spotted a white sedan with a purple and white shirt sleeve at the window parked in the shade under a palm tree, positioned to watch the entrance to the Inn, not the beach across the street.

An older, distinguished looking couple crossed the road and walked out on the short pier to the smaller boat. We hurried to meet them.

"Sir, could I ask a favor?" Bart flashed a friendly smile.

"Yes?" The tall, silver-haired man responded suspiciously.

"Would it trouble you too much to deliver us somewhere near the airport? We've got to catch a flight and our car's conked out."

He looked down at his frowning, diminutive wife. I opened my purse and pulled out a one-hundred-dollar bill.

"We'll gladly pay you for your inconvenience."

A greedy smile spread across her lined face. "We'd love to. We don't have another thing to do all evening," she said with a voice husky from too many cigarettes. She plucked the money from my hand, stuffed it in her purse, and snapped the clasp shut with a resounding click, then tucked the bag securely under her tanned, leathery-looking arm.

I glanced at the restaurant. I couldn't see the parking lot from here, but the boat was clearly visible from the patio. We scrambled aboard and quickly ducked out of sight behind the cabin.

"Can you still see the white sedan in the parking lot?"

Bart peeked around the corner. "Four of them. That color and model seems to be a favorite of car rental agencies. Where was the car you said was driven by the infamous purple-and-white-shirted man?"

"On the right side, away from our car, under the palms in the shade."

"Yes, it's still there." He sat back down beside me.

As the boat pulled away from the little pier, he said hopefully, "Well, we may have done it this time."

"Do you realize I have stuff spread all over this island? And nothing with me except some lotion in my purse. I don't even have a toothbrush."

"It's all right, as long as you have your checkbook. And in answer to your unasked question, one of very few unasked, I might add, I don't usually spend money so lavishly recruiting help. We're playing a different game this time. I know Nate's adopted many of Antonio Scaddono's habits, being his next in command, and one thing Tony did well was spread money around to buy favors. He'd throw a fifty-dollar bill here and there to get what he wanted. By giving the waiter a hundred dollars, we've bought his loyalty and beat Nate to the punch."

The lady returned as we got underway. She immediately began questioning us sharply about where we were from, what we were doing here, then asked point blank, "Do you do this often?"

"No, ma'am." I laughed. "Our car couldn't seem to get us all the way to the airport as quickly as we needed to get there."

"I see." She didn't really, but we both let it go. Before she could question me further, I asked about her and her husband. Were they retired? From what? Where did they live? What do they do now? Do they have family? Grandchildren? She was delighted to talk about her grandchildren, nothing else, and invited us to join her husband.

"He likes to be a part of everything. He'll be very curious about you."

My tactic didn't work as well on our captain. He was not so easily turned aside and pressed us with pointed questions. I gave Bart a look that said, "You're on your own," and turned to our hostess.

"How old are your grandchildren?" I asked.

Bart glared daggers but I smiled sweetly and ignored him, leaving him to try to turn the conversation to the boat, of which the captain seemed very proud. Just then we passed a striking formation in the ocean.

"What's that called?" Bart asked. "I think I saw it in our travel book."

"Chinaman's Hat," he responded.

"Oh, yes. That's the children's story about the huge Chinaman sitting under the sea with just his cone-shaped straw hat visible above. And what's that?"

It worked. They started pointing out rock formations and islands, famous beaches, the lighthouse at Makapuu Point, and Blowhole Lookout where water blows out of a hole in the rock like a geyser. Just after we passed Koko Crater, our captain paused at the mouth of Hanauma Bay. The horseshoe-shaped bay, filled with snorkelers and a cornucopia of colorful fish, was recommended as a must-see-and-do. Our host then throttled up for the famous Diamond Head Crater, pointing out the lighthouse and the World War II battlements still in place on the top.

He named the famous hotels along Waikiki Beach as we passed, and eased the boat into a dock at the harbor.

"Is this close enough? You can catch a cab to the airport."

"Yes, thank you, so much. I hope we didn't take you too far out of your way."

"No, as a matter of fact, we keep our boat not too far from here, and it was your nickel, you know," he added with a throaty laugh.

He pointed out the telephone on the pier, and we waved goodbye. As we turned to leave, I heard the words " . . . idle rich are getting younger. . . ."

Bart loved that. He grabbed my waist and pulled me close. "Did you hear that, 'idle rich'?" He laughed.

"Well, actually, I'm not rich. My mother is. I'm certainly not idle. You keep me busier dodging bad guys than I've ever been in my life!"

"We don't even have to call for a cab. There's one waiting." Bart waved at the driver and he pulled forward.

"Airport, please." We climbed inside, and I nestled in the crook of Bart's arm, relaxing, confident we'd finally shaken whoever was following us.

What did they want? I guess it could be me. Mom (I still found it hard to comprehend!) was worth many millions of dollars. As her only child, I was the natural heir. It was logical they would expect a fortune in ransom, but somehow that scenario just didn't feel right to me. Maybe it was because I wasn't used to having money. Had I been raised as an heiress, would I feel differently?

I shook my head involuntarily.

"Yes?" Bart looked down.

I started to explain, then caught the driver's eye in the rearview mirror.

"Nothing," I said, snuggling closer. "Just some dragons that you'll have to chase away." I settled in for a peaceful ride to the airport.

It would be the last peace I'd enjoy for a long time.

Chapter Seven

It was dusk when we took off for the Big Island with a glorious sunset behind us. As we settled into our seats on the plane, I turned to Bart. He held up his hand.

"I've been waiting for the barrage. I'm sorry, Princess, I don't have any answers for you . . . but I am concerned for your safety." He held my hands in both of his, leaning close. "I couldn't live with myself if I thought I'd brought you into danger, if it were my fault all of this is happening to you."

"I'm not afraid, just puzzled. The more I think about it, the more I have to think they're after ransom. But then, again, why bother stealing my luggage when they could have simply grabbed me anytime they wanted? I'm baffled. And I'm angry they're spoiling my honeymoon."

"I hope that's behind us and we can relax and enjoy ourselves. What do you want to do on Hawaii?"

"I want a hotel room that isn't bugged, and I want to go shopping. And tomorrow I want to fly over the volcano. I *really* want to see it up close."

"The hotel we can take care of immediately. I'm not sure about the shopping until tomorrow."

"But I don't even have a nightgown or a toothbrush."

A wicked smile creased Bart's face. "Tsk, tsk. How terrible."

"If this is an example of what being married to you will be like,

I'd better carry a bag instead of a purse and keep a toothbrush, makeup, and a change of underwear with me at all times."

"Smart girl."

When we landed in Hilo, it was dark and only one car rental agency was still open. Their choice of cars was limited—white sedan or a little yellow convertible.

"No white sedans, please. Let's go for the convertible."

"It's more money, my frugal little princess."

"I don't care. I don't want to see another white sedan, much less drive one! I don't want anything to remind me of the purple and white shirt or Pachy and his portly pal."

"Gotcha. The convertible it is. Decision time again. Do you want the first available hotel room, a resort hotel, or a little Mom-and-Pop we can get lost in?"

"Resort hotels have shops in the lobby. I could buy a toothbrush and a nightshirt."

"Now why would you want to do that?" Bart wiggled his eyebrows playfully.

We found a hotel, registered, explained that our luggage would arrive later, and located the shops before they closed. I selected a loose flowing cotton dress, a necessity in Hawaii's humidity. I also found a pair of shorts and a T-shirt—the other wardrobe essentials—a pair of sandals, and to Bart's dismay, a triple-extra-large T-shirt to sleep in. On impulse, I grabbed a silk scarf. That would be more comfortable than a wig for a quick disguise.

"Aren't you going to get anything?"

"What do I need? I have you."

"A change of clothes for tomorrow."

"You don't like these?"

I pulled a face and pointed to the men's side of the small shop. Two shirts, shorts, and a pair of casual slacks later, plus toiletries, we headed upstairs to discover what kind of accommodations we had for the night. All I really cared about was a hot shower and a bed . . . with no bugs, electronic or otherwise.

Our room boasted a romantic ocean view. Walking straight through to the balcony, I was drenched in moonlight. The silvery reflection of the biggest moon I'd ever seen shimmered on the water, playing peek-a-boo through the black silhouette of waving palms.

I slipped back into the room, crooked my finger to Bart to follow me, turned the lights off, and returned to the moonlight. He followed me to the railing, wrapping me from behind in his arms. I leaned contentedly against him.

"Star light, star bright, first star I see tonight. Wish I may, wish I might, have the wish I wish tonight."

"And what is your wish, Princess?"

"That the world would go away and leave us alone to enjoy each other. That all the bad guys be carted off to an island in shark-infested waters and left without a boat so they couldn't get off. Then I'd have you all to myself."

He turned me to face him and tilted my chin up. Even in the moonlight, the worried expression on the face of this incredibly handsome husband of mine was clear.

"Sorry already you married me?"

"Never. How could I be sorry when it's what I've wanted since I was six years old? I'm just sorry they wouldn't leave us alone long enough to enjoy our honeymoon. I knew what I was getting into when I married an agent. I came in with my eyes wide open. From now on, I guess I'll have to keep them half-closed."

Bart held me close. "Only as far as my faults and failings go. You've got to remember what I told you, Princess—"

I quickly put my fingers across his lips. "Not tonight. We left that on Oahu. Tonight it's just you and me. I only need one thing to make this night absolutely perfect, besides you, of course."

"And that is?"

"A hot shower."

"I have it in my power to grant your fondest wish. I'll even scrub your back."

"I'll reciprocate with pleasure."

Later, once we were clean and refreshed, Bart asked if I'd like to get something to eat.

"I don't want to venture from this room. I'm afraid if we do, the magic spell will be broken."

"How about room service?"

"No, if anyone else came in, it would still break the spell."

"Would you like me to go down and get you something?"

"I don't need anything but you." Suddenly it dawned on me that this big hunk of man was probably starving to death. "I'm sorry, Bart. How selfish of me. Would you like something to eat?"

"As a matter of fact, yes."

"Thanks for being honest. I wouldn't want you to suffer silently because I'm so selfish I didn't want anything to spoil the mood. Some mood if you're starving!"

"I promise I'll set another one just like it, if that will make you happy."

"Granted."

"But let's send for room service so you won't have to get dressed again."

"You don't like what I'm wearing?" I said, holding out my super-sized T-shirt that came almost to my knees.

He grinned wickedly again. "What I'd prefer you wear, or don't wear, wouldn't be appropriate in public."

After room service had delivered sustenance for my hungry husband, we snuggled down together in the dark as moonbeams danced through the open balcony door. I felt totally at peace as I lay in Bart's arms, no longer worried about Nate or Purple-shirt. The two of us were alone, and my world was in perfect order—at least, I thought it was as I drifted off to sleep.

"Wake me just before sunup," I murmured sleepily. "I don't want to miss the emerald fire."

* * * * * * * *

Though the moon was no longer framed in our open door, I could tell it was still high by the moonlight on the palm trees. I'd been sleeping soundly. What had awakened me? Raising up on one elbow to see over Bart's shoulder, I heard a sound on the adjacent balcony. *What are the people next door doing to make such a strange noise?*

There it was again. I started to get up to investigate when Bart stirred, aware that I was no longer cuddled against him. As I rounded the end of the bed, he raised up.

"Something wrong?" he asked quietly.

"There's a weird noise out here. It woke me," I whispered back.

Instantly Bart was on his feet, gun in hand, moving noiselessly into the shadows. And none too soon. An arm reached around the pillar dividing the balconies and grasped the railing. Then a head, and a leg, and the whole body appeared, paused to listen, then swung over the railing onto our balcony. As the intruder turned his back to reach something around the corner, Bart threw him to the patio on his face. Bart had his knee in the middle of the man's back and the trespasser's arms twisted grotesquely toward his shoulders.

"Who are you and what do you want?" Bart demanded quietly.

The intruder moaned and spouted a string of expletives. Bart put his full weight in the man's back and twisted his arms higher.

"Watch your language. There's a lady present. Who are you working for and what are you doing here? Tell me now, or I'll render these arms useless and break your back!"

"Stop! I'll tell you. Nate sent me. He wants it back."

"He wants what back?"

Before he could answer, a muffled pop came from the next balcony. The man went limp. His head thumped to the floor. Bart jumped to his feet and started around the pillar. The door to that room slammed shut. Bart changed directions and flew past me into the corridor.

Everything had happened so fast that we were still without lights. I turned them on. Kneeling, I felt for a pulse. The man was dead, a small bullet hole in the back of his head.

Why didn't the assassin shoot Bart? He was a bigger target. What wasn't this man supposed to tell? What did Nate want back? How did they trace us?

Since I could do nothing for this unfortunate fellow, I hurried to follow Bart. As I turned the knob, the door flew open, nearly bowling me over.

A red-faced Bart entered. "He got away."

"Probably a good thing. It might have been a little embarrassing, chasing through the lobby the way you're dressed."

He nodded ruefully. "It wasn't until I reached the elevator that I discovered I had on heart-covered boxers and nothing more. Not exactly dressed for the public. Is he . . . ?"

"Yes, he's dead."

"I guess we have to call the police again."

"Bart, how did they find us? He said Nate wanted his what back?"

"He didn't get that far."

"We didn't bring anything with us that could have been bugged. All I have is my purse."

"Dump it out while I call Lt. Nakamura on Oahu so he can notify whoever he wants to come and get the body."

I spread the contents of my purse on the bed, examining everything thoroughly. I shook my head at Bart as he reported to Lt. Nakamura.

"What am I looking for?"

Bart put his hand over the mouthpiece. "Anything that looks similar to the electronic devices we found in our room at Turtle Bay . . . maybe smaller."

I examined my wallet, lipstick, pen, mascara, package of gum, fingernail file and clippers, bandages for Bart's cut, extra bandages for my knees, antibiotic salve, and the bottle of lotion Mom had given me. I turned it upside down examining it, twisted the top off, and put some lotion on my shaking hands while I had it handy. Nothing.

"Thanks, Lt. Nakamura. We'll wait for them to come for the body."

"Bart, I can't find anything. You look. You know better what you're looking for."

Bart's search was as fruitless as mine.

"How could they have followed us? I thought we'd lost them. Were they watching us all the time? Were they on the airplane with us? How did they find us if they weren't? Do I have something implanted in me they can tune in to? Our honeymoon has transmogrified into a science fiction movie!" I wailed, the danger of our situation hitting me like a fist, sending shockwaves through my system.

Bart yanked the sheet off the bed, covering the body on the patio—the body I carefully kept my back to. Then he pulled me close to him, wrapping me in his arms to quell the quivering I couldn't seem to stop.

"At this point, Princess, I can't answer even one of your questions. I don't know how they found us. I don't see a bug. We got rid of everything in the hotel room that the de-bugger found. And I don't know why they're following us."

"I can't believe Nate's set on spoiling our honeymoon! Wait till I get my hands on that weasel." I was no longer frightened—I was furious!

Bart rolled me back onto the bed. "What will you do to that weasel, my petite princess?"

It was hard to stay mad with two piercing blue eyes gazing mischievously into mine, above lips that continually interfered with what I was trying to say.

Several minutes later, we were interrupted by a knock on the door.

"Police!"

I was still in my nightshirt, and Bart was in his heart-covered boxers.

"Do we greet the police this way, or get dressed before I open the door?" I laughed nervously.

Bart grabbed at his clothes while I went to the door in my nightshirt.

"Mrs. Allan?" A pleasant-faced detective flashed his badge and introduced himself as Lt. Ishigo. He immediately put me at ease, but something about his companion, Sgt. Luomala, made me uncomfortable. He made my skin crawl, like standing next to someone who has a disease and you're afraid if you get too close, you'll catch it.

"I understand you had an uninvited guest tonight."

I sat on the edge of the bed while Bart recounted the details he had already told Lt. Nakamura in Oahu.

"Any idea what they were after?"

"No, but I wish I knew," I interjected. "I'd be glad to let them have it if they'd just leave us alone."

He turned back to Bart. Bart shrugged.

"We have no idea. He was about to tell us when someone interrupted him."

"Maybe you could venture a guess as to what they'd want bad enough to kill one of their own to keep him from telling you."

"Lieutenant," I started, not even trying to hide the frustration I was feeling, "we left Oahu to get away from these creeps. They tried to take our luggage three different times, in three different cities, broke into our room twice, assaulted my husband, tried to kidnap me, and have been watching us continually. We abandoned our luggage, willing to give them whatever was there, came with nothing except the clothes we had on and my purse, and they still tracked us. We've both gone over every inch of my purse and its contents trying to figure out how they followed us and what they want. If you can find something, be my guest."

Lt. Ishigo tossed my purse to Sgt. Luomala while he continued to question Bart.

Another knock sounded at the door. I looked at Lt. Ishigo.

"Probably the coroner's crew. Would you mind?"

As I let them in, Bart said, "Is there any reason why my wife can't take a shower while they clean up here? She has an aversion to dead bodies."

Gratefully, I escaped into the bathroom with my shopping bag of new clothes. Was this what my life was going to be like married to a special agent? Nothing but bad guys, bugs, and bodies? It sounded like the name of a book. Bart had warned me, and I knew, but I didn't imagine it would be quite so intensive. I scrubbed vigorously. Why did I always feel so dirty when I came into physical contact with one of these low-lifes? As I emerged from the bathroom, dressed and refreshed, the sun was just peeking over the horizon.

"He did it again!" I exclaimed.

"Who did what?" Bart turned to me puzzled.

"The emerald fire. Nate prevented me from seeing the emerald fire."

Lt. Ishigo smiled as he backed toward the door. "I think we're through here. We'll try to stay out of the honeymooners' way if you'll stop delivering bodies to us. You will make sure we can get hold of you?"

"Yes. We promised Nakamura we'd keep him informed, too."

"If you find Nate before we do, try to keep him in one piece so we can get to the bottom of this."

He backed out of the door grinning at Bart. I turned to catch

Bart laughing.

"What's so funny? Did I miss out on a joke?"

"Probably."

"I'll bet he thinks I'm a shrew."

"No, but I think he's a little concerned he might have another murder on his hands if you get to Nate before he does."

I maneuvered to see behind Bart.

"Yes, he's gone. Ready to call it quits, Princess?"

"You mean go home? No way. No one, including Nate, is going to prevent me from seeing this volcano up close, no matter what!"

Chapter Eight

We were booked on the 9:00 helicopter ride over Volcanoes National Park. To say I was excited would be an understatement. Not only was I looking forward to this most spectacular of nature's displays, I was anxious to put Nate and the dead body out of my mind for a while. What could Nate possibly want?

Bart had placed another call to Dad last night to bring him up to date. He wasn't happy at all with the news of the murder, and suggested that he and Mom join us as soon as possible, if we didn't mind, since we didn't appear to be having much of a honeymoon anyway. We both agreed it was a good idea. Maybe they could solve this mystery.

Bart interrupted the silence. "Penny for your thoughts."

"They're not worth a penny today. You wouldn't get your money's worth."

"Does that mean you're not thinking about me, or you are thinking about me?" he teased.

As we arrived at Hilo airport, a dark cloud loomed over us.

"I hope that isn't a portent of things to come."

"What that portends is an upcoming shower." He pulled over to put the top up on the convertible.

We hurried into the terminal in a light shower, but by time we finished all the paperwork for our helicopter ride, the dark cloud had moved on, leaving a deep blue sky full of puffy white clouds in its wake.

We weren't alone on the helicopter. Joining us was a balding, paunchy man in a bright Hawaiian shirt and clashing shorts with black shoes and socks. His wife had thin, straggly hair and wore a garishly colored muumuu, straw hat, and camera. Her shrill, peevish voice whined incessantly at their two children who constantly poked and pinched each other and were generally obnoxious. They were the type of tourists cartoonists draw, the kind you meticulously avoid being near.

I glanced at Bart. "This is not what I had in mind," I whispered.

"It's okay. Once we get in the helicopter, all you'll be able to hear is what comes over your earphones."

He was right. Our pilot introduced himself as Don and gave his pre-flight monologue. We were preparing for take off when he held up one hand. "Wait a minute, folks. We're getting some new instructions here."

He listened a minute on his headphones, then spoke into ours. "I have an emergency call. Everybody sit tight, and I'll be right back." He shut down the engine and ran across the pad to the little brown shack just inside the gate.

Sherrie, the guide who'd oriented and seated us on the helicopter, came running back looking upset.

"Don will be a few minutes. We have another helicopter with two open seats you can take right now if you'd rather not wait," she said to Bart and me. "Pete's our newest pilot, and his charter hasn't been filled up yet."

I smiled with relief as Bart grinned and winked. My volcano trip might be salvaged after all. Sherrie led us to a helicopter already warming up on another pad. It was too noisy to talk, but she motioned us to the front seat. I was thrilled. I'd have a perfect view.

Pete handed us our earphones and welcomed us all on board. I buckled my seatbelt, and as the door slammed, I took stock of the pilot as he gave the lift-off signal. Athletic-looking, early forties, he sported a scar that ran from behind his ear into his shirt collar.

I turned to Bart as the helicopter rose off the pad and could tell by the look on his face he didn't like what he saw behind us. Prickles went up the back of my neck when I checked out the other passengers. Too late. The helicopter was already airborne. Adjusting the fanny pack around his waist that contained his gun, Bart rested his hand lightly on it.

Pete explained about the macadamia nut farms as we flew over, pointing out the smoldering volcano ahead, but my mind was far from the volcano right now. My fellow passengers did not look like men interested in the volcano. What were they doing here? Had we been followed again?

My ears perked up when Pete said we were fortunate—a new lava flow this morning afforded us a view that most people didn't get to see.

Momentarily I forgot the pair in the back and leaned forward, gazing with awe at the white smoke billowing forth from the crater ahead of us. I could do without the canned Hawaiian music piped over my earphones. I'd have preferred to hear more about Pele, the goddess of the volcano. I wanted to know what powers the Hawaiians ascribed to her . . . how they'd come to believe so fiercely in her.

Pete maneuvered the helicopter over the top of the fiery red river coursing slowly from a vent hole in the side of the volcano. It was like nothing I'd ever seen before—liquid fire languidly consuming everything flammable in its path.

But now came the real treat. As Pete flew to the top of the Pu'u O'o vent of Kilauea, he intoned "the world's most active volcano." Nothing had prepared me for this steaming cone of boiling, bubbling 2500-degree fireworks. The bottom of the crater was huge, the size of several footballs fields, but it was obscured by billowing clouds of steam. Pete dipped the helicopter low so we could catch a glimpse of the seething red-hot lava in the bottom.

As I turned to Bart with excitement, I was stunned to see a gun pressed against the bandage behind his ear. When I pivoted to see the man holding the gun, a hard metal object jammed into my temple. Bart carefully, slowly, went for his gun. The steel barrel smashed into Bart's hand. He winced with pain as a hairy hand reached around, relieving Bart of his weapon.

Pete's voice, different now, grimly filled our headphones.

"Folks, there's been a slight change of plans. We're going to do a little detour here. The lady wants a helicopter ride over the volcano, and we're going to make sure she gets a real up-close view, minus excess baggage."

The helicopter dropped down and hovered over the rim, so close I felt I could reach out and grab a handful of ash and cinders. We straddled the rim of the cone.

Suddenly Bart's headphones were jerked off, and the gun barrel crashed against the side of his head. As Bart slumped unconscious against the door, the hairy hands undid his seat belt, opened the door, and shoved his limp body out of the helicopter.

"No!" I screamed, grabbing for Bart in vain. Strong hands pinned me against the seat. I clawed at my seat belt and the hands gripping me as Pete dipped the helicopter to see where Bart's body had landed.

"That was a lousy shot! He was supposed to go *in* the volcano, not straddle the rim," a voice whined in the earphones.

"It's all right," Pete assured him. "When he wakes up and starts moving around on that loose ash, he'll slide right into Pele's waiting arms."

I've got to save Bart, I thought frantically. *But how?* I slumped against the seat, letting my head fall back, as if I'd fainted. They bought the act. The hands relaxed on my shoulders. Through half-shut eyes, I saw one man leaning towards his window to watch Bart.

Pete made another low pass over Bart's still body. Taking my captors by surprise, I lunged for the door and hurled myself out into open space, planning to land next to my unconscious husband. To say I miscalculated would be a gross understatement.

Landing head first in the loose ash and cinders on the rim of the cone, I started slipping down into the crater, creating a landslide I couldn't stop. Grasping, reaching, clawing for any hold to stop the wild plunge toward the seething cauldron below, my arms became a bleeding mass of cuts and scratches from the sharp cinders. My mouth quickly filled with dust and ash.

Right into Pele's waiting arms! I thought as I slid downward into the sulphurous smoke billowing from below. *Does one burn to death slowly, or is the lava so hot you die instantly?* I renewed my frenzied efforts to stop this descent into hell. It seemed forever before I stopped. I lay stunned, fearing to stir. I hurt all over.

Finally I moved gingerly. Then I froze. The small ledge I was lying on, barely wide enough to hold me, began to shift.

But I was being strangled by the leather strap on my purse. In order to have both hands free to get into the helicopter, I'd looped my purse strap across one shoulder with the bag on the opposite hip. It had saved my life. The strap, catching on a sharp piece of cinder, had slowed my fall enough to allow me to stay on this tiny ledge, instead of slipping down past it.

Could I sit up? Each movement brought another shower of cinders down on me. How stable was the ledge? Would it hold, or would any movement send it and me plummeting the rest of the way into the volcano?

I needed to move, to assess my situation, to see how I could get out of here. Bart! Where was Bart?

I moved an inch at a time, rotating very carefully, tucking my legs up and around until I was sitting on the little ledge with my feet hanging over. My lungs burned. I coughed. The sulphur fumes would get me if Pele didn't. The scarf in my purse! I tied it, bandana style, over my nose and mouth.

Twisting slightly so I could look up over my shoulder to the top of the volcano, I tried to see Bart. Had he moved and slid on down past me, or had he managed to roll down the other side to safety? I couldn't see him. I could see the helicopter, could hear its thunder even above the grumbling of the volcano and whistling of the wind. I could feel it as it swept low, vibrating the ledge, causing cinderslides all around me.

I waved the helicopter away. But now there were other helicopters buzzing lower, I'm sure, than their normal tour allowed them. I tried counting through the swirling clouds—three blue and white ones, two yellow and orange, and a shiny black job. Couldn't they see what they were doing? They were loosening the cinders! Would my ledge hold? Pointing to the slides, I motioned the helicopters off. How could they get me out if every time they came close, my precarious perch threatened to slide away, too?

My knees and legs burned, and my hands and elbows were a

mass of shredded flesh. I couldn't see Bart so I focused on picking the sharp cinders from my bleeding skin while I figured out what to do next.

I had been seen. Surely they could figure a way to get me out of here. All they needed was a rope ladder or net or chair like they used to rescue people from floods or mountain ravines. Rescue units had perfected their methods, but then, how often did they have to pluck someone from inside a volcano?

I thought of Mom and Dad. What a short time we'd had together as a family. It wasn't fair. Last week I'd finally seen my dad face-to-face after twenty years of only telepathic images and impressions to let me know he was alive.

Oh, Dad. What would you do if you were here?

He was here! Dad was here! I received a strong image of Mom and Dad in Hawaii. They must have caught the first flight out last night or at oh-dark-thirty this morning. I telepathed my message . . . *trapped on a ledge inside the volcano . . . Bart unconscious somewhere.*

"Ohhhhhhh!" The rock I was sitting on shuddered beneath me, and the whole crater rumbled and seemed to shift. I looked down, past my dangling feet. The bright, orange-red liquid below bubbled higher, leaping in small explosions of color. Thick clouds of sulfurous gas spewed forth, gagging me, even through the bandana I had tied around my face.

She's after me, Dad, I telepathed. *Pele's after me.*

The image of my father was gone as quickly as it had come. My throat burned, as did my eyes. Had I been hallucinating? Was Dad really close, or were the fumes getting to me? The bubbling increased. Eruptions of fiery lava flew higher, Pele throwing her fireballs toward me, her fingers reaching out to me. Moving cautiously, I tucked my feet up on the ledge, leaving the strap around my shoulder and neck, and pulled my purse around so I was sitting on it. My rock was getting hot as the boiling below intensified. The purse was lumpy and uncomfortable, but better than burned buns.

Where was Bart? Had he rolled down the other side? Or had he . . . no! I wouldn't think of that. He would be safe. *Please make him be safe,* I prayed, *and while you're at it, don't let my guardian angels take a Twinkie break right now, God.*

I thought about the faith of those young families as they lay their hands on that tiny infant's head. I heard Michael's simple prayer, remembered the trust in his eyes. *Dear God, help me have that kind of faith, and please get me out of here alive.*

A momentary peace settled over me. My prayer had been acknowledged. Then I heard the helicopter again. A blue and white one this time, coming closer. The rotors stirred the cinders up around me. My precarious perch vibrated violently. I tried to wave the chopper off. It started a landslide on either side of my ledge.

A voice came out of the smoke. "The ladder. Grab the ladder."

Yes, there was a ladder. It was close, but not close enough. The helicopter pulled up, turned and came back again. I watched for it through the smoke. Another rumble came from deep within the bowels of the volcano. I glanced down. Pele was angry. Her fireballs exploded closer now.

The helicopter dipped low. This time I barely missed the ladder. They'd found the range, but who would get me first—Pele or the helicopter?

It pulled away and swung around, once more dangling the ladder tantalizingly close. Again I missed, and again. I didn't dare stand up; I didn't dare move any more than just to reach out. The rumblings shuddered through me, and the smoke thickened. I gasped for air. There was none—only noxious gas. My lungs ached. My throat burned. I could barely see—barely breathe.

What had I read about the legend of Pele? The islanders made offerings to appease her, and she responded. What could I give her? What do women love? I looked at my emerald. If I didn't get out of here, it wouldn't do me any good. If I could appease her . . .

Superstition. It was all superstition. I had a more powerful God who'd heard my prayer. Another rumble and the entire volcano trembled. It was as if Pele had read my mind, knew I had dismissed her as less powerful, and was determined to prove her power. Maybe I'd better cover all avenues here. I pulled the ring from my finger and started to throw it as far as I could into the bubbling cauldron below.

What am I doing? Pele isn't real. She's a pagan goddess. Make believe. She couldn't possibly have the power to save me—or destroy me. I put the ring back on my finger.

"Sorry, Pele. I almost lost my head there for a minute and threw away the most precious possession I have with me. That might have made you happy, but it certainly wouldn't have shown much faith and confidence in God, would it?"

Was it my imagination? Was there one final spectacular explosion of raging liquid fire before the smoke began to thin? Was the boiling mass of hot lava simply simmering now? The bubbling, gurgling, eruptions of lava had subsided. It wasn't my imagination. *Thank you, God.*

Neither was the helicopter merely my imagination. It was very real, and this time the ladder was dangling close. Dare I stand up and reach for it? No. I was dizzy, giddy from the gas. I didn't trust my sense of balance.

Suddenly the smoke cleared enough for the pilot to deliver the ladder right into my hands. Reaching out, I grabbed it, clinging with all my might. I got one leg through a rung. Nothing could shake me loose now!

I heard a whoop and a holler from above, and the helicopter rose straight up into the clear blue sky, out of the heat, out of the smoke, the cinders, and the sulphur. Tears streamed down my face from the gas, but also tears of thanksgiving, tears of joy, though those were tempered by my fear for Bart.

As we cleared the rim of the cone, I searched the edge and the slope of the volcano for him. Where was my husband?

I felt the ladder being hoisted into the helicopter. My eyes burned so badly I could hardly see. My head bumped on the runners, then strong arms reached for me, pulling me, ladder and all into the open cockpit of the helicopter and safety.

I sank into the seat, leaning against my rescuer.

"Thank you. Thank you so much. *Mahalo,*" I croaked, throat raspy and sore.

"That's quite all right, Mrs. Allan. You didn't think for a minute we'd let you get away so easily. Not when we needed you so badly."

Whirling around, I stared straight into the sneering faces of the very men I'd jumped from the helicopter to escape.

Chapter Nine

"This time we'll be takin' no chances. Tie her up good and tight."

I sank weakly back into the seat, allowing them to tie my hands and feet. I had no strength left to fight. My throat hurt too badly to try to make myself heard above the roar of the helicopter.

Did they think they could simply fly away with me? Opening my smarting eyes, I scanned the skies. Half a dozen helicopters hovered nearby. Surely these thugs wouldn't be allowed to cart me off under the very noses of newsmen and charter helicopters filled with tourists who had witnessed my rescue!

My captors waved, thumbs up, pretending they'd successfully accomplished a good deed. One by one the helicopters peeled away to continue their tour of Volcanoes National Park by air, except for one. The paparazzi.

Stick with me, guys. I'll never bad-mouth you again. Stay with me. Then I lost sight of their chopper. *Were they following us?*

A small, skinny guy grabbed my arm and wiped it with a cotton ball.

"No! You can't do that! No!" But already I felt the needle plunge deep into my arm.

A voice, close to my ear said, "It's all right. We'll let the news crew film us rushing you from the helicopter to a waiting ambulance. Only you won't go to no hospital."

Then black velvet covered my eyes, my mind, and I sank into oblivion.

* * * * * *

Pele reached out for me again, drawing her fiery fingers across my skin, burning me with every touch. I thought I'd escaped. Did they throw me back? She tugged at my hand. *You want my emerald, Pele?*

I tried to give it to her, but my hand wouldn't move. Nor would my arm. That was okay. I hurt too much to move anyway. If she wanted it, she could take it.

Men's voices. Not Pele. I struggled to open my eyes. I felt sick, nauseous . . . and I hurt. I hurt everywhere. My mouth was dry and cottony, my tongue so swollen it nearly gagged me.

"Leave her be. She'll come around sooner or later." It was a rough voice—a voice I knew. One I didn't like—a voice associated with noise. A helicopter. I tried again to open my eyes. They wouldn't work. A door banged. It was quiet.

Where was I? Trying again to move, I found my body still would not respond. Was I paralyzed? I wiggled my toes and fingers. They were all right. I was tied to a cot. I felt the canvas with my fingers, and the wooden frame. A camp cot. I struggled to open my eyes, but they were swollen shut, probably from the sulfur dioxide and hydrogen sulfide of the volcano.

I slept, drifting in and out of consciousness, for how long I couldn't tell. Eventually I could open my eyes. They grew accustomed to a light above me, a single dim bulb hanging from the ceiling. The tiny room was empty except for this filthy cot. It was covered with animal hair, and probably fleas. I checked my bindings, which turned out to be strips of grubby, greasy rags. I shuddered involuntarily. The floor was dirt. No windows. One sagging door.

Dad. Can you hear me? I concentrated on sending a message to my father. *I'm not in the volcano anymore.*

The impression I received was of frantic parents.

Dad, I telepathed. *Is Bart okay? Did you find Bart?*

Not words, just images, impressions. They'd heard the report of the rescue, but when news crews arrived at the hospital, there was no ambulance.

Dad, what about Bart? Did you find Bart? Is he okay?

I got the impression of a bandaged hand and head. And worry.

Could I help them find me?

Good question. In my foggy state, I wasn't sure whether I was projecting telepathically, or just hallucinating. Was Dad receiving my jumble of thoughts?

Pete could have made sure Bart landed in the volcano instead of on the rim with a chance to survive. He'd purposely saved Bart's life. Why? And there was something about the little man in the chopper, something in the back of my mind . . .

Yes! He smelled like a hospital and he had on scrubs. He said they had an ambulance waiting. I concentrated on sending that message to Dad. Had he received it? Where was he? Where was I? What would happen when my captors returned?

I couldn't just lie here waiting for them to reappear. Whatever they'd given me was beginning to wear off, and my tendency to claustrophobia was beginning to kick in. I was bound to the cot at my knees, hips, shoulders, and my wrists with strips of dirty cotton fabric. I wiggled and squirmed, but each ankle was individually tied to the legs of the cot with wide strips of rags, as were my hands. I'd have to work from the top down. And quickly. Throat-tightening fear—claustrophobic panic—began to overwhelm me.

Wriggling and scooting as far to the foot of the cot as I could get, in a movement to make a contortionist envious, I laid my head close to my shoulder and squirmed under the rag binding my shoulders. Fear and phobia were powerful motivators. Now for the hips.

I wiggled my way back to the head of the cot as far as I could go, working my bonds down past my hips. Slipping my hands into the holes at the side of the canvas, and with my legs tied to the foot of the cot, a sit-up was easy. Then I surveyed the situation. What good had I done? What had I accomplished besides exhausting myself totally?

I couldn't free my hands. I couldn't free my feet. There was nothing in the room, except this cot and me—and my purse. They'd left my purse on the floor beside me. It had survived a descent into the volcano and the ascent out as well, and it looked it. Its contents were strewn all over the dirt floor and my wallet was open. Oh, well. Maybe the few hundred dollars they'd found would keep them happy long enough for me to get out of here.

With my hands still stuck down in the holes at the side of the cot, I could bend down to the rag tied around my knees. I could probably tear it apart a thread at a time with my teeth. How badly did I need freedom? Bad enough to put that filthy rag in my mouth? Where had it been? What dog had slept on it—or worse? I shuddered.

Okay, girl. This is no time to be squeamish. You've got to get out of this predicament as fast as you can.

Leaning forward, I took the awful rag between my teeth, trying not to touch my lips to it. Grinding my teeth back and forth much as I did to break thread when I sewed a button on, I severed several threads, then had to straighten up and take a deep breath. I didn't want to think what germs might be even now invading my system. Pleasant thoughts. Think of Bart. Picture his smile, his blue eyes, his gentle touch, his arms waiting to hold me. Chew some more rag. Then rest. Chew. Rest.

Think happy thoughts. Think honeymoon without Nate and his mischief-makers. Chew on the rag. Remember pleasant memories. The good feeling in the house of Megan and Tapata—a tiny, modest apartment filled with love. Chew on the dirty rag. Think freedom.

Now there were only a few strands left. I couldn't stifle the urge to be free long enough to bite through the remaining threads. I popped my knees up as high as I could get them, straining against the strands as they painfully cut into my scraped, bloodied knees, which were still filled with cinders. The worn threads broke.

I needed my hands free. Could I shred my bonds against the sharp metal edge of the frame? Maneuvering the grimy fabric into position took a few minutes, then I finally found the right motion— the movement that hooked and broke a thread at a time. Rub and pull. Rub and pull, being careful not to rub my wrists raw or tear my flesh against the metal hinge as I tore the fabric.

My shoulders ached with the movement. I longed to lie down

and rest, but feared the return of my captors. I had no idea how long they'd been gone or when they'd return. At last—one hand was free!

I knew I had a fingernail file in my purse, but the bag wasn't within reach with my left wrist still tied to the cot. I reached out again, leaning all my weight to one side. The cot tipped over, dumping me within range of my purse and the file. I quickly sawed through the bond holding my left hand. But I'd be here all night on the torn T-shirt that tied my feet.

The strips of T-shirt wound around my ankles were knotted under the cot. My fingers, stiff and sore from tight bonds and shredded from trying to stop my fall in the volcano, fumbled unsuccessfully with the knots. I tried the one around my hip, which was knotted under the cot as well. Luckily, this one was a simple matter of rotating the knot from the bottom, sliding it around to my lap. Using my fingernail file as a pry in the folds, I untied the knot.

But how to get to the knots around my ankles? My problem seemed compounded as I writhed on the dirt floor of the shack with the cot whacking me as I struggled. I was tired of bumps and bruises and hurting—and dirt!

What could I use? I rummaged through my purse. Had they missed something when they emptied the contents on the floor? Snagged on the fabric lining of one pocket, I found my fingernail clippers.

A few well-placed snips and I was free. Quickly I scooped my belongings off the dirt floor and back into my purse. As I stooped, my knees cracked and bled. A little lotion would help. Did I dare take the time? From under the cot, I painfully retrieved the pearl-shaped bottle of lotion.

The top quarter of the bottle twisted off, but slipped out of my clumsy fingers and rolled back under the cot. Stooping to get it, I cracked my battered knees further. It was then I heard the first sound since the men left. They were returning.

Abandoning the cap under the cot, I stuffed a tissue in the neck of the bottle and dropped the lotion in my purse, slipping out the drooping door into a jungle. Bushes hugged the shack and trees towered over it. I was grateful for the moonlight that filtered through foliage. Darting behind the nearest tree, I stopped to think.

Where would they be least likely to look for me when they discovered I was gone? Where they had just come from! My best bet would be to head straight for them on the trail, getting as far as I could, and slip off until they passed.

Had the moon been lower, I couldn't have moved so fast, but it was directly overhead so I had no trouble making my way down the narrow little slit through the trees. As I moved, my aching body reminded me, acutely, of what a beating it had taken today.

The voices sounded closer now. I pushed my tired body to get as far down the path as I possibly could before I met them.

The shack had to have been on the top of a good-sized hill. I was descending rapidly—then the little trail took a sharp turn. As lights drew nearer and voices louder, I slipped off the trail into the dense bushes.

"Why didn't he tell us what he wanted? We could have got it the first time and wouldn'ta had to hike back up the stinkin' hill. What does he think we are, a couple of goats?"

I couldn't hear the answer of the softer-voiced one, but the booming-voice one replied, "No, I didn't tell him we were holding her for ransom. He'd kill me!"

They came close enough now to hear the one with the softer voice.

"You don't think he'll find out?"

"Nah," the Boomer almost yelled, puffing from the exertion of the climb. "Nate's headed back to Hong Kong as soon as he gets whatever she's got. Said he's got an emergency to deal with back there that can't wait. He said to take her home after I got it, which we'll do, as soon as her folks cough up the money. He said she's not to be roughed up at all. Good thing he can't see what that volcano did to her."

They moved on up the hill, but I didn't wait to hear anything else. I hurried down the trail as fast as my wobbly, aching legs would take me.

The steeply sloping path leveled abruptly into a clearing. I found myself on the beach before I had time to stop and reconnoiter. Bart's instructions had been "Look before you move." On one side a stretch of sand gleamed in the moonlight with waves lapping gently against the shore. On the other, a high wrought-iron fence with an ornate gate led to gardens and a huge house that seemed out of place on the beach.

As I wavered between seeking friendly forces down the beach or taking a chance with the house, a masculine voice, low and melodious, spoke from somewhere nearby.

"Welcome, Allison. I've been waiting for you. I was sure you could quickly outwit those two."

I whirled to see who was at my elbow, but I was alone in the moonlight. Then lights flooded the area and the wrought-iron gates swung open.

"Come in, my dear. There's a hot bath waiting, a bed with fresh, clean sheets, a change of clothes, medication for your legs and hands, and safety from your pursuers."

"Who are you? Where are you?"

Again the voice, calm, close, comforting, spoke.

"I'm a friend, Allison. Right now, you need a friend. I haven't time to explain because I'm late for a very important appointment. You'll forgive me if I have to leave you alone. Once you enter the gate, you'll be safe. They can't penetrate the electric fence. Please accept my hospitality and my apologies for not being a better host. The house is yours and you'll be alone until I return. What you need most is rest. I assure you, you'll have the utmost privacy and safety. I must be gone for two days, but I hope I've anticipated your every need and provided for it. Don't be frightened. The noise you hear will be my helicopter as I leave. *Sayonara.*"

My hesitation at his invitation disappeared as I heard a shout from the hilltop. They'd discovered I was gone. They'd be here sooner than I cared to think about. Dare I hope this offer was a respite from my abductors? Wherein was the greatest danger—at the calloused hands of my captors or the offer of the anonymous voice?

Another shout. They were running down the hill. My choices were limited—the open beach, the apparent safety of the fenced garden, or back into the jungle. They were at the bottom of the hill.

"Allison, come inside the gate," the voice commanded.

I wanted to run back into the trees and hide, to take my chances on my own. But I couldn't. I felt compelled to obey that captivating voice.

Stepping inside the elaborate wrought-iron enclosure, I was startled when the gate swung shut immediately. I whirled to grasp it when the voice firmly, quietly cautioned, "Don't touch it, Allison. It's electrified. You're safe now. They can't get to you. Come into my house and rest."

The voice was hypnotic. I turned, almost trance-like, toward the house, obediently following the instructions. What an amazing effect that voice had! Who was this man? How did he know so much about me? Was it even a man? The voice seemed to be its own entity, a separate persona from any human body. I began to think of it as such . . . the Voice.

The quiet of the night was shattered by the roar of a helicopter taking off from the other side of the house. Was I walking into another trap or was I being rescued? A wave of weariness swept over me. I was too tired to run, too tired to hide. If this was a trap, I was too tired to worry about it.

Chapter Ten

Lights blazed from every window of the house and the lawns and gardens were dramatically lit. The path wound artistically around trees to a veranda that surrounded the house. It was built in the Polynesian fashion, open to the sea breezes with a high roof to pull the heat up and away from the living area. But this was no thatched hut. This was a showplace right out of *Architectural Digest*.

The library was amazing, a wonderful room filled from floor to ceiling with books encased behind glass. Dark, masculine furniture dominated the large room—forest green leather chairs, a navy blue leather sofa. Lush Oriental carpet in green, navy, and mauve covered gleaming hardwood floors.

The Voice again. "Allison, you should have reached the library if you chose to accept my invitation. I forgot one important thing. I'm sorry to have to ask this of you, knowing how exhausted you must be, but would you please feed cat? Instructions are in the kitchen. Again, forgive me for asking, but we'll both sleep better knowing cat has eaten. Rest well."

This time I knew the Voice had come over a speaker from the helicopter. I could hear the motor in the background. *Feed cat.* Not "the cat." Strange. But so was the Voice. So soft, so refined, yet it had an unearthly quality.

Angry shouts emanated from the beach, but the fence did keep the kidnappers out. I was safe, at least from those two. Was I safe in this house? My mind was still muddled from the drug the men had administered in the helicopter, my powers of reasoning impaired, but for the moment, I felt I'd made the right decision.

Leaving exploration of the house till I had my strength back, I found the kitchen and the instructions. It wasn't cat, it was "Kat." The note on the counter informed me Kat's food was in the pantry.

Opening the nearest door, I entered a well-stocked, room-sized pantry. I would certainly not go hungry while here.

Bags clearly marked "Kat," scribbled in big bold letters with a wide-tipped black marker, were stacked at one end of the room. I filled the ample-sized bowl labeled KAT'S FOOD from one of the bags and replenished the water bowl, then turned to the refrigerator to see what I might have to eat.

At a soft sound behind me, I whirled to stare straight into huge, gorgeous golden eyes. I froze where I stood. Could this be Kat? I hoped it was Kat! If it wasn't, I was in a heap of trouble. Those luminous eyes belonged to the most enormous lion I'd ever seen. I swallowed hard, too afraid to move a muscle.

"Allison, meet Kat, your bodyguard. Kat, this is Allison. You are to watch over our guest and protect her until I come back. Don't be afraid, Allison. He won't hurt you."

The voice made me tingle. I looked for speakers, but saw none. Was I being watched, or was it on tape, electronically activated by movement or sound? Kat approached me.

"Hi, Kat," I said tentatively. He raised his head and stared me straight in the eye. The note said he liked his ears scratched. I cautiously offered my hand. Like my cat at home, he put his nose up to nuzzle it. What incredibly soft fur! I got brave. I put both hands down to pet him and scratched him behind the ears. He did indeed love it. Loud purring rumbled from deep within.

All my life I'd wanted to run my hands through the mane of a lion. Now I was doing it. And I wasn't even afraid. That was as much a surprise as finding Kat.

He turned to his food bowl, and when it was empty, he returned for more scratching. I'd have been happy to oblige but I was close to collapse, my energy utterly depleted.

Normally a hot shower was my saving grace. Tonight my tired

legs could not hold me up. I'd need a long soak in a bathtub. Assuming the bedrooms were to the back of the house, I followed the wide central hall.

Each of the living areas opened into this large hallway with double-wide doors, or in the case of the larger rooms, two or three sets of double-wide doors, all of which were wide open to admit the ocean breeze. Perfume from unseen flowers pervaded the house.

At the end of the hall, a short flight of stairs led to a landing with two wondrous doors. As I labored up the stairs, I hastily examined the elaborately carved ebony, inlaid with ivory, jade, and mother-of-pearl. These doors were closed, locked. To my left and right, doors of the same size stood open. I turned to the one on the right.

"Good work, Allison. You've chosen correctly." The Voice, velvet and seductive, confirmed my choice. "Your bath is drawn and waiting." There must be an electric eye, a laser beam, something, that activated a tape as I passed. I hoped so. The alternative left me cold. I should have been frightened of the Voice, terrified of being in this unusual house, but strangely enough, I was not, and I was too exhausted to question why right now.

The room was lovely, decorated in cream and honey tones, accented with aquamarine and lavender. Soft breezes drifted through the open doors from the veranda. An enticing aroma beckoned me to the bathroom where I found a magnificent sunken tub filled to the brim with bubbles. The water temperature was perfect! How long ago had this bath been drawn?

Again the Voice, soft, soothing, like strokes on a cat's back, "The tub is designed to retain the temperature scientists have decreed as most relaxing and beneficial. As long as you're in the bathtub, it will maintain that ideal temperature. I've supplemented it with special herbs to which natives ascribe curative powers. They should ease your painful wounds and speed the healing process. Soak and enjoy."

Had he anticipated every move I would make? Or was he watching me from some hiding place?

A huge window above the sunken tub opened onto an enclosed garden, which was private and well lit. Was I still affected by the sedative they'd administered on the helicopter, or was I so fatigued that my good sense had evaporated? Could I even consider undressing under these circumstances?

I hesitated only a moment before peeling off my torn, cinder-scorched clothes, discarding them in a heap in the corner. I couldn't stand being filthy a minute longer!

As I lowered my aching body into the bath, the soothing Voice spoke quietly.

"Lie back, Allison. Let your body, your mind, and your spirit work together to heal. Relax. Go deep inside yourself. Will your body to heal. You can achieve miracles when you combine all your inner resources together."

His tones were mesmerizing, hypnotic. As I leaned back, the hauntingly beautiful strains of Beethoven's "Moonlight Sonata" softly filled the air. I let the bubbles envelop me in Elysian softness. I'd expected the scrapes and scratches to burn when they got wet. Instead, I felt as if I were wrapped in tranquilizing balm. Eyes closed, totally relaxed, I gave myself up to the rapturous melody that encircled me and the soothing water.

At first I was too exhausted to even think. Gradually I became aware of the blissful sensation of a massage. Three levels of tiny jets emanated caressing fingers of water so gentle I'd hardly noticed them at first. Their magic banished my aches and pains.

Something stirring in the garden outside my open window shattered my serenity. Adrenalin surged through my body, and my fight-or-flight reflexes kicked in. Flight might be the best tactic since I was not dressed for a fight—nor in any condition for one, for that matter. As I reached for a towel, panic and fear flooding my senses, the Voice spoke again, calmly quiet.

"Allison, Kat is coming. Don't be alarmed."

Kat stepped languidly through the open window and sprawled his enormous length along the wide ledge, one giant paw drooping over the side of the tub. He rested his head on that paw, gazing at me with great golden eyes.

"Hello, Kat. You just scared me to death. I'm glad for your company, though."

Alert now, shaken from my stupor, I realized my every movement was anticipated. I looked around the bathroom. Was I being spied upon? My danger antennae hadn't alerted me, but then I was exhausted. Maybe I was too dazed for them to work. I saw nothing that looked as if it might contain a surveillance camera, but Bart said you could hide one behind the screw hole of a light switch.

My mind was a turmoil of questions. Who was this man? He knew my name. He was aware of my kidnapping. He had anticipated my escaping the shack. He had prepared tapes knowing that I would come . . . or was the helicopter simply a ruse to make me think he had left the island and he was still here, watching me as I disrobed? Were these not recorded messages but live commentaries?

With the peaceful therapy of my bath at an end, my mind was turbulent with questions and fears. I quickly wrapped myself in the huge, cream-colored Turkish towel that had been folded neatly on the vanity chair next to the tub. Was I being paranoid? I wanted to think my mysterious host had, in fact, flown away on the helicopter, and I was truly alone with Kat. But I couldn't be sure.

Turning to the vanity, I discovered a new toothbrush still packaged, a fresh bar of soap, even my brand of moisturizer and deodorant. A draft of dread chilled me. Whoever this was knew more about me than I cared to realize—he had planned to bring me here. This was not a spur-of-the-moment offer of sanctuary.

The Voice came softly almost in my ear. "When you're ready, Allison, you'll find on the vanity a natural antibiotic salve prepared by the local shaman. Spread it generously over your abrasions. By morning your wounds will feel much better."

Eerie! I'd just reached for the bottle of lotion from my purse. Had he seen me, or had he anticipated a woman using lotion after her bath? I didn't want to think anymore. No more questions. I was totally drained. If his salve had medicinal qualities, I'd use it.

As soon as I was through with my toiletry, Kat stood, stretched, yawned, and with one easy, graceful leap, landed at my feet.

"Are you keeping me company tonight, Kat? I think I'll feel safer if you do."

On the bed, which had already been turned down, lay a lovely peignoir set, made of creamy silk and lace, very short and sexy. Very different from my extra large T-shirt of last night.

Last night. It seemed so long ago. I felt I'd lived a lifetime today. I guessed it was still the same day, but I didn't know how long I'd been out from the sedative.

I searched the closet for something less revealing, found nothing in the line of nightwear, and was too exhausted to look further. Donning the creamy silk nightie, I tumbled into bed. At least there wasn't enough of it to irritate my cuts and scratches.

My weary and bruised body sunk deep into the feather mattress. Kat jumped on the other side of the king-sized bed and gently stretched one paw toward me. After all I'd been through, going to bed with a lion didn't seem incongruous at all.

"Goodnight, Kat. I'm rather glad you're here." I stroked the soft fur, then laid back and closed my eyes.

The Voice again. "Goodnight, Allison. Pleasant dreams. I assume you sleep with the lights off." With that, the house went dark.

My brain burst with questions. How? Electronic devices must be triggering pre-recorded messages. But I was too tired to care. I'd found some answers, though. Nate wasn't behind the kidnapping. His men were. But Nate did want something I had. I just couldn't imagine what it could be, and I was still puzzled by how they'd tracked us. And why they'd killed their man on the balcony.

The Voice haunted me. It was compelling, hypnotic. *Oh, Bart! Hurry and find me. There is something very wrong on this island.* I'm not sure I even remembered to say *thanks* for my delivery from the volcano before I was asleep.

I woke in the night from a sound sleep, calling out to Bart. I sat up in bed, my heart pounding. Someone had been in the room—someone had been touching me. I reached for Kat. The bed was empty.

"Kat?" I got out of bed and nearly fell, my legs so weak they could hardly hold me up.

"Kat? Where are you?" Pale moonlight bathed the veranda in a soft glow, casting long shadows into the room from the door frames. I moved into one of the shadows and looked over the veranda and lawns and gardens outside my window. There was no movement, no sound. The breeze cooled my hot, feverish skin and I moved carefully into the open.

What—or who—had been in the room with me? I had an unmistakable impression of a presence here. Something had awakened me. I was so tired I should have slept for days. Sinking gratefully into a chaise lounge right outside my door, I was amazed at how weak I felt.

Sleep fled. My skin was prickly. The Voice had said I'd have privacy and safety, but I'd felt neither with the running commentary every time I turned around.

Get a hold of yourself and think. Who was the mysterious Voice and how had he been able to intervene when Nate arranged the kidnapping? Why had he intervened?

A slight sound in the gardens sent a shiver through me. I sat very still. If someone was coming, they'd have to cross an expanse of well-lit lawn and I'd have plenty of warning. But to do what?

There was a movement in the shadows, but I couldn't move, held in place by fear as much as exhaustion. The shape kept to the bushes instead of crossing the lawn, moving closer, right for the veranda where I sat. Then Kat stepped into the moonlight.

"Kat! You scared me to death!"

He came gracefully, deliberately, up the steps, and laid his huge head in my lap. I scratched his ears, relieved beyond measure that he was back. Burying my fingers deep in his luxurious mane, I felt a cord around his neck which contained a small metal disc. Was that how the Voice knew where Kat was at any given moment? How he could tell when Kat entered a room? That made me feel better—a little.

"You left me alone, Kat. You were supposed to protect me."

Then I had a chilling thought. *What if he had been protecting me? What if he had chased someone away?*

"Is that what you did? Was there someone in there with us?"

Certain there had been, I was more puzzled than ever. Kat stretched, yawned a huge, wide yawn, turned to the bedroom, then looked at me.

"You're right. It is the middle of the night. I haven't had nearly enough rest."

When I was once again in bed, Kat jumped on the other side,

stretched out his paw to me and I relaxed. At least my body did. My mind was busy piecing together impressions. A form, tall, slender, dark, tender. I'd been touched. My legs had been touched. My fingers followed where memory told them to go.

I was surprised to find fresh salve, an ointment that I hadn't put there. A ministering angel? I hardly thought so. This angel left a feeling of unrest. A dark angel.

Chapter Eleven

"Allison. Allison, wake up."

I could hear the Voice, but I chose to ignore it. I wasn't ready to wake up. I wanted more sleep—needed more sleep!

"Allison. Kat has to be fed. You need to be fed. You need nourishment to help you heal."

I stuffed the pillow over my head to shut out the Voice. I might have succeeded but someone pulled my covers off. Furious at being disturbed, I threw the pillow and sat up, incensed that anyone dare uncover me. Even my own mother had never done that when she tried to get me out of bed.

Kat was the culprit. He looked like a huge, playful kitten, sitting on the bed with the covers in his mouth.

"You win, Kat. I'll feed you." I rolled carefully toward him, still stiff and sore in every joint, but amazed at how rapidly my cuts and abrasions were healing. Burying my head in his luxuriant mane, I put my arms around Kat's neck and rubbed his ears while he purred his approval. He licked my arms with a tongue rough as sandpaper.

"Whoa, Kat. I've already lost several layers of skin. You'd better leave that where it is. Come on, let's go find the kitchen."

I pulled on the short silk robe that had been left with the nightie. I really needed to find something more modest to wear—as soon as I'd fed Kat.

The lion leaped gracefully off the bed and stood close to me, waiting for me to get steady on my feet.

"Are you going to make sure I don't fall down, old boy?"

He walked beside me, leading me down the stairs and through the long wide hallway. If I paused to look into a room, he got behind me, nudging me ahead.

"Okay, Kat. I get the message. You're hungry. No detours. Lead me to the kitchen."

He obliged, staying close enough for me to grab hold a couple of times when my weak knees threatened to give way.

Kat fed, I turned to the refrigerator to satisfy my hunger. When had I eaten last? Breakfast yesterday before our flight over the volcano? Our ill-fated flight . . .

My breakfast was delicious—macadamia nut bran muffins, fresh fruit, and coconut-pineapple juice. All my favorite things. A happy coincidence . . . or did the Voice know me that well?

Who was he? Why had he brought me here? Did he also want what Nate wanted? Was he trying a new tack—not force, as Nate's men had, but killing me with kindness? That made sense. The over-riding questions were what did I have, and why did they want it?

"Good morning, Allison." The Voice, beguiling, seductive, interrupted my thoughts. "I trust you slept well and enjoyed your brunch. So sorry to wake you. Kat is extremely well behaved as long as he's well fed. But he is, first of all, a wild animal and as such, no matter how well trained and seemingly docile he is, he can be unpredictable when his routine is disturbed."

I couldn't believe my ears! I sputtered furiously, "You send an unpredictable wild animal to 'guard me' and then tell me if he doesn't eat on time, he could eat me? Thanks a lot! I think I'll take my chances with those two on the outside of the fence! At least they won't—"

The Voice interrupted my tirade, quiet, confident, almost mocking.

"I'm sure this news is very disconcerting. I imagine your green eyes sparkling, your long hair tossed indignantly, and you stomping prettily off to dress and leave my house. Don't, Allison." The tone changed. "You are not safe outside the fence. Not only are your pursuers waiting, the island is inhabited by wild white-lipped peccary. They can tear a man apart in minutes. Kat will protect you until my return. Now go lie in the sunshine and set your mind and energies to healing."

The Voice ended his appeal in conciliatory tones, like a doctor prescribing help for a wayward patient, saying he knows best because he's the doctor.

Who does he think he is? I was, indeed, going to get dressed. Every time that voice spoke, I had the feeling he was sitting in a control room somewhere, pushing buttons, watching my every move, laughing at me, playing with me. Like a cat with a mouse.

But if he was here, why didn't he feed Kat and let me sleep? If he was so anxious for me to heal, why didn't he leave me in the healing slumber I was enjoying when he woke me?

Psychological warfare? Wake me before I'm rested? Set my nerves on edge by telling me I'm not actually safe with Kat? What else? The tapes to make me wonder if I'm being watched? Yes. He was playing with me.

Relax, Allison. Don't get psyched out. Calm down. Think before you act. First, get dressed. You aren't comfortable on his grounds and his terms so get out of this nightie and into something that doesn't make you feel like a stripper. Then find out where you are.

I hurried back to the bedroom, found a cool, cotton dress in the closet, and felt my confidence increase by leaps and bounds. I may be playing on his game board, but I didn't have to play by his rules. Now, if I just knew what the game was.

I found the chaise lounge an ideal spot for a little rest in the sun and liberally applied the balm he left for me. Someone else had been in that jar during the night. The contents were greatly diminished since I'd used it after my bath. Then I remembered my dream. . . .

Or was it a dream? I leaned back on the lounge and closed my eyes, remembering the night—the moonlight—Kat coming back across the lawn. And the hands on my legs. Fingers touching, caressing my arms and legs, stroking the healing ointment gently over lacerated limbs.

Cold chills shivered through me. I was freezing in the hot island sun, feeling violated. This was more disturbing than the attempted kidnapping or being roughed up in the helicopter. It frightened me. I didn't like not having control over myself—over who touched me. Lately, I seemed to have lost that control.

Okay, Allison. Find out where you are, or better yet . . . Dad? Dad, are you there? I tried to reach him by telepathy. No answer. Had I talked to him last night in the shack at the top of the hill, or had that been a dream? No, it was real. I think it was real. Why couldn't I contact him now?

Dad? Please hear me. Where are you, Dad? Nothing. I didn't have much to tell him anyway. When I discovered where I was and the identity of the mysterious voice, I'd have something substantial to report. I missed Bart, needed him, needed his reassurance, his support, his love.

I stood, still weaker than I wanted to be. A search of the house might reveal letters, pictures, files. There had to be something that would give me a clue about my enigmatic host. How about his room?

I went into the hall to the closed doors. Locked. All the windows, actually doors, were open in the house. Slipping back through my room to the veranda and around the house to where his bedroom doors were, I found them closed, curtained and locked. I couldn't see in anywhere. Continuing around the house, I found what had to be a large garden outside his bathroom, a high wall with vines and flowers cascading over the top, similar to the one outside my bathroom window.

Grabbing a handful of vines, I tugged tentatively on them. They seemed strong enough, but was I? My hands were not healed from the cinders yesterday. *Are you going to be a pansy and let a few cuts stop you? If he's watching, this should flush him out.*

Filling both hands with the vine, I pulled myself up the wall, hand over hand, wincing as my cuts burned, till I was on top of the wall, tired limbs quivering from the effort.

I was astounded at the beauty of the Oriental garden below me. Sand raked into lines and curves, fish ponds and fountains, statuary discretely tucked into shaped shrubs and flowers, or pedestaled in the open. I'd never seen anything so pleasing to the eye—and ear. Tiny wind chimes tinkled in the breeze in symphony with the gurgling of the water. Fragrant blossoms gently perfumed the air.

Dropping to the ground, I leaned against the wall for a minute till my legs stopped quivering, then carefully made my way around the waterfall that cascaded from the top of the wall. A white gravel footpath wound artistically around a fishpond with azure blue tile and bright orange goldfish. An ornate concrete park bench in the shade of a small flowering Mimosa tree was too inviting to pass up. I sat down to give my shaking legs a rest.

Leaning back, eyes closed, I let the soothing sounds and peaceful feeling of this enchanted place work their magic. I could stay here and be lulled into complacency by this beauty.

Up, Allison! Don't succumb. You have work to do.

Abandoning the peaceful beauty of the garden, I climbed the veranda stairs to the bathroom window, only to find it also closed and locked. I could break in—there were ample rocks in the garden, but I was averse to breaking things. There must be another way in.

How had my bathroom window latched? I shut my eyes, trying to picture the window. It was a simple gold hook. If I had something to slip between the doors, I might open them.

Pulling a long, slender leaf from an oleander bush, I slipped it in the crack. Not strong enough. I picked three leaves, stacked them together and pushed them toward the hook with an upward movement. I felt the hook release. The windows swung out toward the garden, and I stepped onto the wide tile ledge similar to the one Kat had lounged on in my bathroom last night.

But this was much more elaborate than mine—beautiful though mine was. No expense had been spared to make this the most luxurious bathroom I'd ever seen—with one very strange feature— there were no mirrors in this black marble and gold room.

The inner door led into the darkened bedroom. Sunlight streamed into every other room in the house—doors stood wide open to the outside. But this room was dark, curtained, locked. Why? What was here someone wanted to hide?

I searched for a light switch and found none, so I crossed the room to the double doors and flung them open to flood the room with light.

I was stunned. In the very center of the room, dominating it, circled by half a dozen black marble steps was a huge round bed covered with a black satin comforter and piled with pillows of many shapes and sizes—all black satin.

Two walls, like all other rooms in the house, were made up completely of double doors with beveled glass, but these were covered with heavy black satin drapes, unlike the uncurtained ones throughout the rest of the house.

The walls were covered in black silk linen, the closet doors padded with black leather. The carpet was black. Even the furniture, long dresser, and highboy were ebony trimmed with gold. This room also lacked a mirror.

A search of the dresser drawers disclosed black socks, black shirts, black everything. Granted, there were different styles and fabrics, but the color was same—black.

The closet was full of suits, expensive, very expensive, made in Hong Kong by an elite couture shop. Wools, silks, gabardine—all black. I looked for a safe, but found none, even in the closet.

A selection of robes and smoking jackets hung in another closet—black. Ties, slacks, and jackets. He didn't lack for style. The variety of fabrics was amazing, and the amount of clothes was staggering, but the same color? Astounding. Again, there seemed to be no place a safe could be hidden.

I couldn't believe there wasn't a single scrap of paper anywhere—and no pictures at all.

Should I go back the way I came—or could I do this the easy way and slip out the door into the hall?

Would my host, whoever he was with his strange habits and tastes, be upset if he knew I'd been in his bedroom? Probably. How could he tell? I'd been careful to put everything back exactly where it had been.

I examined the door to the hall, looking for something across both doors as Bart cautioned. There it was at the bottom. A piece of black thread, stuck across the doors when it was wet. If I'd opened these doors, the thread would have fallen to the black carpet and he would have known I'd been here. Rather James Bondish, I thought. Why? Why would it matter if I'd been here?

How did he get out of here? And how would he get back in? Certainly not over the wall! I didn't have time to look for secret entrances—I needed to search the rest of the house before he got back.

Closing the doors and putting the curtains back as I had found them, I shut the bathroom door, dusted my footprints from the black marble bathtub, and backed out the window. I held the gold latch up with the oleander leaves, shut the window, and pulled the leaves through the crack. I heard the latch drop into place, leaving all as I'd found it.

Carefully I smoothed out my footprints in the sand, reshaping the lines and curves as they had been. What a wonderful garden. I felt such peace here—totally opposite to the turmoil I'd felt in the black bedroom. I was loathe to leave the garden. It was a healing place for both body and soul.

Going back over the wall was easy. The stones of the waterfall were like steps. I dropped to the ground on the other side where I obliterated my tracks and returned to my bedroom.

The chaise lounge on the veranda looked so inviting I could hardly pass it by, but I needed to find some clue to my host's identity before he returned.

The kitchen yielded nothing—not even a cookbook or an instruction manual for the appliances. Curious.

The dining room hutch contained silver, napkins, tablecloths, and lovely dishes, but nothing to indicate ownership of any kind.

The library was the same—even the desk drawers were conspicuously empty. I opened a glass case and pulled a book randomly from the shelf—a copy of *The Bay Psalm Book,* the first book published in America. Talk about rare books! There were less than half a dozen of this one in existence. Nothing was written inside—not even a "This belongs in the library of" label.

I examined several others. Some were famous authors, others were obscure to anyone but a bibliophile. All were void of any claim of ownership. Interestingly enough, all seemed to have been read. The backs were supple, not stiff as I had supposed they'd be, and the pages fell open to certain spots—were these favorite passages?

Sandwiched between my room and the kitchen was a lovely lanai. Marble tile the color of the sand on the beach—not quite white, not quite gray—sparkled in the morning sun. Exotic plants of all descriptions filled the room, hanging from the ceiling, from baskets on the walls, in containers of every size and sort. It was a pleasant clutter of flora, a room made to wander and experience nature in without getting sand in your shoes or insects in your hair. The verdigris wrought-iron furniture looked inviting.

Did my host ever sit and relax here and admire this beauty? I couldn't picture him here. But, then, what kind of picture did I have of him?

The living room stretched across the entire front of the house. French doors offered a breathtaking view of the formal gardens leading to a white sand beach and turquoise ocean fringed with very tall, very old palm trees. Picture postcard perfect. Another time I wouldn't have been able to tear myself away from such beauty. Now I felt driven. I had to know where I was, who my "host" was, why he had rescued me from Nate's men, and what he wanted.

The teak end tables were empty, and the drawers in the teak writing table had paper and pens, but nothing else. There were no magazines, no newspapers. The living room was devoid of any clue.

The bedroom across from mine was the only room I hadn't searched yet. It was identical to mine in layout, but with a different color scheme and furniture. And, of course, I found nothing.

Strange. This was like a model home, exquisite in every detail, but there was no personality here—no clue of what the owner might be like or who he was.

If not for Kat and all the plants in the house that required care, and the fact that it was absolutely immaculate without a speck of dust anywhere, I could believe this wasn't really home to anyone—just a convenient place to stop occasionally.

Was that it? Was this an out-of-the-way hideout or meeting place? Maybe it wasn't even on the map—it could be an island so small in the middle of the vast Pacific that no one cared to note its existence.

My next step was clear. I needed to find out what was on the island besides a tiny shack on the hill and this house. And I needed to know if anyone else was here besides my two captors, Kat, and me.

My exertions of the morning had left me exhausted. I hated feeling this way, hated not being full of energy and enthusiasm. Maybe a quick rest in the sun would replenish my depleted vim and vigor.

My host had thoughtfully provided for every need, from my personal brand of moisturizer and toothpaste to a selection of clothes in my size. But not a single pair of shoes. Bizarre. My own were dirty beyond belief, scuffed and scorched from my excursion into the volcano.

Reluctantly retrieving my shoes from the corner in the bathroom where I'd discarded them the night before, I cleaned them as best I could, stuffed them in my purse in case I needed them, picked up the little vial of balm, and retreated to the chaise lounge on my veranda.

My skin absorbed this wondrous medication like a sponge. Another application made all the difference in how my wounds felt. Not only was it healing my cuts, burns, and scrapes amazingly fast, it made me feel good. I didn't hurt as much after an application of this magical elixir. It seemed to penetrate into my bones and muscles and heal them, too.

I reclined on the lounge, willing myself to relax, feeling the tension leave my body.

Bart, where are you? How are you healing from your wounds? What are you doing right now? Do you miss me as much as I miss you? This wasn't the way our honeymoon was supposed to be.

Anger coursed through me. Nate did this! He ruined my honeymoon and separated me from my husband. Adrenaline flooded my system. I had to get out of here and find Bart and my folks. They'd be sick with worry. I grabbed my purse and left the comfort of the lounge. Following the perimeter of the fence might lead me to something.

The formal gardens were a unique pleasure, filled with exotic island plants. The mazes, instead of being precisely trimmed in the European fashion, were free flowing with vines and orchids. It was like a tour through botanical gardens, each plant and tree meticulously labeled with both common and scientific names. The high wrought-iron fence was hidden in most places by a vine growing on a trellis. I followed this to the front of the house where the trellised vine stopped, and I could approach the fence.

Was it really electric? Did I dare touch it to find out? Slowly I put out my hand. What would happen if it was? Would I just get a little shock, or could I get a jolt that would really hurt? Or worse?

You're not very brave, Allison. Get your hand up there. You'll never get out of here if you don't try!

The Voice, again almost at my elbow, startled me so I nearly fell into the fence. It was quiet, impersonal, almost like he was reading a notice.

"The first jolt is a warning—only 10,000 volts. The next is 50,000. Deadly. Leave this area at once."

This time he didn't call me by name. This was a generic warning taped for anyone who got too close, activated by some hidden sensor. He didn't foresee me coming here. That was good.

The fence was probably ten feet tall, with ornate, sharp points on top of each rod, but the rods were too close together to squeeze through if it wasn't electric. Following the fence along the front of the house, all I could see in both directions were waves rolling endlessly on the sandy beach.

Around the other side of the house, where I'd entered last night, I saw the gate that had swung open for me. My former captors were nowhere in sight, and the gate was still shut. As I approached it, the Voice again intoned the warning.

Parting the leaves of the bush nearest me, I found a speaker. The Voice could leave taped messages to be activated by sensors or could use them for his live messages. Very clever.

I'd take him at his word for now. Until I determined there was no other way out, I wouldn't touch the fence. The vine-covered trellis began again right after the gate and continued the length of the house, preventing me from getting near the fence.

Keeping to the sandy path, I'd almost come full circle around the house, passing my host's garden wall, when the path made a sudden unexpected turn, not like the gentle curves found in the rest of the garden. It looped next to the trellis, then immediately headed back to the usual pattern.

I peeked through the leaves. I couldn't see the fence. This was different from the rest. Why?

Grasping the trellis, I pushed, hoping something would happen, but nothing did, nor when I pulled. But the sandy path was also different. This had to be an exit!

Something rattled above my head when I shook the trellis. Feeling up through the leaves, my fingers found a latch—a little hook which I easily undid, then pushed gently on the trellis. A portion swung open, leaves, vines, and all, into a narrow tunnel of green.

Closing the trellis door, I headed into the ivy tunnel, dark even in mid-day from the density of the leaves. Some gardener had worked many hours getting this to grow so perfectly. The tunnel curved gently, as the sandy path had done so I couldn't see the end, but I could tell I was heading away from the house and the beach toward the sound of rushing water.

But it wasn't the pounding of surf I could hear, it was a waterfall. As I progressed into the green tunnel, it got closer, louder, and suddenly the tunnel opened upon a clearing surrounded by a dense jungle. I was free!

Chapter Twelve

A lovely pool filled the clearing. At first glance, it seemed to be a natural pool, but on closer examination, I found that both the waterfall that fed it and the pool were man made, though totally natural looking. The clearing was just big enough to accommodate the pool, probably thirty feet across and fifty or sixty feet long, but not rectangular. It arched and curved and looped with little waterfalls cascading into the pool at intervals. It was truly a scene out of Eden, with exquisite flowers everywhere.

Was this my host's private pool? Anyone who'd gone to this much trouble must use this place for more than an occasional stopover.

I saw no way out of here unless another swinging door was concealed behind the greenery and blossoms that crowded the pool. The waterfall! I'd been able to climb over the wall of my host's garden. Could I do the same here?

The rocks were slippery, mossy, but I climbed to the top with little effort. Looking around, I was amazed to find it was much higher than I thought. I was at least fifty feet in the air and still in the trees.

Jungle pressed in upon the waterfall, which was fed from a stream winding down the mountain. What was on the other side of the mountain?

My climb was no longer effortless. Whoever built the waterfall had placed the rocks almost perfectly for steps. Mother Nature was not so cooperative and the ascent became much more difficult. Sandals weren't substitutes for hiking boots. My hands and knees suffered horribly, and my cuts and scrapes filled with dirt and began to sting.

The terrain got rougher, rockier, and steeper, and the undergrowth became thicker. Stopping to catch my breath, I thought longingly of the chaise lounge and the warm sun, and of being clean. I could go back to that amazing bathtub with its therapeutic water and massage. It was tempting.

No. The Voice had to return from wherever he'd gone—if he'd gone. First of all, I wasn't sure I wanted to meet my mysterious host. And second, I must find out where I was.

Slipping and scrambling over and around the volcanic rocks that formed the mountain, I climbed the hill that rose steeply in front of me. The ground was wet. Apparently it rained frequently, and the foliage was so thick, the sun couldn't dry things out. The air was heavy with the musty smell of wet, decaying vegetation.

Then I remembered my two captors. Where were they? I must be more cautious. My trail was obvious since I'd made no effort to cover my tracks. I definitely did not want to stumble across them again.

It was cooler now, and cloudy, I thought, though I couldn't be sure. I hadn't seen the sun since I entered the jungle, this never-ending world of green darkness.

It began to rain, a steady drizzle, making my climb miserable. I was a muddy mess, but I couldn't stop. I had to reach the top. I remembered reading the height of some of Hawaii's mountains—thirteen thousand plus feet. Surely this wasn't one of them, though my body couldn't be convinced I hadn't clawed my way up at least ten thousand feet already.

Don't exaggerate, Allison. Be positive. Think positive thoughts.

I remembered Bart's face at our wedding, the love in his eyes, the joy I felt realizing that he did love me and that our wedding was not just part of a plan to capture Antonio Scaddono. I thought of Bishop O'Hare. He made me feel good, like the two young families at Sacred Falls.

Michael's little face came into my mind, and his total trust in his Father in Heaven. He had talked to God as if He were there in front of him, just as Bart had when our plane exploded on the Azores, and we desperately needed transportation back to help my injured father in California. Their prayers had been answered dramatically.

I paused in my climb, dropping carefully on bleeding knees. "Dear Father," I began. How easy it was to pour out my heart and my story to Him, though He must already be aware of my situation. But if He was aware, why wasn't He helping?

I needed to know much more about Michael and Bart's God. I was fairly certain He was the same one I'd always prayed to, but Michael and his family, and Bart, seemed on much more intimate terms with Him than I was.

I began again. "Dear Father, please help me get out of here and back to Bart and my parents." I ended with, "And be clean again soon." I wasn't just concerned about my discomfort. I was also concerned about the dirt in my open wounds and the very real possibility of infection.

Reluctantly resuming my climb, I noted green moss on everything, indicating lots of rain and not much sun. Not good. And I was tired. How much higher must I go? I couldn't stop. There was no place to sit or lie down. Everything was miserably wet.

Just as I decided things couldn't get much worse, I suddenly I felt prickles on the back of my neck. I was being watched—or followed. I paused, listening intently.

I *was* being followed. The Voice? No. I hadn't heard a helicopter, unless he'd been hiding all the time, watching me, and knew when I left the garden. No. Somehow his voice led me to believe climbing muddy mountains wasn't his style.

It had to be my captors. They'd heard me and were coming after me. Quickly, quietly, I scrunched down under the leaves of a huge elephant ear plant. I was so covered with mud, face and hair included, I ought to easily blend in with the landscape.

The sound came again, closer—not voices, not even identifiable, but someone was there, headed straight for me. I shrank deeper into the mud, hugging the rock. I couldn't see out. Could they see me behind these leaves?

Barely discernible, it was almost more a sense of someone there than a noise. It couldn't be the Voice. He'd send someone after me. Those bumbling idiots I'd escaped from wouldn't be so quiet. Who could it be? Then I remembered the Voice cautioning me there were wild animals on the island. Peccary, did he say, that could tear a man to shreds in minutes? Peccary were related to wild boar. Extremely dangerous. *Please, no.*

I held my breath, not daring to even breathe. Whoever, whatever, was right where I'd been before I ducked into the elephant ears. I could feel them, feel their presence an arm's length away.

The leaves moved. They'd found me! They were coming directly to my hiding place. I had nowhere to go. Could I run? How far could I get? I was exhausted, bleeding, aching in every muscle and joint. But I wouldn't be captured again. I thought of the filthy flea- and hair-covered cot I'd been tied to in the shack and cringed. I couldn't go back there. I would not!

Tensed to spring, barely moving, I got ready for flight. Closer. Now I could hear breathing. The leaves that hid me parted . . . and Kat stepped into my hiding place.

"Oh! Oh, Kat! You scared me out of my wits! Look at you. You're almost as dirty as I am. What a muddy spectacle we make." I buried my arms in Kat's muddy mane and scratched his ears. Though his wet fur didn't smell wonderful, he was warm and that felt good. I was shaking from the chill.

"Don't suppose you know where I could get a nice hot bath and warm bed, do you?" This was probably as warm as it would get. When it got dark, would the temperature change? I didn't want to be any colder than I was. I snuggled close to Kat and used him for a pillow, a wet, muddy one. He purred contentedly while I scratched his ears.

"Where do you sleep when you're not sharing the guest room with someone? Do you have free run of the island? Do you have a den somewhere, cozy and warm and dry?"

As if Kat actually understood me, he arose, stretched grandly, yawned, and started up the mountain. When I didn't move immediately, he stopped, waiting.

"Am I supposed to come with you? Maybe you do have a nice warm cave somewhere."

Staggering after him, I felt worse than before, cramped and achy from sitting on the cold, wet ground. None of the brochures of Hawaii pictured rain, yet I'd been soaked to the skin twice in only how many days?

Think positive, Allison. Think happy thoughts. You will get out of this. You will find a hot shower and get clean. You will find your husband and have a honeymoon.

That got my adrenaline surging again—that and thinking of all the things I could do to Nate to make him pay for this misery he'd put me through. That gave me renewed energy.

I didn't note the trail if there was one. I simply followed where Kat patiently led. He paused briefly for me to catch him, then leaped gracefully from rock to rock, leaving me to scramble up as best I could.

Rain pelted me when we crossed open spaces, but ran in steady rivulets off the leaves above me most of the time.

"Whoa, Kat. Let me catch my breath for a minute." Sitting on a ledge, a rock jutting out of the mountainside, I held my face and arms up to the rain. It worked. It was raining so hard it was almost as good as a shower.

Kat came back to sit beside me, head on my lap, offering his ears for another scratching. As I rested briefly, I became aware of the sound of rushing, rippling water and realized I'd been conscious of it for some time. We were parallelling a stream cascading down the mountain. The same one that fed the waterfall and pool behind the house?

"Okay, Kat. Lead on. I'm rested, one layer cleaner and think I have my bearings so I could find my way back."

Did Kat understand me? Or was he simply on his way somewhere and liked his ears scratched so much he was bringing me along with him?

We kept close to the sound of the water. I couldn't see it, or much of anything else through the rain and dense green, but we were still climbing.

I'd made it past "the wall," when I knew I absolutely could not take one more step, but I had, and now my energy returned and I experienced the high, the rush athletes get when the endorphins kick in.

I couldn't even guess how long we'd been climbing. Was I paralleling the path I'd taken down the mountain that first night? I didn't remember hearing water then.

Rain slackened, jungle thinned, clouds lifted. I could see a few feet in all directions for the first time since I climbed over the waterfall. Kat hurried now, taking long, loping strides. I pushed forward, staggering with fatigue, afraid I'd lose him.

At the top of the mountain, we suddenly broke into a clearing. It looked like someone had sliced the top off of a perfectly formed peak, gently scooped out the center, and filled it with water. The sky-blue lake, reflecting the remainder of the rain clouds and one puffy white one, was completely surrounded by tall green trees and huge rocks.

Kat hadn't stopped to take in the scenery and was leaving me behind, headed around the lake to the largest of the huge rock formations that protruded into the water.

I followed until I reached his rock, but instead of climbing up after Kat, I sat on the edge of the lake to wash off the mud and clean out my cut and bleeding knees, legs, and hands. The water was warm enough to be inviting, and setting aside shoes and purse, I plunged in, clothes and all. They needed to be cleaned as much as I did.

I rubbed and scrubbed and finally slipped out of my clothes to get clean underneath. What I wouldn't give for some shampoo and a bar of soap! After cleaning my hair as best I could, and scrubbing my clothes, I laid them out on the rocks that now absorbed the heat of the sun, stretching out beside them, relishing the warmth the rocks afforded.

Remembering the jar of ointment in my purse, I applied it liberally to my wounds, hoping they were sufficiently clean to begin healing.

Relatively clean, warm, and rested, I looked for Kat. He'd disappeared into the rocks thirty or forty feet above me. From that height, it might be possible to see over the tree tops and view the rest of the island.

Suddenly the quiet was shattered by the approach of a helicopter, still unseen, but coming this way. I grabbed my clothes and scrambled up the rock, desperate to attain Kat's hiding place before the helicopter arrived. The climb over the steep, smooth rocks was difficult, but I was driven by the dire need to escape the smothering attentiveness, the smooth seduction of the Voice which the helicopter represented.

The roar of the rotors was deafening, the vibration in the rocks terrifying. I slipped and fell, got up and climbed again.

"Kat, where are you?" I called. I didn't know where he'd disappeared; I only knew it was somewhere above me. Then I found it—a small cave barely big enough to hold Kat and me. I rolled into it and snuggled behind Kat just as the helicopter roared into view from behind the rocks.

Had I been spotted? The chopper came from the opposite direction of the house. Was my host just returning? Or were my captors searching for me or a way to get onto the grounds to find me?

It swooped low over the lake, turned, and circled around Kat's rocky hideaway, then made another pass at the foot of the rocks where I'd been lying. Had I left something besides a wet spot on the warm rocks? I took inventory. My purse! Was it in plain sight out there? I didn't dare look to see.

The chopper hovered at the foot of the rocks, then lifted slowly to the level of the cave. At the sight of the rotor blades, I tucked behind Kat, trying to be invisible. I'm sure I could have looked directly into the pilot's eyes if I'd dared peek over the top of Kat.

Could he see me? Was it my mysterious host, or my captors? Caution won over curiosity and I kept my head down. Would it make a difference? Had I been spotted or did they just suspect I might be here?

It seemed like an eternity before the helicopter swooped away, taking the roar and vibration with it. I expected the rocks to tumble down the mountain with Kat and me in them. How could Kat, a wild animal, stand the noise? I'd have expected him to run, which would have left me exposed in more ways than one. I pulled my still-damp clothes on quickly, feeling less vulnerable already.

"Thank you, my friend. You take your duties as my protector

quite seriously, don't you? I'm grateful for that." I rearranged myself behind Kat so I could scratch his ears in appreciation. "Now what?"

Good question. My purpose in coming up here had been to discover where I was, or at least what was on the rest of the island. I had to expose myself to do that. If it was the Voice in the chopper, would he come back as soon as he discovered I was missing from the house? Had he suspected I was here or was he just checking on Kat?

If, on the other hand, it had been my captors, had they merely been checking out the lion in the cave? For some reason, I was afraid of them only physically with their ability to overpower me, not of their acute mental prowess. The Voice, however, was quite another story.

It had been quiet for some time. I ventured a peek out. My purse was nestled in a crevice at the foot of these rocks. Had it been seen? I didn't know.

Time for action. If it was my host, he might come looking for me anytime. I climbed to the top of the rocks above the cave. Kat followed.

The island was small with this peak at its center. I could see the ring of white sand, and one rooftop. If there were other houses, they were snuggled in the green jungle that spread right to the beach. I suspected there were none on the island, only the ramshackle hut I'd been tied in. It sat nestled among the trees halfway down the mountain.

Islands loomed from the water in the distance, but none close enough to do me any good, and none I could identify.

Questions flooded my muddled mind. If this island belonged to the Voice, how and why had my captors brought me here? If my mysterious host had actually saved me from them, what had he done to them? Left them wandering the island? Not likely.

They probably worked for him, snatched me, and brought me here. In my foggy state, I walked right into his arms as he supposed I would when he called them the bad guys and said I'd be safe with him—an age-old ploy for which I'd fallen.

Now what? No way off the island that I could see. Dad? I tried to reach him telepathically, but received no impression that I'd succeeded. What to do?

I retrieved my purse, applied another coat of the soothing balm to my cuts and abrasions, and climbed back up to Kat's cave, just as I heard the helicopter again.

Chapter Thirteen

"Kat! Come back! Come hide me and I'll scratch your ears."

Kat ambled amiably back from the craggy lookout above the cave and settled in front of me.

"Good boy. You're incredible." I rubbed, scratched, and praised my friend and ally while he purred appreciation in his deep-throated voice.

The helicopter was taking its time getting here. In fact, I wasn't sure it was coming at all. It seemed to be flying over all the rest of the island. Had I not been seen, or my errant purse?

Suddenly Kat growled a low warning. I peeked over his broad golden back and saw my captors rounding the lake, striding purposely in this direction. Did they know I was here? Were they searching or just exploring?

Kat continued to growl, and the closer they got, the more intense Kat's irritation became at the interlopers' presence. As the two men approached the foot of the rocks, Kat let out a tremendous roar and sprang from the cave to pose majestic and awesome atop the rocks.

"No, Kat! Come back!" I whispered. "They'll shoot you!"

"AAAIIEE! Get 'im, quick!"

Their screams came from directly below us. I knew they had guns, knew they would use them. I scrambled from the cave to stand beside Kat.

"Don't you dare shoot this magnificent animal. Your boss will kill you if you harm his pet." It was a guess and a gamble.

The looks on their faces were worth disclosing my presence. Their mouths gaped open, hands hanging limply at their sides, guns pointed at the ground.

"Get out of here or I'll send Kat to tear you limb from limb." *Would my bluff work?*

They hesitated.

"Get down here. Scarlotti wants to see you."

"What does he want with me?"

"To make sure you're all right."

"You can see that I am. Go tell Scarlotti I'm just fine."

"We can't go back without you. He'll kill us."

"If you stay here, Kat will do the same, just not as quickly. If you shoot Kat, Scarlotti will kill you for hurting his pet. You're in a no-win situation. You'd better find another line of work, pronto."

They drew back, conversing in quieter tones, trying to solve their dilemma. They were terrified of not accomplishing their mission, and of Kat. Who was Scarlotti? Were he and Nate working together? What could I possibly have that was so valuable anyone would go to these lengths to retrieve it?

Apparently the duo had made a decision. They approached the foot of the rocks again, guns still drawn.

"Come down now or we'll kill the lion."

"You wouldn't dare incur the wrath of Scarlotti. He loves this animal. He's spent his life raising and training Kat." I was guessing, of course, but felt fairly accurate in my assumptions. Someone had obviously invested a lot of time and love. "Kat is far more important to him than I am. Now get out of here, or Kat will have you for dinner."

They didn't bluff as I'd hoped. The tall man with sharp black eyes raised his gun and pointed it at Kat.

"Come down now, or he gets it."

"I warn you. Scarlotti will kill you if you hurt Kat."

"I'll plead self-defense. You've got to the count of ten to be down here, or that's a dead lion."

The gun stayed pointed at Kat, and me. If I sent Kat after

them, it would mean death or injury for him. If I didn't, would this man actually shoot Kat? If he was cold-blooded enough to do that, knowing he had to answer to Scarlotti, what would he do to me for forcing the decision on him and the ultimate punishment?

I stood my ground. I couldn't believe he would actually shoot.

" . . . Eight. Nine. Ten. Get down here now."

Suddenly he fired. The bullet whizzed past my head and ricocheted off the rock above me, sending stinging fragments everywhere. Kat roared and crouched to spring. I grabbed his mane.

"No, Kat. Stay."

At that moment the helicopter that had remained a background din throughout this confrontation erupted in noise over the lake. A machine gun sprayed death in a deafening staccato accompaniment to the roar of the rotors.

Two bodies flew through the air like rag dolls, landing in a twisted, grotesque heap. The rocks were stained red with blood.

I sank weakly to my knees, buried my head in Kat's mane and hugged him, trembling all over. Now what?

The helicopter landed near the edge of the lake on a smooth rock barely big enough to accommodate it. It perched there precariously while a tall, slender man with long, dark hair stepped down and motioned to us.

"Kat. Allison. Come."

It was the Voice. Kat immediately started down the rocks. I did not.

"Kat. Bring Allison," the Voice commanded. He stood in the shadow of the helicopter so I couldn't see his face, but his voice clearly meant business. Apparently, he was not used to being ignored or disobeyed.

Kat stopped and turned to me. Would he actually come after me and take me to his master? What would I gain by being obstinate? I had no means of protection, nowhere to run, nowhere to hide. And the man had an automatic weapon. Resigned, I climbed down the rocks after Kat.

The man, clad totally in black, returned to his seat in the helicopter, leaving the door open. Kat jumped in the front seat beside his master. No wonder the noise directly outside the cave hadn't bothered him. He was used to it. I climbed into the back seat and donned the headset he indicated on the seat next to me.

"I'm sorry you must sit in back. This is Kat's favorite spot and he thinks it belongs to him. I'm disappointed in you, Allison, that you didn't take advantage of my hospitality to heal and get well, and instead chose to escape. You've wasted a tremendous amount of energy. However, you are rather more clever than I gave you credit for. I'm awed that you found your way out and amazed at your courage in wandering the island with the wild peccary loose, and in facing up to those two bumblers. Thank you for defending Kat."

No introductions. No remorse at killing two human beings. So matter of fact about it. I shivered at his cold-blooded nonchalance.

"Are you cold, Allison, or is that an emotional reaction to the scene you just viewed?"

Was he psychic?

"I couldn't permit them to harm Kat. He's been the one loyal, loving constant in my life here. Would you have had me allow that worthless riffraff to live at the expense of this extraordinary, well-trained, devoted beast?"

He didn't turn to me for an answer, but I knew he was waiting for one.

"I'll not debate the moral dilemma you had, nor the decision you made. The gun was pointed at me, as well as Kat, and I'd received anything but tender, loving care from those two before. Kat has been far more helpful and sympathetic than they were. There might have been some other solution, however. You have the advantage of knowing my name, but I don't know yours. What do I call you? Do you have a phone I can use to call my family?"

He pretended to be occupied with landing the helicopter on the pad beside the house, and gave me no answer. I couldn't see his face. Long, black, silky hair hid it from me, falling over his face as he moved, and he was careful not to turn enough to reveal his features.

"I'm sure there's nothing you'd like more than another therapeutic bath . . ."

"Actually," I interrupted him, "I'd like to call my husband more than anything else."

He continued as if I'd never spoken. "I've taken the liberty of preparing your bath and left more of the healing balm for your wounds. Can you clean them properly or will you require assistance? I'm disappointed that you must start the healing process all over again." His voice, sensual, soothing, and hypnotic, frightened and distressed me. It was too convincing, too compelling.

"I'll be fine, thank you, especially when I return to my husband and my honeymoon." Aware that he wasn't going to give me any answers, I jumped down from the chopper and crossed the pad to the wrought-iron gate. It swung open as I approached, and I went through without a backward look, straight across the lawn to my bedroom, over this same lawn Kat had crossed last night when someone had applied the balm to my wounds.

Was that just last night? How long had I been on this island? At least twenty-four hours, plus however long I'd been unconscious after the sedative. Bart must be frantic, Mom and Dad, too. *Oh, Bart, please find me, quickly. I don't like this man or anything about him. I'm afraid. There's something dark and sinister about him. I don't want to be here with him. I want to be with you.*

I concentrated again on contacting Dad. I had no impression that I'd reached him, but I kept explaining where I was, what the island was like, where I'd seen other islands, and told him of my mysterious, frightening host. I prayed my message reached him.

Antiseptic had been left on the bathroom vanity. I used it to carefully clean my wounds, all the while telepathing my message to Dad.

I lost concentration when I climbed into the tub. Something soothing and relaxing happened as I breathed deeply of the aromatic herbs dissolved in the bath and in crystal bowls at the side of the tub. Incense burned on the window ledge.

It was as if deep thought were banished, too much trouble, too much energy involved. I relaxed into a state of vapidity as I submitted to the therapy of gentle water massage, aroma, and soft, haunting music.

I was startled back to reality by a sound that intruded on my subconscious, pulling me back from whatever dream-like fantasy land I'd entered.

"Kat!" I sat up abruptly as Kat draped himself across the ample window ledge, one paw again in my bath.

"I'll gladly surrender my bath to you if you'd like. I think I've been in here long enough anyway." Remembering I'd forgotten to get a clean towel from the linen closet and would have to drip across the floor to get one, I was unnerved to see a neatly folded bath towel at arm's reach on the vanity stool. That wasn't there when I got in the bath! Had he actually entered my bathroom while I relaxed in the tub? I hadn't heard a sound until Kat came. I shivered uncontrollably, frightened that he could come and go so stealthily that I had not even heard him, hadn't been aware of his presence.

I didn't like not being in control, didn't like having to react instead of act. Now it seemed a very long time since I'd actually had any control over my life, or my privacy.

Quickly I dried, applied balm, and, wrapped securely in the robe hanging on the chair, went to find clothes. I felt vulnerable, exposed, and needed the comforting security that a long-sleeved turtleneck shirt and long pants could give me right now.

There were no such things to be found in the wardrobe, but on the bed lay fresh night clothes. Thankfully, they were not as skimpy and revealing as the ones last night. My dinner was on a tray next to the bed.

The Voice drifted softly, apologetically, from a speaker somewhere in the room.

"I'm sorry I can't join you for dinner. However, I've prepared something very special. I keep the peccary on the island for three reasons. They keep away trespassers—they're as ferocious as wild boar. They also keep my hunting skills finely honed, and the meat of the white-lipped peccary is delectable. I'm sure you'll agree. I'll see you upon my return in the morning. Kat has already had his dinner so you may go to bed immediately after you've finished yours. Just leave your tray until morning. Rest well, Allison, and heal."

I was relieved to hear the helicopter take off, relished the quiet it left behind, and the privacy.

"Well, Kat. Looks like it's just you and me again. That makes me happy."

Kat ambled over to sniff my dinner and enjoy a scratch behind the ears. I accommodated the scratch, but didn't share my dinner, not sure of the strictness of his diet.

If the Voice—Scarlotti?—had prepared this himself, he was an excellent cook. It was delicious, as he said it would be. I felt drowsy as I finished, curiously satiated and languid. *He wouldn't have put something in my food. . . .*

I shook off the thought. He'd realize the exertions of the day would leave me too tired for mischief. That wouldn't be necessary. But I needed to take advantage of the time alone to discover who he was and what he wanted with me.

"Now what, Kat? Another exploratory mission, or bed?" What did I hope to find when I'd already searched?

The library. I needed to check the books he read and see what he had on exotic herbs. He was either an expert himself or had access to someone who was well-versed in the ancient art of herbal medicine. The balm he'd given me for my cuts and abrasions could be classified as a miracle drug, its healing powers were so phenomenal. The herbs in the bath, too. They made not only topical hurts disappear, but vanquished aches and pains deep within as well.

My limbs felt heavy, awkward, and I had to fight to keep my eyes open. I sat on the edge of the bed. *Had he put something in my food? Or was the trauma and exhaustion of the last few days merely catching up with me?*

I had to check the library before I succumbed to sleep. Stumbling clumsily down the hall, with Kat at my side to cling to for support, I made it to the library, but was so exhausted from the effort, I dropped into a green leather chair to recoup my strength. I'd never felt so tired before, but then I'd never fallen into a volcano before either. Kat rested his massive head on the chair arm to be scratched.

With great effort, I forced myself to the bookshelves, scanning the titles until I came to a section on herbs. I pulled out a few to read, then dropped back into the chair, alarmed that I had not even the energy to stand. *With what did he lace my dinner that made me feel this way? There was no doubt he'd given me something. Was it merely to make me rest better, to heal quicker, or was there another reason?*

I'd go to bed as soon as I'd checked the books . . . I'd check the books as soon as I rested my eyes for just a minute . . . .

Chapter Fourteen

The bright moon cast shadows into my bedroom, long fingers of darkness reaching, menacing, threatening. Lying very still in my bed, my mind groped upward to consciousness. *Where am I?* Gradually I climbed out of the foggy state of a drugged sleep. *I'm in bed! How did I get here?* The last thing I remembered was being in the library, so tired I couldn't stand up, hold a book, or keep my eyes open. I could not possibly have made it down the long hallway and up the short staircase to this room.

The slightest movement in the shadows, the vague impression of fingers lingering on my uncovered legs and arms, shocked me into full wakefulness. I reached for Kat, felt the soft warmth of fur on the other side of the bed, all the while keeping my eyes on the shadow I was sure had moved.

I turned on the lamp on the night stand, but before my eyes adjusted to the light and without seeing or hearing movement, I sensed I was now alone. But I hadn't been. The balm had not yet absorbed into my skin, it was so recently applied.

I pulled the covers up close, clutched them tightly, and turned off the light. With it on, I might as well have had a spotlight on me. With it off, moonlight would reveal anyone entering my room through the open French doors. But he couldn't see me. Or could he? Could he see in the dark? It was easy to ascribe all sorts of unearthly attributes to my elusive host.

There was no doubt whom it had been. My dark angel of last night . . . the Voice. He'd lied about coming back in the morning. Or had he? "I'll see you upon my return in the morning" had led me to believe he would not be back until morning. It was morning now . . . very early morning.

"I'll see you . . ." Did that mean I was actually going to see his face, talk with him? Could I find out, finally, what everyone thought I had in my possession, what everyone wanted so badly? In the morning . . .

Drifting in and out of sleep, I clutched the covers to me each time I awoke, until dawn finally flooded my room with golden streams of sunbeams. Kat was gone. I hadn't been aware of his departure so I'd slept more than I thought.

I jumped out of bed, swooned dizzily, and sat back down. Whatever he'd given me last night hadn't worn off completely. I'd have to be more careful about what I ate. When my head cleared, I dressed quickly in the most modest attire I could find, a long flowing jade green dress nearly hidden in the back of the closet.

As I stood in front of the mirror brushing my hair, I remembered his mirrorless bathroom. Why? There were no mirrors anywhere in the house, except the small ones in the two guest rooms. The house had no windows—just French doors everywhere that all stood open, night and day. An open door could give no reflection at night. His bedroom had curtains on the doors. There would never be any glass to reflect.

What an imagination! My mysterious host was probably a very normal person with some peculiar quirks. *Stop blowing everything out of proportion, Allison.*

I stepped into the brilliance of the early morning island sun, basking in its warmth as I settled onto the chaise lounge. Closing my eyes, I thought longingly of Bart, and wiped an involuntary tear from my cheek. *Where are you? What are you doing this minute? Staring across this same ocean, wondering, worrying about me? Have you healed from your injuries? I miss you. I need you.*

I tried again to reach Dad by telepathy. Still no impression that he'd received my message. If only I could tell him where I was. *If only I knew.*

"Why are you crying, Allison?" I jumped, startled. The Voice, entrancing, solicitous, spoke directly behind me. I hadn't heard his approach. He moved like a ghost.

His long, silky hair fell over my face as he bent over, his hands firmly pressing me back onto the lounge, preventing me from turning to see him as he spoke in dulcet tones.

"No. Don't move. This is the best thing you can do for yourself."

"Who are you? Why am I here?"

"Lie quietly, Allison, and concentrate your mind and your heart and your soul on healing. Think only of that while I prepare your breakfast."

I leaped off the lounge and turned to face him indignantly. He was gone! Had I imagined the voice? The hands on my shoulders? No. I could still feel where he'd touched me, still smell the lingering scent of masculine cologne.

Bart! Dad! Find me, please! I don't like this!

Who was he? Why had he brought me here? What could he possibly want? I'd asked these questions before, but they had a totally different nuance now.

I lay back on the lounge and concentrated, though not as he had instructed. I concentrated on Dad with every fiber of my being, calling out to him across the endless miles of blue ocean that separated us. He must receive my message. He must find me. Quickly.

I opened my eyes. Enticing aromas emanated from a silver tray on the table at my elbow. A single perfect dark red rose in a shining silver vase adorned the tray.

I whirled to see my elusive host, but his hands caught my shoulders, held me against the chair so I couldn't turn.

"No. Eat while it's hot. I'll stay and talk as long as you don't turn around. If you do, I'll be gone."

"Why can't I see you?"

"Not yet. Later, I promise you will."

"I won't eat a bite until you tell me who you are and why I'm here, and when I can leave."

"Please eat. No more questions now. I've provided those things your body requires to replenish itself. You have not treated it well,

Allison, jumping into a volcano, shredding your flesh, flooding your system with noxious, toxic gases."

His voice was hypnotic. I felt drawn to it, lured by the lyrical, luscious tones, his elegant manner of speaking. Mustering every ounce of self-restraint I could find, I managed to keep from turning to look at him. I needed desperately to know what that voice had to tell me.

"Why am I here? What do I have that Nate wants so badly? I need answers, now!"

"You cannot talk and eat, too, and you must have this nourishment. I want you perfectly well as soon as possible. If you'll eat, I'll talk."

Alarms went off in my head. He wanted me to eat. He was too obvious about it. *Not on your life will I eat your tainted food! But why did you make it look so appetizing?* I was starving, and it smelled so good! I picked up the fork and faked taking a tiny bite to initiate his narration.

"Nate secreted a valuable jewel with your belongings. If he were to be apprehended, he didn't want it in his possession. He felt sure he could easily repossess it at any time and he'd let you spirit it away for him."

"But there was nothing in my luggage. We searched, over and over."

"You overlooked the obvious." He sat on the lounge behind me, pressed close, his arm circling my shoulder, long, slender fingers extending my pearl lotion bottle in front of me. His hair fell across my shoulder as he held it out for me to see.

I jerked away, repulsed at his touch. Grasping his wrist, I turned to look at him, but he pulled me tight against him, his arms holding me in place.

"Don't, Allison. I am not ready for you to see me yet. Give me your promise you will not turn, or I'll leave you now, with all your questions unanswered. And please eat. You need the nourishment."

His closeness was repugnant and frightening, and yet . . . *Bart! Please come and take me away from here!*

I answered as calmly as I could. "I promise, if you won't sit so close."

His laugh was low, musical, beguiling. He moved slightly, his arms releasing me, but he remained close, the bottle extended in front of me.

"I thought that was a present Mom slipped into my luggage."

"As it turned out, it *is* a present, from Nate to me. Finish your breakfast while I prepare the gift. You may watch."

I was so hungry, the food smelled so delicious, and he was so persuasive. But I would not be drugged again, even if I had to starve to death. I made a pretense of cutting and eating, but avoided putting the delicious smelling morsels in my mouth, palming them and carefully stuffing each bite under the cushion.

He moved to the side, arms extended so I could watch as he turned the pearl-shaped bottle upside down, inserted a coin in a small indentation in the flat bottom, and twisted. He lifted the bottom off, put a long finger in the lotion, and pulled out a plastic bag.

Using my napkin, he wiped the bag, opened it, and revealed a huge oblong pearl in a magnificent, intricate gold setting.

"This is what Nate wanted. It's part of the state jewel collection of Thailand, rumored to have been worn by each of the wives of the King of Siam on their wedding day, and offered to Anna, as well. It's one of the most precious biwa pearls in the world because of its size, unique shape, and nacreous nature. And now it's mine. You may wear it if you like. Imagine, wearing something so beautiful, so valuable, so historical."

"No, thanks! I want to leave now. I must find my husband. He was hurt . . ." I pulled away and tried to stand up. He held me back.

"Don't you want answers to your questions? Relax, finish your breakfast, and I'll finish the story." Like a sorcerer, he wove enchantment with his voice. I didn't want to wear the pearl, but I did want to hear what he had to say, more than he knew. He slipped the ring on my finger and held up my hand so I could see its luminescence in the sun.

"When Tony kidnapped the grandchildren of the Thai king, he also stole some valuable jewels. You foiled their plans when you spirited the children and the jewels away, with the exception of this magnificent gem Nate had hidden. Nate saw their plan unraveling.

Tony did not. He was blinded by his drive for revenge, his lust for Margo's estate and her millions. Revenge and greed killed Tony as much as you did."

Icy daggers of dread danced up and down my spine. What did he know? What did he mean?

"My father wanted me to see how clever he was, wanted me to observe his disposal of his nemesis of twenty years. He brought me with him to Margo's estate the day she was to finally make an appearance so I could watch her die. I was watching from the house when the golf carts exploded. His idiots bungled it. Your whole wedding party was to have been blown to bits on the way back up to the house, but the ceremony took too long."

Terror tingled through my body. I didn't like where this was going.

"Fortunately, he had a backup plan. He'd planted explosives around the patio, just in case, for the little reception your mothers had put together. Either way, he was going to make sure there were no survivors. In the end, he was the only one who didn't survive."

"You saw . . ."

"I saw you bash in the head of my father to prevent him from killing your husband. I'm curious to know your feelings as his skull caved in under the board. You've experienced something rare I have not . . . yet."

His words swirled harmlessly through the air like falling blossoms. I knew I should care about what he was saying, but I didn't. I felt myself going into shock, felt detached from my surroundings, from myself, from him . . . Antonio Scaddono's son. He continued.

"I allowed Nate to kidnap you to recover the pearl. I gave him permission to have his men bring you here to my island, knowing you could elude them and find my house. I didn't anticipate your impetuous jump from the helicopter to save your husband, nor your unfortunate descent into the volcano. Bart was supposed to die in that volcano as you watched, and you were to be the lure to bring your parents into my hands.

"Nate believes you lost the pearl in the volcano since his men found only the top of the bottle containing the tracking device in the shack. Nate returned to the Orient without the precious pearl, thinking it was gone forever. I hurried him back there by arranging an 'emergency' he needed to take care of. His men are dead, and no one else on earth knows where you are."

"But why? Why are you going to so much trouble to get us here? If you want my family dead, why don't you just shoot us?"

"You killed my father. Your mother had made him a fugitive so we could not return to the United States. Your father tracked him, pestered him, drove him underground all those years. I am going to destroy each one of you, in front of the others. It will be my exquisite pleasure to introduce you to mind-altering, body-ravaging drugs that will have you screaming, begging for mercy until you go stark-raving mad."

At that terrifying announcement, I shoved my elbow back into Scarlotti's midsection with all my might, knocking the wind from him. As he crumpled forward in pain, I slammed the heavy silver vase down on the back of his head, hard, and fled to the mountain without looking back.

Chapter Fifteen

I opened my eyes. *Where am I?* My head wouldn't move, nor would any of my limbs. I saw a dark ceiling above, a dark interior before me, and out of the corner of my eye, a curious scene a la Merlin. An old man, bent with age, white hair flowing past his shoulders, busied himself mixing ingredients from an array of bottles and bowls on a cluttered table.

I tried to speak, but my mouth wouldn't form the words. Elephantine shadows loomed at me, moving, swaying, reaching in the flickering candlelight. I quickly shut my eyes. *What am I doing here? How did I get here? Where is here? Why can't I move or speak? Why do I have this excruciating pain in my head?*

I'd been dreaming, curious colorful dreams of incredible scents and sensations, of flitting among the flowers with a butterfly, swooping and swirling above the ocean spray with a seagull. It was an absurd, implausible dream, but the impressions lingered, making it seem real. I relished the memory, wouldn't let it escape, reveling in the freedom of floating, drifting on the wind, gliding, hovering at will.

The old man's presence at my side brought me crashing back to earth. I gazed into eyes the shade of morning glory, deep set in walnut-colored, wrinkled skin. With his hand under my neck, he lifted my heavy head and put a vile smelling liquid to my lips, expecting me to drink. My hands wouldn't respond to my command to push it away. I couldn't turn my head to escape. He poured the odious liquid into my mouth, and I was forced to swallow it.

My body was heavy, burdensome, too unwieldy to manage. My head lolled back on his arm and he propped a pillow behind me, leaving me in a sitting position, then shuffled to his table to resume mixing his potions.

Bottles, jars, and containers lined the walls of the small, dark, windowless room, which, after further examination, I decided was actually a cave. Entire branches, individual leaves, and bunches of flowers hung upside down to dry from ropes crisscrossing the cave that were tied to tall tree limbs wedged tight against the curved ceiling.

The only light in the room emanated from the stub of a candle on the table. *We must not be near the entrance to the cave,* I decided.

Shutting my eyes, I tried to recall, to relive, the floating, drifting, soaring sensations that had been so pleasurable, so joyous.

The old man came to me again, this time with bowl instead of cup. He held my arm up to the candlelight, rubbed salve across a long gash in my forearm and over my hands, and applied it liberally to fresh scrapes, cuts, and scratches all over my legs, then returned to his table.

My body looked like I'd been in a fight with a pyracantha bush and lost. The strange thing was I felt no pain. In fact, I did not feel the old man's touch, only a tremendous heaviness of limb, diametrically opposed to the total weightlessness I'd been enjoying in my dream, the complete freedom from the pull of gravity.

I tried again to speak, but my mouth simply would not move to form the words. Unintelligible sounds, a soft sort of moaning grunt in my throat, was all I could manage.

Once more the old man turned from his mixing and stirring with a bowl in his dark hands. He knelt at the foot of the bed and spread a murky-looking mess all over my feet. I didn't feel a thing, which was odd. My feet were normally extremely sensitive. I could never stand to have anyone touch them. But I didn't feel his hand holding my foot, didn't feel his fingers smearing something dark and gooey-looking over the bottom of my foot, between my toes, over the instep, and around my ankle. *Why couldn't I feel anything except this agonizing pain in my head?*

I couldn't feel, but I could certainly hear. A helicopter, so close its tremendous vibration made the plants hanging overhead sway and dance, rattled jars and bottles on shelves, and sent cacophonous sounds echoing through the cave and my head.

"Allison! Where are you?"

The Voice, warped by a loudspeaker, reverberated through the cave, through my mind, sending waves of terror through my body as the helicopter sent vibrations through the earth.

The old man looked up from his muddy ministrations at my feet, staring into my eyes, analyzing, inquiring, probing.

"You don't want him to find you?" he asked gently, his low voice warm, comforting.

How could I tell him? I couldn't speak, couldn't shake my head. The sounds that came from my throat were indecipherable.

"I understand. Your eyes speak for you. He won't find you here." There was a lengthy pause as he continued to look at me. He dropped his head and resumed smearing the smelly substance on my feet. When he finished, he took long, wide leaves from a stack on the table and carefully wrapped my feet, encasing them completely in neat green booties, tucking the ends under as I'd seen basket weavers do.

He shuffled off behind me and soon I could no longer hear him, just songs of birds echoing through the cave and the sometimes near, sometimes distant, roar of the helicopter as it crisscrossed the island, spiraling the pain in my head to new heights when it approached.

I jerked awake, brought out of a dream of gliding weightless over the treetops by the old man pressing the cup to my lips again, urging me to drink.

"This will soothe the pain you're probably feeling and make you sleep for many hours. Kat came to keep you company. He seems to think he's your personal bodyguard. Rest well."

He removed the pillow, leaving me flat on the bed, applied another coat of salve to my arms and legs, and turned to leave.

"Kat, I'm counting on you to keep your master away. Don't let him find her and take her back. Watch carefully."

He snuffed out the candle and padded softly off, leaving me in the darkness with Kat's huge head resting on the bed by my hand. I couldn't even pick up my hand to scratch his ears.

Several sudden thoughts sent terror pulsing through my body. What if Kat hadn't eaten recently? Would I be his next meal? Who was the little old man? Why was he willing to hide me? Or was he only pretending to hide me until I was well, then he would give me back to Scarlotti? What was the matter with me?

Depression as black as the cave in which I lay shrouded me, wrapped its hideous arms about me, and clutched me to its breast. I'd never been subject to depression, never felt its smothering effects. But now I felt totally helpless, worthless, and quite alone, and was sure I would spend the rest of my short life on this miserable island, in this wretched cave, drinking these appalling liquids. I was mired in self-pity. Tears flowed unchecked down my cheeks, filling my ears, soaking my hair and the bed.

Every sound made my heart skip a beat. If my body were mobile, I'd have jumped a foot every few seconds. Kat nudged my hand, laid his huge head against my leg as if to reassure me, but it didn't work. If I couldn't raise my hand to scratch his ears, would he revert to his wild nature and eat it?

I drifted into a troubled sleep, feeling hands stroking and caressing me. I woke to find Kat's rough tongue licking my arm.

The glowing candle revealed the little old man mixing his noxious-smelling potions again. This time he also brought me something to eat.

"Is the pain gone?"

I thought about it a minute. Yes, it was gone. And so was the overpowering heaviness in my limbs. I could raise my hand, could scratch Kat's ears. I could even speak.

"Where am I? Who are you?"

Kindly blue eyes sparkled as a fatherly, tolerant smile creased his wrinkled brown face.

"You're safe. When Scarlotti asked for more of his drugs, I feared he'd give them to you, instead of using them himself. I watched as you climbed the hill, running from him barefoot through the underbrush. Scarlotti cornered you on the peak above Kat's den.

You jumped off the ledge rather than let him catch you. Fortunately, you landed in the water instead of on the rocks, though just barely. Kat saved you from drowning."

"Thank you, Kat." I scratched behind his ears and rubbed his head in gratitude. He put his head on my lap, ready for more.

"Why did I have such a headache? And why couldn't I talk or move when I first woke up?"

"You had a nasty bump on the head. I wasn't sure how severe your injuries were, or whether you had any broken bones. I gave you an herb that causes temporary muscle paralysis until I could determine your injuries. That was my excuse for getting you away from Scarlotti. Then I told him you'd run away when you woke."

"Side effects from the herb?"

"It's harmless. Hospitals use a form of it on trauma patients and burn patients to keep them from moving while skin grafts take hold. Here. You must have a bite to eat. I know you won't eat much, but you need a little something. Then you may sleep as long as you'd like. Scarlotti won't find you."

He offered a plate of fruit and bread, but I shook my head and pushed it away. Gently he insisted, breaking a piece of bread, putting it to my mouth.

"Thank you, but I can't eat. My system is too upset. I'm so depressed I could cry."

"What you're experiencing is probably caused by a drug Scarlotti gave you in your food. You may undergo mood swings, depression, and nervousness until it's out of your system. You were brought to this island against your will, held captive, and given drugs you'd never take intentionally. You mustn't blame yourself for any of this. I promise when the drugs have worn off, you won't feel so bad. Eat just a bite or two. Then sleep."

More to placate the kindly old man than anything else, I ate the bit of bread he offered. It was good. I accepted more, and some banana, mango, and papaya cut up on the plate. It did make me feel better.

"Thank you. You knew better than I what I needed."

"We witch doctors are very good at that, you know," he said with a wink and a smile. "Kat, are you staying? I must get back to

Scarlotti so I'll know his plans. I'll see that he doesn't bother you again until we can get you off the island. Sleep now." He patted my hand, scratched Kat's head, and turned to snuff out the candle.

"Wait. Don't go!" I struggled to sit up. "I can't stay here. He mustn't find me again. I've got to get off this island right away. Please help me."

He gently urged me back onto the pillow and pulled the blanket around my shoulders.

"I'll help you, but you can't leave now. The only way off the island is an outrigger I have hidden. But you aren't strong enough to use it yet, and Scarlotti is watching too closely. He doesn't know about this cave, so he won't find you here. The entrance is carefully concealed and he's never found it in all these years."

"Tell me about him."

"Scarlotti is the only son of Antonio Scaddono. I met Antonio many years ago in the Orient when I was working as a gardener on an estate he bought. I was developing new strains of exotic plants, and I stayed on when the estate changed hands. Scarlotti was just a boy, but very curious and interested in growing things so he spent many hours with me in my greenhouses. Antonio was a ruthless, evil man, but he loved his son very much, and took him with him whenever he could. One day, someone with a grudge—probably a life destroyed because of the drugs he dealt with—threw acid at Antonio. He managed to avoid it, but it caught young Scarlotti full in the face. The only thing that saved his eyesight was his thin arm flung across his eyes.

"Antonio paid European specialists hundreds of thousands of dollars for skin grafts, then for plastic surgery to make Scarlotti presentable. But they couldn't do all Antonio wanted for his son. He tried for years to get Scarlotti into the United States to specialists with new techniques in plastic surgery. Apparently Antonio had been seen when he killed someone. He couldn't go back to America for fear he'd get caught."

I understood things more clearly now. "My mother witnessed that killing. She had to change her identity to protect her life from him." What a strange chain of events. No wonder Antonio hated my mother so much. She prevented him from getting the medical help his son needed.

The old man shook his head sadly. "The evil men do return to haunt the children. Scarlotti was a brilliant child. He loved learning and experimenting, but his pain and ugly face warped his soul. He experimented with drugs to ease the pain and to forget what he looked like. I found a mixture of herbs that produced a tranquilizing effect on Scarlotti, made him able to control his rages, to keep his mind on his studies. Antonio paid me to produce new and better drugs that would keep Scarlotti from destroying everything around him, and himself. A few years ago, Scarlotti found this island, built the house, and created a paradise where he could read and study until his operations were complete and he had the face he now has."

"And where there were no mirrors to remind him of his looks. Does he live here all the time?"

"Most of the time. Scarlotti turned his considerable talents to his father's illegal drug business, increasing crop yield and profits from new markets. He brought me here to produce his personal prescription and built a little cottage for me near the beach with a wonderful greenhouse and laboratory. He thinks I mix his special formula there. I wouldn't dare leave it where he could find it. I come here to mix it in secret, then give him only one day's dose at a time. An overdose could kill him. I suspected he gave you a portion of yesterday's ration when he asked for more."

"How am I going to get off the island without him seeing me?"

"Tomorrow he has a meeting on the Big Island. You should have your strength back by then. As soon as he leaves, we'll put you in the outrigger. You should reach safety before he returns with the men he's bringing back to find you." He waved his hand around the shadowy cave. "I'll have to hide all of this before they get here, and you'll have to be safely away."

I shuddered at the thought of Scarlotti finding me.

"Now sleep. I must be at my cottage or Scarlotti may suspect I've hidden you. He'd kill me first, then worry about his drugs later. Don't leave here. I'll see you in the morning."

He patted my hand, put out the candle, and left me in the dark with more questions than usual on my mind. My brain shut down before I had done much thinking, however, and I slept, a dream-filled sleep of curious colors and shapes and sounds and smells that left me doubting my sanity until I opened my eyes on a now-familiar scene.

Kat sat at my side, the flickering candle created strange configurations on the wall of the cave, and my benefactor was mixing potions again at the little table.

"Is it morning?"

"Ah, yes. Good morning. How do you feel?"

"I'll tell you after I try to stand up."

He produced a plate of fruit and bread like the one he provided yesterday. I ate every bite.

"Scarlotti's ready to leave. As soon as we hear the helicopter clear the island, you must be on your way."

"I don't know your name, or how I can possibly thank you."

"It's better that you don't know. There. He's leaving. Come quickly."

As the noise of the hated helicopter faded in the distance, I followed the old man from the dark cave, through a narrow tunnel, and into the verdant green overgrowth covering the entrance. I was temporarily blinded by the dazzling island sun.

"Help me with the canoe," he commanded, uncovering a small outrigger he had stashed in the lush green plants outside the cave. We carried it to the water's edge.

"Have you ever used one of these?"

"No. I've paddled a canoe, but never an outrigger."

"Outriggers are easier, more stable."

He produced a jar of ointment and began spreading it over my arms and face.

"Put this all over your skin, wherever you are exposed to the sun. It will prevent sunburn."

The old man put two canteens of water in the boat while I spread the concoction over my skin. I noticed with surprise the pearl ring on a string around my neck and the leaves still wrapped around my feet.

"Leave them there until you arrive on Maui. Your bare feet were badly cut climbing the hill and the herbs on them will help them heal. See that island?" He pointed to a distant shape on the horizon. "It isn't as far as it looks. Keep your eyes on that and navigate straight for it. Here is an old, faded muumuu to pull on over your torn dress, and a hat, both for protection from the sun and to cover yourself in case Scarlotti is searching the sea on his return."

I turned to the old man, overwhelmed by gratitude for his help.

"Thank you doesn't quite cover how I feel."

"Go," he said, turning me toward the outrigger.

Kat strolled to the water's edge and eyed the canoe. I knelt and buried my face in his luxurious mane.

"Goodbye, dear Kat. I'll miss you."

"Go quickly. You haven't a minute to waste."

I rose, kissed the walnut cheek of the old man, and stepped gingerly into the outrigger. As he pushed me into the oncoming waves, I paddled hard into the open ocean, keeping my eyes on the distant island that was my destination, a seemingly unreachable goal.

Chapter Sixteen

What am I doing here in the middle of the ocean? I know nothing about outriggers or navigation.

I remembered reading about a woman, an experienced sailor, who fell asleep in her boat off the islands. The currents had taken her out to sea far from land. She drifted for days. Nearly died. *Am I going to die?*

Once again I tried to telepath my predicament to Dad. Concentrating, I explained I was in the water somewhere between the Big Island of Hawaii and Maui, a tiny speck in an immense body of blue. Hopelessness washed over me. He couldn't hear me. They'd never find me.

Stop it, Allison! Be positive!

Okay. I could do this. All I had to do was keep my eyes on that island and paddle. And paddle. And paddle. I did so for what seemed hours, listening the whole time for the dreaded sound of Scarlotti Scaddono's helicopter.

My arms began to ache with the unaccustomed exercise, then my back. My choice of exercise was running, making my legs and lungs my strong suits. I stopped paddling long enough for a drink of water, never taking my eyes from the island ahead of me, afraid it might disappear.

I thought of Bart. That made me feel better, imagining him sitting in front of me, his blue eyes encouraging, his banter urging me on. How I loved Bart. I replayed games of hide and seek as we grew up, using Margo's entire estate as our playground. Long California grasses swayed in the ocean breeze as we ran golden hills, climbed giant oaks, raced on the beach, built fantastic sand castles and watched them wash away with the tide. What an idyllic childhood I'd had with Bart at my side as my best friend, big brother, protector, knight in shining armor.

We had talked for hours on end, about every subject under the sun. Our discussions were lively or serious depending on the topic. We'd discussed at length where we'd come from, why we were here on the earth, a purpose for our existence, and what would happen when we died. Where would we go from here? What became of the spirit when the body was in the grave? Deep subjects. Bart said he'd found the answers in that prison in Tibet. I wanted desperately to know those answers.

I remembered the years after our graduations, his from college, mine from high school, after his first proposal, just before he'd completely disappeared from my life. I remembered the pain at finding myself abandoned again, first by my father at age five when he was supposed to have been killed in an explosion, then by Bart. The two men I loved most in my life had left me. I pulled harder on the paddle. But there had been a happy ending when Bart came back, even though I hadn't believed at first he still loved me.

I pictured him now trying to find me. He was a professional. He'd check the hospitals, track the helicopter numbers, find the pilot and question him. He and Dad would be working together. They'd issue an all-points bulletin on Nate, have everyone in this part of the world looking for him. And they'd be grilling the men who tried to kidnap me back on Oahu.

When his image faded, I pictured Mom, her dark hair blowing in the wind. She'd remove the pins that held her hair twisted in a bun, shake it out, let the wind blow it free across her face. She always believed I could do anything I set my mind to do. I'd learned more than a dozen languages with an ease that surprised even her. Now she encouraged me again, imploring me to keep paddling, keep an eye on the island.

The island didn't seem to be getting any closer though I'd been paddling forever. I stopped for another drink, just a sip. If I got lost, if I drifted, if I couldn't make it to the island today, I'd need to conserve my water.

Would the old man send me out here in the middle of the ocean if it would take me more than one day to get to the island? If I slept, if I couldn't see the island in the dark, I could drift and miss it completely. Would he take that chance on a novice, an inexperienced sailor? Or was he just trying to get me off the island so Scarlotti Scaddono wouldn't punish him—or kill him—for helping me?

You're being negative again. There's no room in this outrigger for that. Stop it.

I thought of Dad. When they had told me he was dead, I wouldn't believe them. My five-year-old brain just would not process that kind of information about someone I loved so very much, and who loved me as I knew he did. Then strange flashes of knowledge, images, impressions, my father's messages when I was in danger, convinced me he was indeed alive.

But I hadn't seen him face to face until the week of my wedding—just last week. I pictured his piercing gray eyes, heard his heartening cadence, *Paddle right, paddle left. Keep it up, Bunny. You can do it. Stroke right, stroke left.*

How many times in his career as an Interpol agent had he been caught in impossible situations? Probably more than he could remember.

I thought of the cruel scars criss-crossing Bart's back from his imprisonment in Tibet. How had he endured the constant beatings? He said Emile's God helped him through it all, but we'd never had time to discuss it. *Bart, I need to know what you found out.*

Michael's little face filled my thoughts. He believed in God that same way. When he talked—and it seemed more like talking than praying—to God, he knew He was there listening and would respond. I'd prayed all my life, but it wasn't to a God I felt was waiting to help whenever I asked. My God was omniscient, omnipotent, the power of the universe, very important. I'd always just hoped that He wasn't too busy to hear me, and that for some reason, maybe I or my problem would be significant enough at that moment for my petition to be heard and answered.

Bart and Michael prayed to a God who knew them personally, who responded because they were important to Him, one they felt comfortable calling "Father."

I'd hardly taken my eyes off the island, had looked neither to the right nor the left for fear I'd head in the wrong direction, but a movement in the water caught my eye and I looked toward it.

Shark! Oh, no! Dear God, Father, please be with me now. It was about fifty feet from my outrigger, slightly ahead, and keeping pace with me. I stopped paddling and watched it. It disappeared. *Thank heaven.*

Resuming the tiresome paddling, I kept my eyes on the island, now and again scanning the seas around me for the dreaded fin. I was just beginning to relax my vigil when I felt a bump on the outrigger, right under my feet. The shark was under me!

I quickened my strokes to match the frantic thumping of my heart. *Outrun a shark? You're kidding yourself.* I slowed again to my former rhythm. *Mustn't use up all my energy uselessly,* I reminded myself sternly.

The bump came again on the bottom of the outrigger, gently, just a reminder he was there. I know! I know! How can I forget?

Then as if having a shark for a companion wasn't bad enough, I heard the thud, thud, thud, thud of a helicopter behind me, louder and louder, till I felt it right over me. The noise was deafening. The down draft of the rotors stirred up the waters around me, making progress difficult, and nearly whipped my big straw hat from my head. I stared straight ahead at the island, didn't dare look up so he could see my face, hoping the hat and roomy muumuu shielded and disguised me enough so my pursuer wouldn't recognize me.

What if it isn't Scarlotti? What if it's someone else, someone who could rescue me from this predicament? I must look. I can't turn down a chance for help.

Tipping my head slightly, I peeked around the corner of the hat. It was the same black and silver design as Scarlotti's. Could there be more than one like his in this area? I couldn't see in the tinted window, but he could see out. I'd have to assume it was Scarlotti, have to wave him off like an islander would do who was just on an inter-island trip.

As I raised my hand in what I hoped was a friendly gesture, I suddenly noticed the color of my skin. I couldn't possibly be sunburned already. This wasn't red. My skin was a lovely shade of brown. As long as he couldn't see my face or my clothes, Scarlotti would have no clue I was anything other than a native islander.

The helicopter swooped low over the front of the outrigger one more time, so low the runners skimmed the tops of the waves, as though he were trying to look under the large brim of my straw hat into my eyes. I ducked my head, pretending to reach for a canteen, lingered over opening it. The old man hadn't mentioned the cream he gave me for sunburn would also change the color of my skin. I said a silent thank-you to my benefactor.

Finally the helicopter left. I fervently hoped I hadn't made a mistake and sent away someone who could have taken me to safety or arranged it for me.

After my drink, when I started paddling again, the island seemed closer. How long had I been out here? I checked the sun and found it high overhead. Its brightness burned my eyes. It must be about noon. The old man hadn't said how long it would take to reach the island, but I'd probably been paddling about four hours. At this rate, it would be nightfall before I reached my destination.

Then what? What if I landed on an uninhabited area? How far would I have to go for help? *That's a discouraging thought. Discouraging thoughts are not allowed in this outrigger. Think positive thoughts. Your friendly shark has apparently been scared away by the helicopter.*

Something good came from that. *Always look for the good in a situation. I'm building great muscles in my arms. I'm learning a new skill—maneuvering an outrigger.* What else? There must be something else good from this. *I escaped from Scarlotti.*

Suddenly a jarring jolt against the canoe almost knocked me off balance. The shark was back. It came again, harder this time. How much battering could this little boat take before it started leaking? Outriggers were known for their sturdiness, but could mine withstand this kind of pummeling?

Help me, dear God! I can't do this on my own. If you're really interested in me, if you really love me, as Bart said, you know what's going on right here, right now. Please help me.

Another bump, this one even harder. Adrenaline surged through my body. I braced the green frond booties against the sides of the boat and increased my paddling stroke, not hoping to outdistance the shark, but simply to take advantage of the new energy flowing through my body.

Suddenly I remembered a movie based on an actual incident a couple of years before about a family whose big yacht, battered by killer whales, had sunk in minutes. They drifted for weeks in a life raft with sharks all around. I had no life raft. When my little craft sank, I'd be lunch—all five-foot-four, one hundred and twenty pounds of me. Bart would never know what happened, never have a clue as to what became of me.

What a black thought. Why did I have to remember that movie just now? Surely I'd seen movies with happy endings. Why couldn't I remember any of them?

The shark became more aggressive. He surfaced a couple of times, then disappeared. I increased my stroke and braced for another battering. It came. All was quiet for a minute. I searched the seas but couldn't see him. I kept paddling, stroking hard, digging the paddle deep into the water, arms and back aching with each stroke. Then I spotted him, cutting great circles around me, coming closer with each lap.

My throat tightened. My stomach tied itself in knots, and my arms tingled all the way to my fingertips. I prepared for the final onslaught I knew was inevitable.

Please, God. Help me. One final prayer. I looked around, wanting to see where the attack would come from, wanting to know when it happened. He was advancing from the left, fast, his great fin slicing the water, leaving a wake behind him.

I dropped the paddle in the bottom of the outrigger and clung tightly to the sides, hoping, praying the little boat could withstand this ramming.

Suddenly the water was alive with fins. Sleek gray bodies swarmed around the boat, churning the water around me. There were more than I could count, twisting and twirling in the water. A feeding frenzy? On me?

Hopelessness washed over me, blocking out the sun, clouding my vision. I was drained, physically and emotionally. The dolor I felt plunged me into the deepest, darkest abyss of despair I'd ever known. Dolor. I'd found that word years ago when Bart disappeared. It aptly described all the things I felt then: anguish, grief, heartache, misery, mourning, sorrow. I felt all of these now, and more. I'd finally found my father, and my family was together again. Bart had come back to me . . . and now I would die.

Chapter Seventeen

The air was a blur of graceful, glossy, gray forms, gamboling, gliding through the air, splashing playfully back into the water beside me.

Dolphins!

Dolphins everywhere! Two, three, four leaped in unison eight feet out of the water, then another half dozen copied the act. They circled my boat, frolicking, rejoicing with me, it seemed, in having driven the shark away. Their perpetual smiles sparked a celebratory mood. How could I not be happy just watching them? No wonder sailors considered dolphins a good omen. In seconds they'd brought me from the depths of despair to jubilation and hope.

Hope. Hope leads to faith. Faith brings miracles. *Thank you, dear God, for sending the dolphins. Thank you.* I bowed my head in gratitude. He had just given me my life back.

The dolphins continued cavorting around the outrigger, their blowholes spraying a cool, refreshing mist on me. Rejuvenated, I picked up the paddle and, assisted by the dolphins cutting through the waves in front of me, resumed the laborious stroke.

As I paddled, I telepathed once again my repetitious message to Dad. I didn't know where I was, much less where he was. Could I reach him?

That's okay, I told myself. *God appears to be listening to you, and he is interested in your welfare. He's more powerful than your earthly father, and He knows where you are.* That was a comforting thought. Then I had another even more comforting thought. Bart and Michael spoke to Him as "Father," their Father in Heaven. If He were truly my Heavenly Father, He would be vitally interested in my welfare. He'd care as much, or more than, my earthly father. It was a new and exciting insight and gave me renewed confidence that I would survive this ordeal.

After the dolphins disappeared, I diverted myself from the tedious paddling by singing all the Greek songs I could remember, then all the French, Spanish, and Italian songs I knew. I'd never learned any songs in Mandarin. That was strange. I thought I'd learned folk songs in every language I'd studied. Doing research with Mom into the native folklore and music of different cultures around the world, I remember learning the songs before anything else.

I thought again of the wizened old man. He'd given me his only means of escaping the island. What would he do now for transportation when he wanted . . . or needed . . . to leave? I realized suddenly how much he had sacrificed for me and how dangerous it had been for him to help me. What would Scarlotti do to him if he knew? How else could I completely disappear from that island without help? What help was there, besides the kindly old man? It would all point directly to him. I felt very selfish, and grateful, and offered prayers on his behalf. Would Scarlotti's dependence on the drugs be enough to save the old man from his wrath? I hoped so.

I didn't know how long I'd paddled after the dolphins left me. I was in a daze, moving automatically, when suddenly I realized I was very near an island. I'd made it! The water ahead teemed with sail boats, yachts, cruise ships, and fishing boats. Colorful parasails punctuated the deep blue sky. It felt good to see people, lots of people. I felt I'd been isolated forever.

My hands had blistered, the blisters popped, and now they were bleeding. I could hardly hold the paddle. Strange, I hadn't felt the pain until now. Gritting my teeth, I kept paddling. Only half a mile or so to go. My problem would be keeping out of the way of all the bigger boats who thought I was more maneuverable than they were.

One last pull on the paddle, one last effort, steeling myself for the pulse of pain as I pulled. The outrigger coasted on a wave, rushed toward the beach, and drove onto the sand. I couldn't move. My back ached, my arms were leaden. I didn't even want to look at my hands. I just sat in the little boat, quivering from head to toe. *I made it! Thank you, dear God!*

Waves pounding on the shore, then ebbing back, threatened to carry me back out to sea, but I couldn't stand up. My trembling legs wouldn't hold me.

A couple of burly teenage boys were running on the beach, throwing a ball between them. They cautiously approached as I sat numbly looking around, trying to force my body to move, my legs to stand up and get out of the boat.

"You okay, lady? Need some help?"

"Yes, please. Will you pull this up on the beach, and help me out? I seem to be having a hard time standing up."

They dragged the outrigger above the water line, then each taking an arm, helped me stand, and assisted me out of the boat.

"Look at your hands! Is that from paddling?"

"Yes. Could you get me to a telephone, please? Is there somewhere we could put the canoe for safekeeping? I need to return it."

They passed knowing looks between them. "It's okay," one said. "This part of the beach is ours. Nobody'll bother it."

They held on to my arms until I could walk steadily by myself, leading me down the beach to a little hut that rented snorkeling equipment and beach and water paraphernalia, and also sported the nearest available telephone.

I called the police in Hilo, and when I told the dispatcher who I was, he immediately put me through to Lt. Ishigo. I asked him to notify my family that I was okay and tell them to please come and get me. He asked where I was.

I turned to my young benefactors who were listening wide-eyed to my conversation.

"Exactly where am I? And is there somewhere close I can get something for my hands?" Pain throbbed through both of them.

"There's a first-aid station down the beach." They recited the name of a beach I couldn't pronounce, so I passed the phone to one of them to give directions to Lt. Ishigo. He handed it back after a moment.

"I'll be at the first-aid station. Is that detailed enough or do you need an exact location?" Lt. Ishigo assured me they could find me. I hung up and turned to the boys.

"I'll need your help some more, I'm afraid. Could you get me to that first-aid station?"

The boys were more than willing to help. They assisted me to the station about half a mile down the beach, holding me up when I stumbled wearily in the sand.

We entered a neat little room with cots against two walls, an examining table in the center, and a desk, filing cabinets, medicine chest, and bookcase against the back wall. Nestled in one corner was a shining stainless steel sink. Big windows in front afforded a clear view of the beach.

A petite, dark-eyed islander greeted my escorts as we entered.

"Hi, Tono, Jeremy. What did you bring me to patch up today?"

She didn't look much older than they were, obviously knew them well, and was glad to see them. They boosted me onto the examining table and held up my hands for her to see. I felt like a puppet someone else was manipulating. I was literally too tired to hold my hands out myself. All I wanted was something to make them feel better, and sleep. And Bart.

"We found her on the beach, Leilani," one explained.

The smile disappeared from her perky face, and Leilani quickly became a concerned professional health-care giver. I didn't care whether she was a doctor, a nurse, or was only adept at putting on a Band-aid as long as she could make my hands stop hurting.

Tono stood on one side of the examining table to support me. Jeremy held a large stainless steel pan while Leilani poured antiseptic soap liberally on my blood-stained hands. I winced with pain as she gently cleansed them to assess the damage underneath.

"You've had quite a workout today, haven't you?" she asked quietly, looking closely at me for the first time. "You're not from around here." It was a statement, not a question, and it slowly dawned on me through my fog of fatigue that she'd just noticed I was not a native. With my dark hair, and now darkened skin, it would have been a natural assumption.

She took off my cumbersome straw hat and handed it to Tono,

told me to lie down on the table, then turned her attention back to my hands. She scrubbed my wrists and arms, and we all watched as my beautiful brown skin turned white again, revealing cuts, scratches and bruises that weren't noticeable before. The three of them exchanged glances, but I was too exhausted to care what they were thinking.

She was thorough. I thought she'd never stop scrubbing and cleaning and dabbing at my hands and arms. This cleansing process, though necessary, was extremely painful. I longed for the gentle touch of the old man and his numbing medicine.

Finally she finished and proceeded to medicate and bandage me. I watched, detached from the whole process, disassociated from my hands. They were simply two appendages at the end of my arms, now swathed in bandages, looking like catcher's mitts, and no longer painful, just heavy.

Leilani motioned to Tono and Jeremy.

"Unwrap her feet. They may also need some attention."

The boys eagerly fell to their task. The once green, supple fronds were now stiff and turning tan, and frankly, uncomfortable, but since my other discomforts were much more acute, I'd ignored the scratchy, prickly ones on my feet. It felt wonderful to get them off, inducing a feeling of lightness and freedom.

"Get me another bowl of soap and water and we'll clean this off so we can have a look." She looked at me as she scrubbed the dried mud off my feet.

"Who put this on you?"

"An old man."

She turned back silently to her work, masking an expression that flitted across her face. Fear? Of what? Island medicine? No. I was wrong. I was too tired to make any assessments, any judgments at all. Nothing was computing correctly.

When she was satisfied she'd cleansed them sufficiently, Leilani applied something soothing to the bottom of my feet, around my toes, to my ankles, and up my legs. What had I done? Run through the jungle, up the mountain and over the sharp, volcanic rocks bare-footed and hadn't even noticed it? Not good. But there was no pain connected to my feet. Whatever the old man put on them had been a muddy medical miracle. The white bandages were more comfortable than the fronds, but just as binding. My sense of freedom evaporated.

Leilani motioned to Tono and Jeremy to move me to a bed while she went to the medicine cabinet and came back with two little white pills and a glass of water.

"A couple of aspirin will help. Go ahead and rest for a while."

Gratefully I took the aspirin, without even thanking her or the boys, and fell back onto a most welcome clean, white pillow. As I closed my eyes and felt myself sink into the seductive arms of sleep, some part of me registered that Leilani had gone immediately to the telephone, turned her back and was speaking softly into the receiver. If I hadn't been so drained, so completely worn out, my danger antennae would have been tingling, would, in fact, have been sounding off like a five-alarm fire.

The noise of a helicopter very near roused me from a deep, exhausted sleep. A frisson of fear flushed through me, jolting me wide awake. Scarlotti! I sat up, ready to run.

No! Bart, Mom, and Dad could come in a helicopter. I tried to calm my wildly beating heart, settle my frazzled nerves, bring my disjointed world back into focus. I must look a mess. Bart didn't need to see me like this.

I stood up, shakily at first, then hurried to the sink in the corner, ignoring Leilani, who looked up from papers on her desk. I had intended to wash my face, but my hands were bandaged. I couldn't even comb my hair, if I'd had a comb.

The helicopter was right outside, setting down on the beach. I didn't care how I looked. All I wanted was the safety of Bart's arms around me, the security of his love to make my world sane again. I hurried to the door, noticing for the first time it was dark outside.

The bright landing light shining directly into my face prevented me from seeing the helicopter. Sand swirled everywhere as the chopper settled on the beach, creating a miniature sandstorm. Palm trees waved wildly and somewhere a dog barked at the noisy intruder.

I waited for the noise to stop, for the engine to die away, but it didn't. Sand whipped in a frenzy as the rotors spun a hundred feet from the door. A figure emerged silhouetted against the bright light, shielded its face from the blowing sand, and ran up the beach toward the open door.

I started out to meet him, feeling Bart's arms around me already, crying in relief at finally being safely back with him. Then I stopped. Even through my tears, I could see it wasn't Bart.

Long hair blew wildly in the wind. Scarlotti! It was Scarlotti, not Bart that had come for me. No!

I whirled back toward the open door, then veered sharply and ran around the building. *Get off the beach, out of the sand so you can run!*

My bandaged feet slushed awkwardly through loose sand which sucked me in to my ankles. I felt like I was running in slow motion, making all the right moves, but not getting anywhere.

"Allison, it's useless to run. I'll catch you wherever you go." I could hear Scarlotti as the helicopter's engine whined down. It propelled me forward. He would not catch me again!

Suddenly my feet hit solid ground, the road's edge. I ran blindly down the road, frantically trying to decide whether I would be safer in the darkness or whether I should run toward lights and people. Scarlotti could tell someone a convincing lie, and I'd be right back in his clutches.

I ducked into the shadow of the trees lining the side of the road and tried to keep moving away from the seductive voice that followed. He was closing the distance between us, getting closer each second.

The trees opened into a clearing in which a waterfall cascaded down the hill and water tumbled over rocks in front of me. I turned quickly to follow the water, knowing full well it was headed straight back to the road and the beach. I'd be in the light, but I'd be caught in the dark anyway. Scarlotti was right behind me.

I burst into the road as a car careened around a corner and crossed the bridge, its lights blinding me. Brakes screeched. Horns honked. People screamed and jumped out of the car, shouting at me. I raced across the road with Scarlotti at my heels.

"Stop her!" he shouted. "She's on drugs. Just escaped from the hospital. She's dangerous!"

The people from the car chased me, yelling at me, staying between me and the bridge. I had no place to go but toward the beach. Bad choice. No choice.

Footsteps pounded closer and closer behind me, but not Scarlotti's. He'd done it. One convincing lie and now someone would catch me and take me back to him.

It was too cruel, to be so close to freedom, then have it snatched away. I fled as fast as I could, using the last ounce of strength I could muster to scramble up over the rocks that suddenly appeared in front of me.

A strong hand grabbed my ankle and pulled me over backwards. I fell straight into the waiting arms of a strange man.

Chapter Eighteen

How could I convince my captor Scarlotti was lying and I was not a suicidal druggie, a danger to society needing to be put behind bars?

"Please, listen. Don't let him take me. Call Lt. Ishigo of the Hilo police. He'll tell you who I am. Please." I pled for my very life which would be worth nothing if Scarlotti took me back to his island.

The man holding me stood indecisive, wavering between Scarlotti's authoritative declaration and my own pleading.

"That man's held me captive on an island. I escaped. The police are coming with my husband and parents to get me. Will you wait with me until they arrive and not let that man come near me? Please. I'm terrified of him."

Scarlotti had been standing in the darkness, just outside the beam of headlights with the small circle of people from the cars. When it became apparent my captor wasn't hurrying me back to him, Scarlotti turned from his audience and started toward us. What lies had he been telling them? What stories had he conjured up to convince them I needed to return with him?

"Please don't let him take me back. Call the police first and verify who I am."

The big man hesitated, not yet convinced. Scarlotti approached us in the darkness, his mesmerizing voice calm and seductive.

"Allison, you know you must come back to the hospital with me so we can treat you properly. You're not well enough to be out on your own just yet."

"He's lying," I whispered. "Don't let him take me. Stand between us so he can't touch me. Please. He wants to kill me."

I wriggled out of my captor's arms and stood behind his bulk, feeling very much like a little girl hiding from a monster in a bad dream.

"Tell him you're waiting for the police to decide what to do with me," I prompted. "Tell him you'll take responsibility until they get here."

I knew immediately I'd said the wrong thing. Some people don't like responsibility, especially when they don't know what it entails. My would-be benefactor's stiff, defensive bearing slumped into an apologetic posture, and he turned to grab me.

"Then keep him away while I find the police. At least you can do that." I tore loose from his grasp and ran as fast and hard as my bandaged feet would allow, avoiding the big rocks where I'd been captured and stumbling over the smaller ones on the stream's edge.

Scarlotti shouted in protest, and the formerly indecisive fellow took up the chase once more, following closely on the heels of Scarlotti.

Clearing the rocky area without mishap, I looked frantically up and down the moonlit beach as I ran for safety. *Where could I go? Who would help me?* It was only a matter of seconds before Scarlotti or his newly recruited helper caught me again.

I hit the hard sand close to the water and felt the adrenaline flow as my fight-or-flee responses kicked in. With bandaged hands, I wouldn't be much of a fighter. By the same token, with bandaged feet I wasn't doing too well fleeing either.

Two figures emerged dripping from the moonlit surf just ahead of me, surfboards in hand. They stopped to watch the race approaching them.

"Help me," I called. "Don't let them catch me."

Without a flicker of hesitation, they ran forward. It was Tono and Jeremy, my benefactors of this afternoon.

"Keep them away until the police get here!" I didn't stop, just kept running as fast as I could, glancing back once to see if they would help. Yes! Scarlotti and my captor were so close behind me, the boys had time only to position themselves between us. The surf-boards served as an effective moving barricade, frustrating Scarlotti's efforts for the moment. It gave me valuable time to gain some distance.

Up ahead, lights of restaurants and shops glowed through the darkness, and I could see people mingling and moving around. If I could get there before they caught me, I might survive until Bart could come for me. *Where was he? Why was it taking so long for them to get here? How had Scarlotti Scaddono found me so quickly?*

I hurried past shops, restaurants, and clubs where people laughed and talked and milled about on the sidewalk, spilling onto the beach. Slipping into the crowd, I pressed toward the liveliest cafe crammed with people inside and out, hoping to get lost in the sea of bodies moving and swaying to loud, live music emanating from the wide open structure designed to resemble an island cave.

Elbowing my way through the packed throng, I pushed toward the rear of the cafe, all the while unwinding my bandaged hands. The further in I got, the darker and more atmospheric it became, with booths and tiny, intimate tables in little spaces surrounded by bamboo screens and lots of lush, green plants that provided a measure of privacy.

By time I reached the ladies room, I had both hands unwrapped. The yards of gauze were easily disposed of in the waste-basket and I locked myself in the furthest stall to release my feet from their once-white prison. I felt like a claustrophobic just liberated from a sarcophagus without all the bindings on my hands and feet.

Should I stay here and hide, or put in another phone call to Lt. Ishigo? I didn't really like my chances of Bart stumbling across me in my current hiding place, but neither was I anxious to come out of hiding and face Scarlotti and his pernicious lies that could send me back with him to his island of terror.

What to do! What to do? Bart's voice came into my mind. *"God doesn't want us to fail. He wants us to succeed. All we need to do is ask. He's waiting to help us."* I certainly needed help and it looked like He was the only one who could possibly get me out of this spot.

I didn't feel comfortable praying in a stall in the ladies room, but I was sure He'd been asked for help from worse places than this. I poured out my soul to the loving God Bart had been introduced to by a Frenchman in a Red Chinese prison in Tibet.

I didn't get any sweeping revelations, or any voices from heaven telling me how to get out of my dire predicament, but I did feel the calm assurance that somehow I would be all right. The question was, how?

My first priority was to inform Bart of my whereabouts. I needed a telephone. The Ritz-Carlton this wasn't, so, of course, there were no phones in the restroom.

Taking a deep breath to fortify my courage, and with a silent prayer in my heart, I reluctantly left my hiding place as soon as the room was quiet and everyone had gone. The first thing I saw as I emerged from the iron gray cubicle was a door marked "Employees Only."

I tried the knob. It turned in my hand and the door opened into a dark void. Voices and laughter outside preceded someone into the ladies room. Slipping into the dark room, I quickly shut the door behind me and felt along the wall for a light switch. There was nothing on either side of the door. I didn't dare move for fear of making a noise and calling attention to myself. I'd have to wait until the restroom was empty, then open the door to shed light on where I was and with what I was sharing space.

The waiting seemed endless. The outer room wasn't clearing. I carefully reached out again, hoping I wouldn't knock over a broom or a can of cleaner off a shelf. As I moved, something touched my face. I stifled a scream. Cobwebs? I hadn't thought about spiders. Instinctively ducking, I reached up to brush it away, touching instead a string dangling from the ceiling. A light?

I pulled the cord and a single bare bulb lit up the small room, apparently a dressing room for waitresses who worked here. Freshly laundered sarongs hung neatly folded on wire hangers on a rod along one wall. Silk flower leis adorned plastic hooks surrounding the mirror above a small dressing table which was cluttered with lipsticks, makeup, perfume, and hair spray cans.

Perfect. I slipped out of my clothes—the once brightly colored muumuu the old man had given me to cover my torn dress, and the dress itself which revealed more than it concealed because of rips and tears suffered in my climb up the mountain. Choosing a green sarong, I wrapped and tied it the way I'd seen it done, hoping I was doing it right and it would stay put. I donned a silk lei of large passion flowers, and matching wrist and ankle bracelets, secured my hair on top of my head with plenty of bobby pins, and tucked a flower over each ear.

Usually I was averse to using anyone else's makeup, but necessity overcomes a lot of aversions. Too bad the suntan lotion/stain the old man had rubbed on me which made me look like an islander had been washed off at the first aid station. At least this makeup was dark. I applied it liberally, with plenty of rouge and eye make-up, then stood back to take in the full effect in the mirror.

At first glance, it didn't look like me at all. If Scarlotti scanned the crowd looking for the person he'd been chasing and just caught a glimpse of me, he probably wouldn't recognize me. Good. Now to find a telephone that didn't require money.

There would be one located at the cashier's station, but that was probably all the way up at the front of the cafe. I didn't want to go back there if I didn't have to. Maybe there was one in the kitchen, wherever that was.

I followed a similarly dressed waitress carrying an empty tray as she wound through a maze of little tables filled with noisy, animated people. She led me to a busy, bustling kitchen with a noise level close to that of a jet engine warming up, with pots and pans banging and clanging, cooks yelling at each other, and waitresses calling out orders.

I spotted a telephone just inside the door and reached for it as a waitress grabbed at my sarong.

"Hey, that's my dress! What are you doing in it?"

"Hiding. Do you know the number of the police here? I'm being chased and your dress became my disguise. Do you mind terribly? Will you help me?"

She softened immediately and her eyes brightened. "What can I do?"

"I've got to tell the police where I am, then stay out of sight until they get here. The man chasing me is telling everyone I've escaped from a hospital where I was recovering from drug abuse. He's very convincing."

"Make your call, then you can help me with the tables in the back. I'll tell everyone I'm training you. I may need your help more than you need mine. We're short-handed tonight and the place is packed. I'm Lisa. Welcome to the Coconut Club."

I made the call, informing the dispatcher to direct Lt. Ishigo and my family to the Coconut Club instead of the first aid station. I was about to call the first aid station, in case Bart was there, when I suddenly remembered the phone call the nurse had made as I settled onto the bed. That was how Scarlotti Scaddono had found me so quickly! What was Leilani's tie to him?

Lisa was back. She thrust an order pad into my hand and motioned toward the water station.

"Table thirty-seven needs five waters, then take their order. Menus are already on their table. Hurry."

"Thirty-seven? Which one is that?"

"Very back corner. All the way back."

Balancing five glasses of water on a tray, I threaded my way around tables, and between the press of people talking animatedly in the narrow spaces between tables. How I made it to the table in the far corner without spilling a single drop was a miracle. I smiled brightly at the silver-haired group of tourists studying the menus.

"Hi. I'm Melanie. Are you ready to order?" As I placed the water on the table, I kept my back to the front of the cafe. I'd be concealed from view by hanging baskets of greenery, unless someone came all the way back looking for me. That would be like Scarlotti. He wouldn't give up easily.

I took their order back to the kitchen and grabbed Lisa on her way out with a tray loaded with luscious-smelling food. *How long had it been since I had eaten?* I was suddenly starving.

"What do I do with the order?"

"Call 'order in,' make sure one of the cooks hears you, and clip it on the string hanging in front of the grill. Grab that filled tray on the carousel and follow me, then take the order for the table next to them."

Lisa kept me so busy for the next thirty minutes I didn't have time to worry about Scaddono or why Bart hadn't come for me yet or my very empty stomach.

Finally we caught up and the pace slowed for a few minutes. Lisa looked at me.

"You don't look so good. Are you okay?"

"Exhausted and starving. Do you suppose I could have something to eat?"

"Of course. What do you want?"

"What are my choices?"

"Anything on the menu."

"Really? I'd like a piece of that tantalizing chicken everyone's been ordering and the Hawaiian bread and fruit plate."

"Just tell Koko. In fact, tell him to make it two, then bring it out this back door. I'll be waiting. I've got to get off my feet for a few minutes."

Koko dished up two plates of the most popular items on the menu, and I followed Lisa's directions out the open door to a garbage area masquerading as a dimly lit patio. One round wooden table and six plastic patio chairs shared the small enclosure with overflowing garbage cans. A bamboo divider failed to separate the two sufficiently. I chose the chair furthest from the offensive sight and smells, and watched a cat furtively return to its search through the refuse.

Lisa afforded me time to devour the delicious meal before beginning her barrage of questions.

"What happened to your hands and arms and legs? You look like you've been in a fight with a rosebush."

"I climbed a mountain in a hurry."

"Who's after you?"

"A very adept liar who could convince my own grandmother that I needed to go with him for my own good. Why haven't the police come? They should have been here by now."

Lisa opened her mouth to reply when the tiger-striped alley cat that had been feasting on the garbage behind us suddenly yowled loudly as it vaulted the bamboo divider, landing on my empty plate. With another bound, it disappeared into the darkness beyond us. Someone or something had scared that cat.

An explosion of terror knocked the breath from my lungs and twisted my stomach in knots. I sprang from the table, poised for flight, with the dreadful knowledge that I knew what had frightened the cat.

Chapter Nineteen

"Don't move, Allison." His voice reached from the darkness with soft, seductive fingers, stroking dissonant chords that sent chills through my body. Softly spoken, it was nevertheless a command, but to the ears of a stranger, the mesmerizing sensuous tone would convey love and caring. I knew what terrors that tonality masked.

Fleeing through the kitchen, I slammed the door behind me to gain a few precious seconds. Where could I go? Scarlotti probably had someone out front waiting for me. Where was Bart? Where were the police? Where were my folks?

Exiting the kitchen, I slowed to a walk, grabbing an empty tray as I went, hoping to look more like a waitress and less like someone on the run. I ducked into the ladies room, and then into the dressing room. Where could I hide? Was I safer in here than running in the open?

There were no other doors, no closets, no obvious nooks or crannies that afforded even a small hiding place. I grabbed the faded flowered skirt of the little dressing table. Maybe, just maybe I could squeeze into the tiny space that seemed barely big enough to accommodate two knees.

I flipped off the light, plunging the room into darkness again, then folded myself pretzel-like under the dressing table. This was one time I was glad I didn't have long legs. I pulled the chair close to the skirt, then straightened the fabric to make sure it hung straight down and hid me.

Then I prayed. With all the fervor of my heart and soul, I poured out a frantic plea for heavenly help.

Why wasn't Bart here? Where were the police? Even if Bart and Mom and Dad were on another island, surely the local police had located them when I called from the first aid station. They would have had time to get here from anywhere in the islands—wouldn't they? It had been hours since I called. How long had I slept at the first aid station? I only knew it was light when I fell into an exhausted sleep, and dark when I awoke.

Then I had a thought that made me sick. *What if the dispatcher hadn't relayed the call? What if Bart had never received my message and still didn't know where I was? What if the police were not on their way?*

Someone was on their way. The door opened and light flooded the little room, illuminating every corner, but hopefully not me.

"Melanie? Are you here?"

Lisa. Was she still on my side or had Scarlotti persuaded her I needed to go with him? Should I answer or stay hidden? *What if Bart or the police had come?* If no one knew where I was, they'd leave without me. Scarlotti could wait me out. I had to come out sometime.

I opened my mouth to answer when Lisa spoke again, this time to someone outside.

"She's not in here. I've checked all the stalls in the ladies room and you can see, there's nowhere to hide in our little dressing room."

"Thank you, Lisa. She has to be here somewhere. She didn't leave by the front entrance. I appreciate your help. It's imperative we find her and get her back to the hospital. Her medication will soon run out and she'll need her next dosage. She becomes extremely paranoid, afraid everyone is trying to harm her. She's usually not dangerous, but could become so if she's cornered."

Lisa turned off the light, shut the door, and left me trembling in the dark. I'd come so close to answering. I'd come so close to walking right back into his hands. He'd even come into the rest room with Lisa! Was there nowhere safe from Scarlotti Scaddono?

Maybe the police had already come. He was so persuasive, he might have convinced them he *was* my doctor and I *had* escaped from his hospital. If I came out expecting to throw myself on them for protection, they could very well turn me over to him. The thought turned my stomach upside down.

My muscles screamed for release from their cramped posture. I couldn't stay in this twisted position any longer, but neither could I move. I was exhausted. I felt like someone had punched a hole in my big toe and drained every ounce of energy from my body.

Dear Father, I'm in a great deal of trouble. Please help me. If you love me as much as Bart said, you won't allow that satanic sadist to catch me again. Help me escape him and guide Bart to me, please.

Unwinding my body from the contortions it performed, I stretched out on the floor for a minute to think. My only allies had been Jeremy and Tono. Were they still believers in my innocence and need, or had Scarlotti hoodwinked them, too?

Now what? If I could get out of here without being seen (fat chance!), and find Jeremy and Tono (another big if), and if they were still willing to help (unknown quantity), I just might have a chance.

I sat up and looked around the tiny dressing room. What was here that could help? Only sarongs, leis, and make-up, which I'd already used. Wait. I'd been scrunched between drawers under the skirt of that dressing table.

I flipped up the gathered faded fabric and found four drawers, each with a name taped on the front. I opened Lisa's first. A pair of cutoffs, a T-shirt and leather sandals completed the sparse inventory.

The second drawer hadn't much to offer . . . a hairbrush, toothbrush and toothpaste, a jar of moisturizer, and a pair of thick-lensed glasses with tortoise shell rims. Did Gina need these to put on her make-up?

The third drawer, Janie's, contained an interesting collection of island jewelry. Kukui nut, pearl, and shell necklaces with earrings to match were all tossed inside. No help.

My last hope was Monique's drawer. I pulled it open slowly, almost afraid to look, afraid I'd find nothing but the end of my rope.

Voila! I'd struck paydirt! Smashed together in the drawer were half a dozen wigs of as many different styles, colors, and lengths. I'd come in with my dark hair down and pinned it up trying to disguise myself, which hadn't fooled Scarlotti. Or had my voice given me away instead of my appearance? Would a long blonde wig do the trick, or a short red one? What could I possibly do that would allow me to walk unrecognized right past my pursuer?

I laughed out loud when I thought of it! It was just preposterous enough to work. I removed the flowers from my hair and donned a pageboy-length frosted wig with a lot of blonde highlights.

Discarding Lisa's borrowed green sarong, I found the largest of the remaining sarongs that comprised about four yards of fabric, bright orange flowers on a black background. Just the ticket. I searched in vain for a piece of string, or even a scarf, then finally unwound a wire hanger and tried it above my waist. It would work!

Three of the sarongs should be sufficient, folded and bunched properly over the wire just under my breasts. Finally, I wrapped the fabric around me a couple of times and tied it behind my neck. I put on the thick glasses and looked in the little mirror.

Ay caramba! A very pregnant, nearly blind, blonde. I scooted the glasses down on my nose so I could actually see my reflection. It would work! Even Bart or my own mother would not recognize me! Now if only Scarlotti wouldn't see through my disguise.

I hung Lisa's green sarong back on the hanger and put everything back where I'd found it, trying not to leave any trace of me behind. Then I turned out the light and waited in a stall in the ladies room for someone to come in. I needed to leave with a group of people, not alone, so there wouldn't be so much attention on just me.

Presently lively chatter filled the ladies room, and I gave up my stall to a little blue-haired lady bedecked with wilting leis. I washed my hands and asked another, obviously with the same group, how she was enjoying the islands and where she was from. By time they were ready to go, we were deep in conversation.

I took the frailest of the elderly quartet by the arm and guided her out the door, keeping my face toward her and away from anyone looking for me. I felt rather secure. Who pays any attention to a bunch of elderly tourists and a very pregnant lady? If you aren't one of the beautiful people, you can be almost invisible, except to avid people watchers who collect characters like bird watchers collect birds.

Their table was in a circular booth near the front of the cafe.

Three older pleasant-looking men stood as the ladies returned to the table. What our younger generation could learn in manners and chivalry!

"We're just ordering dessert. Won't you join us while you finish telling me about the volcano? I was afraid to take that part of the tour, but if you think it's safe, and worth it, maybe I'll be daring this time and try it. I'm Sarah, by the way, and this is Mable, Harriet, Ruth, Evan, Hugh, and Howard."

I nodded and smiled, needing to downplay introductions and just be a part of this group for a while, until either the police or Bart arrived, or I could find Tono and Jeremy. And I wanted to see if I could spot Scarlotti waiting for me or one of the helpers he seemed adept at recruiting on the spot.

Then I saw him, making his way to the front of the cafe, examining the occupants of each table as he came. I turned my back to him, made sure my arms were beneath the table so he couldn't see the scratches there, and pretended to give all my attention to the little lady sitting next to me.

I didn't dare look up to check his progress, didn't dare appear to be paying any attention to him at all. But every thought was of him. How close is he? Where is he? Will he see through my disguise?

Suddenly long silky hair fell over my shoulder, cascaded down my arm. Hands gripped my elbows.

"Allison. I'm so glad I found you. I've missed you, my darling. You'll come with me now."

I turned slowly to face him and gazed into a strange, handsome face I'd never seen before, one that matched perfectly the hauntingly beautiful voice. With a face like that, why wouldn't he let me see him? Why were there no mirrors in the house?

"Hello. I guess I didn't have an opportunity to thank you for your hospitality before I left. I did appreciate it, but I won't be going back with you."

Turning to the people at the table, I asked Hugh to please call the police and tell them Allison Allan was waiting for them at the Coconut Club, and to inform her husband and parents, and Lt. Ishigo, to hurry.

Hugh didn't move from his seat, looking confused and uncertain. I hadn't asked a great deal, just that he make a phone call. Was that so hard?

I repeated my request. "There's a telephone at the cashier's counter right behind you on the other side of this booth. Will you please go to it, ask the cashier to give you the number of the police, and call them. Allison Allan is waiting for them at the Coconut Club. Lt. Ishigo needs to be informed immediately."

Hugh looked from me to Scarlotti, still bending over me, still gripping my elbows. I turned and looked up to find Scarlotti staring at Hugh, gently shaking his head, signaling to him not to call. I didn't need a showdown right here in front of all these people, but I certainly wasn't going to go quietly.

I turned again to the seven senior citizens who had befriended me.

"Will one of you please go call the police? This man wants to take me away from my husband to his island and keep me there against my will. It's called kidnapping. He's planning to kill me and my family. I escaped from his island in a canoe I found. I rowed all day. See the blisters on my hands?" I held up my hands, which were a mass of broken blisters.

Scarlotti started in with his smooth-as-molasses voice, calmly telling of my neurotic state, of my paranoia, of my mental illness which he had been treating at his island hospital.

I clenched the table as he tugged at my arms, his fingers digging painfully into my pressure points.

"Sarah, do you believe me? If I'm a mental patient, don't you think the police will want me to go with him? Someone please call the police and check out my story."

Sarah looked at me, then at Scarlotti. She turned to Hugh, sitting on the end of the curve.

"Hugh, you get up and call the police. I've never trusted anyone who didn't have a decent haircut." She turned to Scarlotti. "Young man, you take your hands off this girl right now. We'll just wait for the police to sort this whole thing out."

But Scarlotti wasn't about to be thwarted by a little old blue-haired lady. Retaining his grip on my right elbow, he produced a small pearl-handled pistol in his left hand, pointing it directly at

Sarah, but keeping it discreetly hidden from general view.

"You don't understand, Madam. Allison can be extremely dangerous if excited. You could be injured. I must take her with me and get her back on medication."

"Don't threaten me, young man. Hugh, go call the police, or I will. And put that gun away or I'll scream for help."

Scarlotti Scaddono may not have frightened Sarah, but I knew what he was capable of and he scared me to death. I needed to protect the well-meaning group from this warped, depraved man, but what could I do, short of actually going with him? Nothing.

"Don't hurt these people, Scarlotti. I'll go if you'll promise not to hurt them."

The long, slender fingers gripping my elbow relaxed the tiniest bit, and the gun disappeared back into his pocket. Scarlotti's left hand slipped around my waist, or what should have been my waist, lifting me off the bench and onto my feet.

"Clever disguise, Allison. It would have worked if I hadn't seen this garish sarong hanging in the dressing room. Stay close to me and walk toward the entrance. Unless you come quietly, I'll shoot our way out of here and not care who gets hurt."

Chapter Twenty

I had no doubt that Scarlotti had help waiting out front for us. He'd had plenty of time to call for reinforcements and probably had connections I couldn't even imagine all over the islands. I thought of Leilani, who had so carefully tended my wounds, then called Scarlotti to come and get me.

Who else was on his payroll? It didn't matter. Even if they'd never seen him before, he could still charm them into believing every word he said. What chance did I have of getting away unless Bart and my parents showed up? It would be helpful if they brought the police with them, but I felt short on miracles at the moment.

Scarlotti's grip on my elbow caused a severe shooting pain down my arm. He stayed closer than my shadow, his body brushing mine as we walked. I hated the touch of him. The possibility of going back to the island with him loomed greater with each agonizing step.

Now, Allison, do something now. A waitress approached carrying a tray of steaming hot food. I paused and turned slightly.

"Please, my arm is absolutely numb. Can you hold it somewhere else? Or not at all? I can't get away from you, you know."

"I'm glad you finally realize that. It was so foolish of you to try."

I turned back as the waitress placed the tray of food on a cart immediately in front of us. When she lifted the first steaming plate, I grabbed it, pivoted, and smashed it into Scarlotti's face. I darted out of his grasp as he tore at the sizzling hot food clinging to his face.

Wasting no time or sympathy, I ran to the entrance, checking out the men standing alone and apart in the sand beyond the crowd as I moved. There were three. Scarlotti's men, waiting for me? Were they looking for someone with bandages? As I threaded my way through patrons waiting to get in, the biggest man, looking like he'd been hired more for muscle than for speed, watched me intently. He glanced at the two who were gazing in another direction, and then back at me, as if needing verification that I was not his quarry.

A ruckus started behind me, probably Scarlotti urging sympathetic spectators to catch me. I cleared the cashier's desk, a shoulder-high bamboo structure about the size of a piano with a petite islander perched on a stool behind it. A telephone sat within arm's reach, enticing me to stop and call the police myself, but there was no time.

The muscle-bound man took an uncertain step forward.

"A man needs help in there with someone in bandages," I called, hoping to get rid of Atlas before his suspicions led him to grab me.

It worked. Not only did Atlas respond, but the other two raced for the entrance, too, shouldering aside the late dinner crowd waiting outside.

That was my cue to run as fast as I could. Shouts behind me sent a surge of adrenaline to assist my flying feet through the sand. But where could I go? I couldn't outrun everyone, and I didn't want to leave the area. I needed to be where Bart could find me when he came.

Two figures loomed ahead of me on the moonlit beach. *No! Please, dear God, don't let them stop me!*

I ran on the hard sand at water's edge. If I veered to avoid them, I'd be back in the deep, loose sand where it was hard to make any distance or speed. I'd have to take a chance it wasn't somebody Scarlotti had enlisted to help him. Plunging ahead, I tried to decide whether I could safely pass them or needed to change direction at the last minute.

Frantic shouts from the cafe advised me Scarlotti had recovered and was directing the chase once more. I determined to take my chance in the ocean rather than be caught again. Then I spotted the surf boards. Could it be? Tono and Jeremy!

"Lady! Is that you? Are you still running from that guy? Oh, sorry. Thought you were someone else."

They were close enough now they could see me and thought they'd made a mistake.

"It's me. Help me, again!"

The boys dropped their surf boards in the sand, grabbed my hands and started running with me toward the buildings on the beach. My feet barely touched the ground as their muscular young legs powered them through the sand.

"Take her to the cave!" Tono shouted as we hit the sidewalk. "I'll slow down the posse." He let go and headed for the muscle man rumbling down the sidewalk toward us.

There was no time, nor breath, to warn him to be careful. Jeremy towed me through yards, alleyways, a park, and behind stores. We zigzagged and looped till I was completely lost and totally exhausted.

We'd left the noise behind, the shouting and scuffling I'd heard take place as Tono met Atlas. Poor Tono. I hoped he wasn't hurt.

But I was. My lungs were bursting and my heart felt like it would explode. I couldn't run another step.

"It's okay. We're almost there. Don't stop now," Jeremy urged.

We ran into an alley behind a well-lit building with music blaring—familiar music. Then I saw the little patio with palm trees trying to disguise the garbage and give credence to the picnic table. We were behind the Coconut Club. Right back into Scarlotti's arms.

Moonlight highlighted a rock formation just beyond the building. In fact, the cafe was nestled against it and had been built to look like a projection of the rock. Jeremy led me to the corner of the cafe and we slipped into a narrow opening just big enough to squeeze through.

"Duck your head."

I ducked.

"Now get on your hands and knees. We have to crawl about ten feet. Don't worry. There's nothing in here but us and sand."

Obediently, but reluctantly, I dropped to my knees and followed Jeremy. It was so dark I couldn't see a thing, but he apparently knew the territory well. He didn't hesitate a minute, just crawled through a winding, ascending tunnel barely big enough for him to get through. I held my breath and followed, willing my claustrophobia away.

We emerged from the narrow tunnel into an area we could stand up in, and not a minute too soon. My claustrophobic tendencies had flared into a full blown phobia in the cramped confines of that dark tunnel.

Light from a large rectangular window cast an eerie green glow in the hollowed out rock room where we stood. I could clearly see the interior of the Coconut Club and the general activity going on below us.

"It's a two-way mirror. We can see them but they can't see us. From the other side, it looks like an island scene painted on a mirror," Jeremy explained.

"What's it for?"

"The guy who originally built the club was a real weirdo. He had a drop-dead gorgeous wife who was a social butterfly. He figured sooner or later he'd catch her trying to cheat on him, and he'd be armed with evidence so he wouldn't have to pay her any alimony."

"What happened?"

"One of his spies fell in love with the lady and told her about this room. She turned the tables on her husband, and ended up with damaging evidence against him, so he had to cough up a bundle when she accused him of infidelity and filed for divorce. My dad was her attorney, and when Tono and I found the tunnel and told him about the room, he told us her story. There's a door into an office in the club, but we never use it. The tunnel's fine for us."

"Now what?"

"I figure sooner or later, the police will show up with your husband. You can watch from here. When you see them, I'll take you out."

"Jeremy, I don't know that the police ever got my first message. They should have been here hours ago, no matter where in the islands they were. If the dispatcher didn't pass the message along, they could still have no idea where I am."

"Then I'd better go call to make sure. What was the name of the guy in Hilo you wanted notified?"

"Lt. Ishigo. He should know how to get hold of my husband and parents. I don't have any idea where they are, but he should. Thanks, Jeremy. I don't know what I would have done without you and Tono."

An easy smile creased his face in the dim, green glow from the window. "It's all right, lady. You did pretty good with that disguise. I'd never have recognized you."

"Too bad it didn't work with Scarlotti Scaddono."

The smile vanished from Jeremy's face. "That was Scarlotti Scaddono? Wow!"

"Do you know him?"

"No. Only about him. I've heard my dad talk about him. They think he's behind the drugs coming into the islands, but they've never been able to catch him. They also think he's smuggling Asians onto the mainland. They say he demands payment in exotic shaped pearls and has quite a collection now."

I felt for the pearl. It was still there.

"Like this?" I held it up for Jeremy to see.

"Wowee! Where did you get that?"

"Scarlotti gave it to me. It's a long story. My husband and I were kidnapped, I ended up in a volcano . . ."

"That was you! Wowoo! I saw them bring you out on television. But you never showed at the hospital, and everybody's been in an uproar trying to figure out what happened to you."

"The same guys that I jumped from the helicopter to escape from were the ones who 'saved' me."

"You jumped into Pele's arms? Wowaa!"

"Not on purpose. I hoped to land beside my unconscious husband and save him from rolling into the volcano. I misjudged and ended up there myself. Scarlotti 'rescued' me from the guys who grabbed us, and kept me prisoner in his house on an island somewhere out there. I'd been rowing most of the day to escape when you found me on the beach. My family must be beside themselves by now, not knowing what's happened to me."

"I'll go call right now. Lt. Ishigo?"

"Right. Thanks, Jeremy. You've been a godsend."

Jeremy scrunched through the narrow tunnel, leaving me alone in the eerie green darkness. I scanned the faces in the cafe below, searching for Scarlotti and the long, silky hair that fell across his face. It was the hair I'd recognize first, and his tall, slender, graceful, silhouette. That dreaded silhouette.

At that point, my knees simply gave out. I dropped to the floor, spent. It had taken all I had to get this far, and I could go no further. *Please, dear God, bring Bart here for me. I've done as much as I can. It's all up to you now.*

I slumped against the wall in a heap, too tired to even raise my head to look out the window.

What if Bart comes and doesn't see me? He could leave without me. Scarlotti won't leave without me. He'll wait me out. Bart doesn't know what Scarlotti looks like, does he? But Scarlotti will recognize Bart. He was at the estate and watched us.

I mustered the strength to raise my head and peer over the rough stone sill at the scene below. Sarah and her party were leaving, slowly. They appeared reluctant to exit, probably wanted to see if anything else exciting would happen. They'd have one interesting tale to tell their friends back home anyway.

Just as they reached the cashier's counter, four policemen appeared at the door. Sarah ran to them and began an animated conversation, with her friends gathering to join in the report. So one of them had called the police. Jeremy hadn't been gone long enough to reach a phone yet.

Bless their hearts. It was gratifying to know there were still people who were willing to get involved.

Movement toward the back of the cafe caught my eye. A heavy man elbowed people out of his way, heading in a hurry toward the restrooms. Atlas! I watched until he disappeared behind a bamboo divider. Was he going out the back way? Or was he going to warn Scarlotti the gendarmes had arrived? Would Scarlotti have stayed here after I doused him with that plate of hot food?

Why not? He could have gone back to the men's room to clean himself off, leaving the chase to the others. I'd made him angry, had insulted and embarrassed him in front of a crowd. He'd really want to kill me now.

Jeremy, Tono, Bart, somebody! Where are you? I can't take a chance on going back down there alone. Somebody has to tell the police Scarlotti may be in the men's room.

Sarah pointed to the rear of the cafe. She could identify Scarlotti as the man I told them had kidnapped me. Sarah had believed me. Would the police believe her, or would Scarlotti persuade them otherwise? He had the capability, the power to convince them I was the one that was lying and he was the one telling the truth.

I had to get down there. If I reached them first and told the police who he was, surely they'd arrest him before his mesmerizing voice could influence their judgment.

I tried to stand up. My legs wouldn't hold me. I crawled to the tunnel entrance, but I couldn't go in. Between exhaustion and claustrophobia, I could not force myself down that dark tight tunnel. I kept telling myself I could get out the other end—there wasn't anything in there to stop me. I *could* get out. I *must* get out. I must get to the police before they got to Scarlotti. Or before his forked tongue got to them.

Slowly, reluctantly, I entered the black hole. I wanted to scream, to run, to go back, to be anywhere but here. I couldn't breathe. Panic started, grew, took over. I couldn't move. I was paralyzed with fear of this tiny, suffocating hole. But I couldn't stay there.

Please get me through this, Father. Get me out of here! I can't stand it!

Suddenly a warm, peaceful feeling enveloped me. My wildly beating heart slowed, and my normal breathing resumed. It was as if I'd had a heavenly hug, a reassurance that someone heard who cared for me, someone who had the power to help. Someone who could give me the power I no longer had to help myself.

With a prayer of gratitude on my lips, I forged ahead through the no-longer-formidable darkness. Would I get to the police before they got to Scarlotti? Whom would they believe? Him or me?

A wisp of fresh air told me I was close to the entrance. Finally, the merest shading of light signaled the well-hidden mouth of the tunnel. I scurried to the opening as fast as my hands and knees would carry me, and breathed deeply of the fresh night air.

Rejuvenated, I raced to the back door of the cafe, scaring the daylights out of the cat again feasting in the garbage cans. The restrooms were just around the corner from the kitchen door. The police had to make their way through the crowded tables. I could probably intercept them just before they reached the restroom area.

There was never a doubt in my mind that Scarlotti would face the police and pull his usual bluff, painting me as mentally unhinged and needing hospitalization, that he was my caring doctor.

I wasn't prepared, therefore, to run smack into him and Atlas beating a hasty retreat through the kitchen. We both stopped . . . and stared . . . for the briefest of moments, though it seemed an entire eternity.

My body moved, but it was in slow motion. I wheeled, tried to run, to flee from his presence, from his voice. It was like a nightmare, when you're running and running and not getting anywhere, and the pursuer comes closer and closer, and there's nothing you can do to stop him.

I heard a scream, bloodcurdling, frightening. *Was that me?* Then his voice, that hypnotic, tantalizing, sensuous voice, calling softly, close behind me.

"Allison. You can't run from me. I'll get you no matter where you go."

His hands grabbed at my arms, my dress, and pulled me back against his body, taking me prisoner once more.

Chapter Twenty-One

"My dear Allison. Did you really think you could escape me? How I shall delight in dispensing doses of agonizing pain designed especially for you."

Scarlotti's sensuous voice dripped with deadly venom. His threats were not idle. I would not, could not let him take me back to his island of evil.

I slumped against him in a gesture of submission. Surprised, he stepped backward to catch his balance, loosening his grip on me for an instant and I bolted out of his reach. Could it buy me the time I needed for the police to get here, for Tono and Jeremy to return, for Bart to find me?

Suddenly a body hurtled out of the darkness with a savage shout, crushing Scarlotti against Atlas. They went down like dominos, splintering the table, scattering chairs and garbage cans with a terrible din.

All I could see in the melee were arms and legs of tables and chairs and men. But there was no doubt who my benefactor was this time. It was *déjà vu,* exactly how Bart had rescued me from Scarlotti's father. And Bart would kill Scarlotti. He was like a wild animal, tearing into his prey with ferocious fervor. All his pent-up frustration at not knowing where I was or how I was, or if I was still alive, burst forth in infinite intensity. Even muscle-bound Atlas couldn't save Scarlotti from Bart's furious onslaught.

It was Dad, rushing on the scene with the police in tow, who stopped Bart's out-of-control attack on Scarlotti, probably saving his malevolent life. Even Atlas welcomed the arrival of the police and an end to the beating Bart had bestowed on both of them.

Mom laughed and cried and smothered me with hugs, but Dad couldn't get close once Bart finally was pulled from the pile. Bart's arms encircled me, barring every evil thing from touching me, blocking out the whole world. Neither of us spoke a word. We just clung to each other, afraid to let go, fearful that something would separate us again.

When I could finally speak without crying tears of relief, I tilted my head back and looked up at Bart.

"Once more you fly to my rescue in the nick of time. Thank you. I was afraid you'd given up on me and found someone else to honeymoon with."

A laugh caught in Bart's throat and came out a half sob. His eyes glistened with unshed tears as he held me away from him, a teasing smile on his face.

"There's a little more here in front than when I saw you last, but a little less in back, Princess."

"I tried to disguise myself so Scarlotti Scaddono wouldn't recognize me while I waited for you to find me. I thought a wig and being obviously pregnant would throw him off, but he figured it out. Oh, Bart, I was so afraid you wouldn't get here in time and he'd take me back to his island."

Bart hugged me again, the best medicine in the whole world.

Dad stepped up and planted a kiss on my forehead. "Do you feel like telling us about it, Bunny?"

"Where is he?"

"The police are taking him to the station."

"Dad, that's Antonio Scaddono's son—the one he wanted to get medical help for in the United States. The police suspect he's bringing drugs into the islands and smuggling illegal aliens to the mainland. He'll talk himself right out of their hands in five minutes and be gone before they even know who he is. Someone needs to tell them to not let him talk until he's locked up. He can convince them to drive him to his helicopter and wish him well as they send him on his way."

Dad turned to Lt. Ishigo who was waiting patiently to get a word in. Mom was not so patient.

"Allison, what happened to your hands, your arms? And look at your legs! What did he do to you?"

"I climbed a mountain barefoot to escape, and paddled a canoe from his island to here. They're just scratches and blisters."

"My poor darling!"

I saw two familiar figures standing just outside the circle of light on the patio.

"Tono! Jeremy! Come here. Come meet my family so they can thank you. If it hadn't been for these two heros, Scarlotti would've caught me. They took me to the first aid station to get me patched up, slowed Scarlotti down when he came for me so I could get away, then hid me when he saw through my disguise."

The boys were a little embarrassed by the attention and thanks they received from Mom and Dad, and especially Bart.

"You may want to tell your dad the police have Scarlotti Scaddono in custody. I'm sure he'll be glad to hear that bit of news." Tono and Jeremy left on the run. With them went my last ounce of energy.

"Does anyone care if we sit down for a minute? I'm afraid I can't stand up any longer."

Bart tenderly lifted me off my feet and cradled me in his arms. "Sorry, Princess. I wasn't thinking."

I put my arms around his neck and snuggled against him, feeling safe and secure for the first time in . . . I couldn't remember how long.

As Bart kissed me, Lt. Ishigo cleared his throat.

"Ahem. I'd like to get your statement, if you don't mind, then you two can get on with your honeymoon. I think we can use the office here in the Coconut Club, unless you feel up to flying back to Hilo to do it."

"Let's do it here," Bart interjected. "I think Allison may be just about at the end of her rope."

Bart had no idea how right he was. I could easily have gone to sleep in his arms as he carried me through the crowded cafe to the office. As we neared the front of the cafe, I saw Sarah and her group standing anxiously on the sidewalk just outside the entrance.

"Mom, would you ask that group of elderly people to come into the office for a minute? They deserve a special thanks, too."

Bart settled into the sofa, still cradling me in his arms.

"I think everyone else would be more comfortable if I sat beside you."

"Would you be more comfortable?"

"No, but we're in the minority, so I'll snuggle next to you for now." I nestled in the protective curve of Bart's arm, felt the reassuring warmth of his body next to mine, reveling in his protective, possessive responses.

"You're such an elusive thing, I may have to handcuff you to me so I don't lose you again while we finish this honeymoon," Bart teased.

Sarah and her friends filed eagerly into the office. I started to get up, but Bart held me back. "No, you don't. You can thank them just as well from right here!"

"Sarah, I'd like you to meet my husband, Bart; my parents, Margaret and Jack Alexander; and Lt. Ishigo of the Hilo Police Department. This is Sarah, Mable, Harriet, Ruth, Evan, Hugh, and Howard. Did I get them all right?"

Sarah beamed. "Perfect. Did they catch the man with the awful hair?"

"Yes, thanks to you good people. Thank you for believing me, and for being brave enough to call his bluff and the police. It's nice to know people who aren't afraid to get involved and help."

Dad shook each of their hands and Mom gave them all a hug, asking where they were from.

"You wouldn't have heard of it. It's a little town in the high desert above Los Angeles—Quartz Hill. We live in Mayflower Gardens, a retirement complex there."

"That's wonderful! When we get this settled, you'll all be our guests at our estate near Santa Barbara. We'll celebrate Allison's safe return, and the resolution of this nasty business. If you'll give me your phone number, I'll call to see when it would be convenient for you to come. We can't thank you enough for your help."

Lt. Ishigo guided them to the door and shook their hands as they filed out. *"Mahalo.* You can go back and tell your friends you helped apprehend a dangerous criminal. Thank you very much. *Mahalo."*

He instructed the policeman at the door to keep everyone out until he was through. Sgt. Luomala's face was dark with disappointment as Lt. Ishigo indicated he was to do it from the other side of the door. Luomala would miss the report. I didn't like him any better now than the first time I had seen him in our hotel room, but I still couldn't have said why.

Ishigo closed the door and settled into the big maroon leather chair behind the desk. "Now, can we get to your report?" At his signal, the officer with him turned on the tape recorder. I obliged with a big yawn to begin the interview.

Dad started the interrogation. "What happened in the helicopter?"

"They hit Bart over the head and dumped him out of the chopper. The pilot was supposed to put him in the volcano, but I'm sure he purposely hovered right on the rim so Bart wouldn't go in. Thank heaven!" I reached up and kissed Bart's cheek. His arms wrapped securely around me.

"I couldn't let Bart slide into the volcano, so I faked fainting. When they were off guard I jumped out, thinking I could land next to Bart. I overshot my mark just a little and ended up sliding down into Pele's waiting arms. I almost sacrificed my emerald to Pele as an offering so she'd let me go."

"If it could've enticed her on your behalf, it would've been a very good investment, I'd say," Bart said. "We may have to go back and leave an offering just to thank her again for letting you go."

I shuddered involuntarily, noting Lt. Ishigo's solemn nod at the suggestion. He seemed to think that was a good idea.

Dad picked up the questioning. "What happened when they lifted you out of the volcano? Do you know who they were and what they wanted?"

"They immediately gave me a shot of something and I woke up tied to a cot on a little island. They were Nate's men. He hid this pearl in a bottle of lotion in my luggage before the wedding, then he disappeared from the estate. It was going to be his cut of the jewels from Thailand." I pulled the string from beneath the sarong and showed them the magnificent pearl ring.

"After three unsuccessful attempts to reclaim it, Nate decided to get rid of Bart, who kept getting in his way. There was a unique transistor we didn't find in the lid of the pearl bottle that kept him in touch with us. His men were instructed to get the pearl, then let me go. Nate didn't want you on his tail for harming your only daughter."

"Where did Scarlotti come in?" Bart asked.

"He'd been working with Nate developing new growing areas for the drug cartel and new strains of opium. Dad, Scarlotti was at the estate. He saw everything. He saw me hit his father over the head with the two-by-four. He decided we'd all pay for his father's death— me for killing him, Mom for keeping him a fugitive, and you for pursuing him all those years."

"You didn't kill him, Princess. The FBI agent's bullet through the heart did it. Of course, the two-by-four didn't do him any good, either." Bart's humor lightened the moment a bit.

"Go on," Dad prompted.

"Scarlotti knew about the pearl. He had Nate's men bring me to his island, then locked me in his estate so they couldn't get to me. He planned on Nate getting rid of Bart in the volcano, then using me as bait to get you two to his island so he could kill us, in some very special way he'd devised just for us."

"Do you know where you were being held prisoner?" Lt. Ishigo asked.

"Only that it was a tiny green island with a mountain in the center and a lake on the top of the mountain. I paddled most of the day to get here, if that helps."

"What's on the island?"

"From the top of the mountain, I could only see Scarlotti's house. The gardener has a small house somewhere, and his secret cave where he mixes Scarlotti's drugs. That's all I could see, but the vegetation is very heavy and there may be something else."

"How many people are on the island?" Dad queried.

"Scarlotti killed the two men who took me there, leaving the old gardener, Scarlotti, and Kat, his pet lion. Oh, and some wild peccary. The old man doles out daily doses of drugs for Scarlotti. He'll probably need to bring some while Scarlotti's in custody."

The phone rang on the desk. The uniformed officer answered the call, then handed it to Lt. Ishigo.

Before he said a word, before he looked at me, before he hung up the phone and cleared his throat, I knew. I knew what the phone call reported. Terror strangled the air from me, leaving me gasping for breath. Panic pulsed through my body.

"No!"

Bart's arms circled me protectively and I buried my face in his shirt, clinging tightly to him.

"Scarlotti Scaddono escaped, flew out of here in his helicopter about five minutes ago. We had people on his tail, but they've lost him."

Chapter Twenty-Two

Dad leaped to his feet and leaned over the desk into Lt. Ishigo's face. "What happened? How could he get away?"

"Just as Mrs. Allan said, Scaddono is very persuasive. He somehow convinced the officers taking him into custody to return him to his helicopter for something, and he escaped. They've dispatched a chopper for us; it should land momentarily in the parking lot."

Dad turned to Mom. "Margaret, get Allison hidden somewhere Scarlotti can't find her, in case he comes after her."

Lt. Ishigo called the policeman in from outside the door.

"Luomala, guard these women. You're responsible for their safety. Take them somewhere you can protect them."

"No!" Everyone looked at me.

"If you leave me here, you'll be worried the whole time that Scarlotti's come back for me. You won't be focused one hundred percent on finding him. He *will* come back for me, and he'll find me. He has eyes and ears everywhere. If I'm with you, he'll know that, too. He wants revenge. He wants to kill all of us, in his own time and in his own way. He believes he's smarter than all of you, superior to everyone. Don't you see? If I'm with you, he'll come to you. If I'm not, you'll never see me again."

The helicopter roared over the club, blocking out Dad's answer, but the resignation in his eyes, and the resolve on Bart's face told me their decision.

"Can you find Scarlotti's island again?" Dad asked as the noise abated.

"All I can tell you is it's somewhere between here and the Big Island, and that the sun was to my back most of the day as I paddled from there to here. I think I'd recognize it from the air."

"Where do you think Scarlotti is right now?" Mom asked.

I thought for a minute. "He'll probably go back to his island while he figures out where I am, leave a phony trail for you to follow, and double back after me. I imagine he'll be delighted that he'll have a chance to show you how brilliant he is by taking me right out of your hands."

"Then let's find that island. Everyone, into the chopper."

As one we rose, Bart scooping me off my bare feet into his arms again. Lt. Ishigo led the way to the helicopter.

"Sir, is there room for all of us in there?" Sgt. Luomala asked.

"We're all going, Luomala, even if it's a little cramped."

I was glad Lt. Ishigo didn't let him stay behind. I was suspicious of everyone, particularly Luomala. I imagined him going immediately to report our plans to Scarlotti, who'd find out sooner or later, but I hoped it would be later, after he was in custody again.

The palm trees in the parking lot swayed wildly in the wind. I wearily dismissed it and boarded the noisy chopper.

As Lt. Ishigo and Dad conferred over a map, I snuggled contentedly into Bart's protective embrace, and though I struggled valiantly to stay awake, exhaustion overcame me and the rhythmic roar of the rotors promptly put me to sleep.

Violent pitching of the helicopter being buffeted by high winds shook me awake.

"What's happening?"

"A tropical storm's blowing through. Lt. Ishigo thinks he knows which is Scarlotti's island and we're trying to make it there before the storm tears the chopper apart. The wind increased in intensity so fast there wasn't time to turn around and go back."

The bright beam of the searchlight revealed, not far enough below us, the roughest seas I'd ever seen—huge white-capped waves rolling and tumbling over each other. Nothing could survive long in that maelstrom.

A heavy downdraft slammed against the helicopter, forcing it down toward the angry arms of the turbulent seas. Not another ditching at sea—and not in this tempest! Bart, Mother and I had barely survived when we'd had to ditch the amphibian in the Mediterranean with the United States Navy standing by. This time no one was standing by and I was sure this helicopter didn't float. Nothing would stay afloat long in this storm.

Suddenly a strip of white sand appeared out of the black night and a mountain loomed in the light ahead of us. The pilot veered sharply to miss it, then turned and flew back toward the beach.

Dad handed me a set of headphones and when I had them on, asked if there was some place we could land.

"Scarlotti has a helipad near the house. If we locate the house, we'll find the pad. And we'll know if he's here." I shuddered just thinking about him, his mesmerizing voice, his malevolent plans.

Suddenly the searchlight illuminated the house and just beyond it, the helipad containing Scarlotti's helicopter. *He was here.* Waiting for us to come?

The pilot struggled to keep the helicopter over the windblown helipad. He'd set the chopper down and the wind would take us back up again. With the earphones on, I was privy to conversations I'd otherwise miss. When the pilot, Lt. Abreu, radioed for a weather update, he was told to set down fast and ride out the storm. It was going to be a bad one.

Hadn't they known that when we took off? Hadn't anyone checked on the weather? Or was this one of those storms born over an isolated area that blows quickly through and is just as quickly forgotten?

"Get out of here, fast, and take cover," Lt. Abreu ordered. "This chopper isn't going to stay put long."

He was right. We jumped from the helicopter while he struggled to hold it as low and steady as he could before he shut it down and jumped himself. He was barely clear when a blast of wind picked it up and smashed it into Scarlotti's, hurling them both into the trees fifty feet from the helipad.

We raced for what little shelter the wildly swaying trees

afforded, fighting our way to the house against the gale forces the wind had achieved. For every step we took forward, it blew us back a half a dozen, drenching us in the process. Palm fronds crashed around us as we dodged flying debris. Monstrous waves conquered the beach and now invaded higher ground. How long before they overran the house?

It took forever to reach the gate which stood wide open, banging against the wrought iron fence. Scarlotti was not careless. Had he simply locked the gate, we'd have been denied entrance because of the electrified fence. *Come into my parlor, said the spider to the fly.*

Bart kept me from blowing away in the wind, propelling me forward. I grabbed at Dad and pulled him close to us, so I could yell at both of them at the same time. I didn't have enough energy to repeat it twice.

"Fence is electric—gate's always locked. Scarlotti's waiting. Be careful!"

Dad nodded, vainly wiping the rain from his face. Mom clung to his belt, trying to keep her feet under her, bending into the wind.

We approached the house on the side nearest the kitchen. All the big double doors were closed except this one. One door stood ominously open to the wind and the rain . . . and us.

Lt. Ishigo cautiously led the way up the steps, motioning to his two men to each take a side of the house and go around it. Dad and Bart proceeded, guns drawn, with Mom and I sandwiched between them. The armed pilot, Lt. Abreu, brought up the rear.

We're walking straight into Scarlotti's arrogant arms. I know he's watching. What's he planning?

We stood, dripping in the middle of the kitchen floor, listening. There was no sound in the house. I expected to hear Scarlotti's mocking voice, taunting, teasing us, tearing away self-confidence.

"Where is he?" Dad asked quietly. "I'm sure it's a trap, but since we outnumber him, I think our chances are better in here than out in the storm."

Before I could answer, it came. That haunting, sensuous voice I'd come to fear, to hate, filled the kitchen.

"Welcome to my house. Please make yourself at home and take

shelter from the storm. I'm sorry I can't be a proper host and prepare a suitable repast for you, but I'm sure you agree, it would be a bit awkward if I were to show myself. However, my dear Allison knows her way around the house quite well, and can make you appropriately comfortable. You will show them around and take care of their needs, won't you, my precious?"

His tone, his voice, his innuendos sent chills through my system. I was mortified by his use of intimate names for me, appalled that he would do so in front of Bart and my parents, but not surprised at his tactics. This would be not just physical, but psychological warfare, to the ultimate degree.

I stepped instinctively back into the safety of Bart's arms, which went immediately around me. The absolute silence in the house was intensified by the severity of the storm outside. No one moved or spoke. Then Mom broke the spell.

"Allison, I think that's a wonderful idea. I don't remember the last time we ate, or were able to sit and relax for a few minutes. Since we seem to be prisoners of the storm, let's make the most of our host's kind hospitality. If you'll show me where everything is, I'll help you fix a bite to eat."

It was brilliant. Mom broke the spell Scarlotti had spun so effectively around us, holding us hostage simply with his puissant voice.

I jumped on the bandwagon. "Wonderful idea! But first, let me show you the house. It's spectacular. Mom, you'll love the garden room. You might consider something like it when you start rebuilding the estate. Dad, we'll never get you out of the library once you see it. It contains the most amazing collection of books I've ever seen in a private library."

Dad winked at me and nodded approval. Lt. Ishigo, standing nearest the hall, suddenly motioned for silence. He'd heard something moving in the house, someone quietly approaching the kitchen. He waved us to hide behind the island in the center of the kitchen and motioned for Lt. Abreu to take one side of the door. He took the other.

"No! It's Kat, I'm sure. Don't shoot. He's my friend! Kat?" I called. "Are you hungry?"

The faint "clip, clip" Lt. Ishigo had heard amplified as it advanced. Then Kat strolled in, filling the doorway with his huge golden mane and glittering amber eyes.

"Kat! I've missed you!" I sunk to my knees and he ambled into my arms, purring loudly as I rubbed behind his ears.

"This is Kat, everyone. He slept with me, watched over me, and even saved my life a couple of times. He's incredible!"

"And he's hungry. I purposely haven't fed him since you left, hoping he'd find something juicier to eat when your friends came looking for me. I must remember to reprimand him for assisting you off the island, instead of keeping you here, as I expected him to do." Scarlotti's voice shattered the lighter mood we'd tried to create.

"Then I'll feed him. And after that, if you'll join us, we'll eat. We can call a truce, you know."

Bart frowned at my invitation, then realized what I was doing.

"I'd like to meet you, Scarlotti," he said. "Allison tells me you know each of us quite well, having spent some time observing us on the estate. We appreciate your hospitality and wouldn't think of depriving you of the comforts of your own home. Please join us."

An awkward silence prevailed for a minute, then I filled it. "Come on, Kat. Of necessity, you get to eat first. Then, if our host will join us, we'll eat, too." I wasn't about to put a single morsel of anything in my mouth unless I could be assured it wasn't tainted.

I opened the pantry and filled the over-sized bowl with Kat's food. Bart hovered at my side, unsure of the temperament of the beast beside me, ready to protect me, if necessary.

"How did you and Kat get acquainted?" he asked.

"The first five minutes I was in the house, he found me and I fed him, guided, of course, by the omnipresent voice of our host."

Bart enveloped me securely with his arms, pressing me possessively against his body. "I can't even imagine what horrors you've been through, from the looks of your hands and legs. I feel awful that I didn't, or couldn't, protect you from all this."

I traced his worried frown with my fingertip. "I guess I'll just have to find a husband who can remain conscious through a blow to the head like you had. Wonder if Superman is still around?"

I kissed the worry from his face, relishing the security I felt in his nearness, the protective warmth of his body next to mine, the love and concern I sensed at his touch. I didn't want to leave the seclusion of the pantry or the protective circle of Bart's embrace.

Kat finished eating and nudged me for more attention, our cue to exit the pantry.

Mom was at the refrigerator, searching for something quick and easy to fix. She produced a beautiful plateful of hors d'oeuvres, already prepared.

"Mr. Scaddono, are you planning a social gathering, or are these for us?"

"They're especially for you, Mrs. Alexander. Please enjoy them."

"Shall I assume they are perfectly healthy, or do I need to use Kat as our taster?"

"Please, Mrs. Alexander." Scarlotti's voice sounded offended. "I would not stoop to such a trivial trick. I've offered my hospitality. I will not violate that ancient custom with chicanery. You may be assured you are completely safe within these walls."

"Thank you, Mr. Scaddono. We would offer the same assurance to you."

I remained silent through the conversation, waiting to hear what Scarlotti's reply would be, then whispered to Mom that we couldn't eat any of the food. I was sure it would be drugged, just as my dinner had been, and as I suspected the breakfast he tried to get me to eat had been.

Silence again. He simply would not reply to our overtures. Did they surprise him? Did it leave him at a loss for words? That wasn't likely. He seemed to excel at repartee.

The two men Lt. Ishigo had sent around the house burst through the door, dripping and exhausted from fighting the wind.

"Man, it's wild out there," Sgt. Luomala said. "If it gets much worse, the house'll be flooded. We'll have to find higher ground soon." Sgt. Luomala was the was one who wanted to stay behind at the Coconut Club. I didn't like him. Sgt. Fabia hadn't uttered a word.

"Find some towels and dry off. We'll keep an eye on the storm," Lt. Ishigo instructed.

We attempted to make light conversation, aware Scarlotti was listening to every word. How incongruous it seemed, sitting so calmly at the table while the storm battered the house without and Scarlotti plotted within. Kat spread at my feet, relishing the occasional scratching I gave him behind his ears.

"I'm sorry to intrude. At the risk of being accused of haruspication, I must warn you, high tide is imminent and the gale is reaching hurricane proportions. The house will no longer be a safe haven. I suggest an immediate departure to the mountain." Scarlotti's usually calm, soothing, voice was filled with urgency.

Bart whispered in my ear, "Haruspication?"

"Predicting the future," I replied.

"I urge you to leave immediately."

"Are you coming, too?" I asked, curious as to whether he would try to ride out the storm here or would also take to the hills.

"Exit through the library. Hurry."

Scarlotti ignored my question. Was there immediate danger of the house washing away? Though flying branches and palm fronds continually crashed against the windows, none had yet broken. The house seemed extremely well-built, and barring a *tsunami,* could probably withstand such a storm as this. Was he sending us into the storm at this point more to endanger our lives than to save them? With Scarlotti, anything was possible. How could we tell the difference?

I voiced my concerns to Dad and Bart while Lt. Ishigo checked outside.

"Allison, you doubt me." Scarlotti didn't miss a thing. Petulance replaced the urgency in his voice.

"Of course, I doubt you. I don't trust you at all."

"Would I send you into that maelstrom if it were safer in the house? I'd never subject you to such danger and discomfort as you'll encounter out there if it were not even more dangerous to stay inside." The chameleon tones changed again, first persuasive, then authoritative.

"Go through the library, follow the path to the gate, and you'll find the trail up the mountain just outside the fence. The hut at the top may give you some shelter, if it's still standing. Depart now."

I led the procession from the kitchen into the hall, unhurried, pointing out pieces I'd admired in the house, beautiful paintings, showing Mom the garden room, and finally, reluctantly, reaching the library. I was loath to leave the safety the house afforded to venture into a wild, turbulent storm before it was necessary. Granted, water was clearly visible, rushing, swirling on the veranda that surrounded the house; still, it hadn't come in. The roof was intact, and incredibly, as yet no windows had been broken.

"Scarlotti, what will happen to your impressive library if the water gets in? You have so many first editions, so many marvelous books. Isn't there something you can do to protect them?" I was genuinely concerned. Books were precious, especially these, and should never be damaged or destroyed.

"I appreciate your concern, Allison, but the bookcases are water-tight. If the house stands, they should weather the storm without damage. Alas, if the house goes, I will suffer a terrible loss."

He was silent for a minute. We waited, not anxious to leave the apparent safety of our sanctuary. Mom leaned against Dad as they stood at the double glass doors watching the storm, his arms circled protectively around her. Bart never left my side, for which I was grateful. The four policemen lined the second set of glass doors, spellbound by the storm. We quietly contemplated the tempest Scarlotti was attempting to send us into.

Suddenly the sound of breaking glass shattered the spell. Scarlotti's truculent shout reverberated through the house. "Get out! The house is going! Get up the mountain to high ground! Don't worry about the fence. The power's off."

As we burst through the doors, the full force of the storm hurled us back against the house. Veranda, steps, and path were obscured by angry, swirling water. Blinding rain driven sideways by the velocity of the gale stung our bare skin, drenching us again immediately.

We staggered forward, propelled into the turbulence by the urgency of Scarlotti's command, stumbling into bushes, clinging to the trees for support. The short distance to the gate was attained only by an exhaustive effort, fighting waters that were waist deep by time we reached the fence.

I vaguely remembered the beach being lower than the grounds surrounding the house. We'd be swimming once we went through the gate. I signaled Bart, dragging me behind him, that we needed to hold on to the fence until it hit the tree line. He passed the word forward to Dad, who led our bedraggled procession.

The going was much easier with the fence to cling to, though the force of the wind battered me into the wrought iron time and again. We finally reached the trees—actually, jungle would be a more appropriate term. We'd barely left the fence, holding on now to trees and vegetation whipping wildly in the wind, when Scarlotti's laughter, transmogrified by the blare of the speakers, halted us in our tracks.

"How easy it was to discomfit you! I'm disappointed that you're no smarter than the rest of them, despite your reputations! This shall be no contest at all. Welcome to my version of 'The Hunt.' We'll see who gets to you first—my specially developed peccary, the storm, or me. I'll see you again, Allison."

His laughter pierced the storm. I did not doubt that my father and Bart were brilliant strategists, but were they a match for a deranged, sedulous mind that had nothing better to do than plot revenge-filled schemes?

As the demented laughter died away in the intensity of the storm, a loud noise emanated from the house. I turned, expecting to see it wash away in a wild wave. Instead, metal louvers rolled from under the roof, enclosing the entire house in a protecting sheaf of steel. All lights vanished and the house disappeared into the darkness of the storm.

He'd tricked us! He'd driven us from the safety of the house out into the storm with all its dangers, plus some of his own creation.

Sgt. Luomala turned, grasping the wrought-iron fence, and screamed, "No! You promised you'd take care of me!"

"And I shall. I always keep my promises," Scarlotti's voice thundered over the loudspeakers.

The night was suddenly lit with electricity arcing from the body of Sgt. Luomala. Tortured screams blew away on turbulent winds.

"Now it commences." With this final ominous statement from Scarlotti, the gate swung shut with a loud clang, before his insane laughter drove us up the mountain.

Chapter Twenty-Three

The trail was a slippery, muddy mess with water running in rivulets everywhere. The jungle was no easier. The wind whipped the trees and bushes savagely, turning dry palm fronds into dangerous projectiles that bombarded us on every hand.

We struggled upward with Lt. Abreu in the lead and Dad close behind him, progressing more because of the gale at our backs than our own agility in the mud. Suddenly a single bright red beam of light sliced the inky night in front of us. Lt. Abreu's death scream was carried away on the wind that propelled us toward the deadly laser.

Dad staggered backward, stunned. We huddled together for strength against the wind, fearing another step would activate the lethal laser again. Scarlotti had wasted no time in beginning the evil game. Dad pulled us into a tight circle, heads together so we could hear each other over the clamor of the storm.

"Path's apparently booby-trapped. Better dig in somewhere and ride out the storm. Any reason for us to try for the hut?" he asked.

"No. Probably blown away by now," I yelled.

"We can't get any more wet. Let's stay put," Mom ventured.

"If we can wait till morning, we'll have a better chance to see traps before we fall into them." Bart's arms went protectively around me.

Lt. Ishigo agreed and moved off the path into the heavy undergrowth. We crawled under the bushes, certainly not out of reach of the storm, but hopefully out of Scarlotti's reach, for the time being.

"He could have microphones or sensors along the trail, and through the jungle, tracking us," I said when we were safely ensconced in a small hollow under a wildly waving elephant ear plant. "He seemed to anticipate every move I made. I envisioned him sitting at a control panel, watching me on monitors. I decided that was too far-fetched. Now I'm not so sure."

"Sounds to me he's planning to get rid of us in a deadly game of hide and seek," Lt. Ishigo offered.

"He's got a good start—two out of eight in as many minutes," the quiet Sgt. Fabia added nervously.

Our attempt at solving our dilemma was cut short by the uprooting of the tree next to us. The wind increased, if that was possible. Rain pelted our exposed skin with the force of hail. We huddled closer together, not that it afforded protection, but probably because the instinct to cling to one another in time of stress was so strong.

The noise of the storm precluded small talk, so we lapsed into an uneasy silence, each, I'm sure, wondering what was next. I was too tired to think, my brain addled from stress and fatigue. My sole comfort was being cradled in Bart's arms as he tried to protect me from the storm, as well as Scarlotti.

What atrocities had Scarlotti planned? Did he really think we would just stumble into his traps and he could eliminate everyone?

But I was so tired, I couldn't think. I felt like Scarlett O'Hara. Everything could wait until tomorrow. Now I would let the storm rage around us and Scarlotti plot his diabolical schemes and the world go on while I slept in the security of Bart's arms.

I was jolted awake when Bart threw me on the ground and rolled on top of me.

"What are you . . ." He covered my mouth with his to muffle my question and made me forget my discomfort as he warmed to the kiss. I'd missed him so much. For a brief moment, I forgot Scarlotti, the storm, the mud, and the danger.

Then Mom brought us back to earth and the reality of our situation.

"Allison? Bart? Are you okay?" she whispered, feeling for us in the dark.

Bart whispered a "shhh" in my ear and reached silently to reassure her we were fine. I stretched out my hand to touch her, and felt something warm, liquid, and sticky on the still body next to me. I stiffened, grasping Bart's arms.

"Stay still," he whispered close to my ear. "Scarlotti picked off Lt. Ishigo. Probably has a night scope on us."

I was quiet, suddenly feeling the dead weight of Bart still on top of me.

"You're squishing me," I whispered.

"You weren't complaining a minute ago," he replied with a quick kiss, sliding off between me and the dead man beside us.

Three down. Scarlotti really was picking us off one by one and with a different method each time. Of course! His ego would preclude anything routine, mundane, and repetitive. He would pride himself on his ingenuity. He had a different death planned for each of us. And he'd left the safety of the house. He was out here in the storm with us.

I sat up, struggling against Bart's efforts to keep me prone.

"War council," I announced. "Heads together. It's okay, Bart. Scarlotti's saving me for last. He won't shoot me."

We groped in the wet, muddy darkness for each other while the storm thundered around us, whipping branches wildly, uprooting trees, and stripping dry boughs, sending them flying. It was difficult to hear over the roar of the wind.

Heads together, finally, we lay in the mud and debris, close enough to talk without shouting.

"Scarlotti has some unique torture planned for me. I don't think he'll shoot any of you either. He's already used that method. Whatever else he's planned, it'll be different for everyone. He's too vain to use the same method each time. He'll flaunt his cunning and creativity to dispose of us, thinking we're too dull-witted to figure it out."

"Or do anything about it if we do figure it out," Bart added. "Okay, he's used electrocution, laser, and rifle. What can we expect next?"

"Anything," Dad said. "He was raised in the Far East. He'd be familiar with everything used in the jungles of Viet Nam, as well as ancient Oriental methods of torture and assassination, which can get pretty gruesome and sophisticated." Dad paused and Mom added her thoughts.

"We can avoid tripping wires by staying off the paths, but if he's tracking us, he can use darts, knives, spears, or other advanced apparatus I'm not even familiar with. I don't like this game, or our odds."

"With a night scope, he can see us in the dark, and even through the storm, he can see us right now. I wouldn't bet he can hear us though. The storm would interfere with a parabolic mike," Bart said thoughtfully. "The storm could also affect his aim. That may be our saving grace right now."

Bart rolled away and busied himself for a minute, then rolled back and pressed a gun into my hand.

"This is Lt. Ishigo's. Unfortunately, he doesn't need it anymore, but you do."

Another tree crashed to the ground nearby. Darkness prevented us from seeing how close the trees were, prevented us from seeing what kind of danger we were in from the storm—or Scarlotti.

Sgt. Fabia jumped up with a shout. "That tree nearly got me."

"Get down!" my father ordered. Too late. An agonized scream pierced the storm. Bart pulled me tight against him, trying to shelter me.

"What happened?" he asked Dad.

It took a minute for Dad's report. "Dart in the face. Not the paralyzing tip you used to dispose of Tony's gang last week. Fabia's dead."

The crashing of another tree punctuated Dad's declaration. I shuddered in Bart's arms. There were only four of us left. Scarlotti had easily disposed of the four policemen, saving my family for last. Which of us had he picked for his next victim?

"Margaret, here's Fabia's gun."

"Thanks, though it seems worthless in the dark. I feel like a duck in an arcade, waiting in line for the next shot."

Another blast of wind brought a cry from Mom's direction.

"Margaret! What's the matter?" Dad's frantic question almost blew away in the increased turbulence. Bart and I both reached for Mom. My hand hit a shaft—an arrow sticking up where none had been moments ago—where Mom should have been.

"Mom!" Sickening dread swept through my body as my hand followed the shaft downward to a liquid warmth already spreading across the prone torso of my mother.

"No! No! Scarlotti, you animal!" I screamed into the wind. "You vicious, barbarous scum! You killed her! You've killed my mother!" I collapsed in an agonized heap in the mud, sobbing uncontrollably. Bart's arms offered solace and comfort, but that wasn't adequate to quench the unbearable pain I felt, the anguish that tore at my heart, punched the air from my lungs leaving me gasping for breath.

Vaguely aware of Bart pulling me to my feet, of movement but not direction, I was numb, unbelieving. I stumbled blindly in the dark and fell. Bart put me back on my feet and we moved again. I don't know how far we'd gone before I stepped on something sharp with my bare feet and fell to my knees in pain.

Pain. That was all I could feel. Pain at my mother's death. Pain so deep it seemed without origin. Pain in my lacerated feet, in my blistered hands, my head, pain in my arms and my shoulders from hours of paddling. Pain eclipsed everything else in my world.

Where was the loving Father Bart had promised was watching so carefully over us? That Father who knew us and all we were going through—that loved us so much? Where was He for my mother? Why didn't He protect her? Why was He allowing Scarlotti to achieve his depraved designs, to get away with multiple murder? We were the good guys. Wasn't good supposed to prevail over evil? *Where are you? Why aren't you helping us? Why are you allowing Scarlotti to do this?* I screamed silently.

More pain . . . branches slapping me viciously in the wind as Bart carried me. Bart fell, and Dad on top of us.

"What happened?" Dad's question was terse as I was buried under multiple arms and legs. Additional pain.

"I stepped in a hole—twisted my ankle," Bart muttered through clenched teeth.

"Can you walk?"

"Give me a minute."

Bart's hands pulling at my sarong brought me out of the mist of misery that enveloped me.

"What are you doing?" I asked, grasping at the sarong Bart tugged on, threatening to undress me.

"I need a strip of your fabric to bind my ankle. You'll never miss it."

The tugging was punctuated by tearing, and I felt the fabric give way. I shifted so Bart could have the portion I was sitting on. He tore a strip from the bottom, all the way around, muddy and wet as it was.

"How's your ankle?" I asked, ashamed I'd been wallowing in self-pity deeper than the mud we were struggling through.

"I think it'll be okay with a little reinforcement here. How are you doing?"

I was about to tell him how miserable I really was when I suddenly thought of Dad—of his loss. I reached out in the darkness, feeling for the arms and legs I'd just been mixed up with a minute ago.

"Dad? Where are you?"

"Here, Bunny. Are you okay?"

I found his strong, hairy arms, cradling Mom, rocking her back and forth.

"I couldn't leave her," he said softly, answering my unasked question.

"I'm ready," Bart said, getting to his feet. "Do you need help?"

I felt for him, found his outstretched hands and he pulled me up.

"I can manage. How about you? Can you walk on that ankle?"

"If you'll support me. How are your feet?"

"Mangled, like my soul, my very existence. What are we doing? Where are we going?"

"We're moving. A moving target's harder to hit. No sense sitting there making things easy for Scarlotti. Might as well offer him a little . . ."

Bart's sentence was cut short by Dad's cry directly behind us.

Chapter Twenty-Four

"Dad? Answer me! Talk to me! Bart, I can't find him. Dad, where are you?" He didn't answer even my telepathic pleas.

Bart's arms pulled me close, then held me tightly against him when he felt the uncontrollable shaking of my body. I was freezing, frightened, fatigued beyond measure, convinced both my parents were now dead, and numb with grief. Bart had an injured ankle, God had lost us in the storm, and Scarlotti had the upper hand. *Would this nightmare never end? Would this night never end?*

Suddenly Kat burst out of the storm's fury, knocking us over, almost squashing us with his enormous body before he lay squarely on top of Bart.

"Get him off me!" Bart's quiet voice was tinged with panic.

"It's okay. He won't hurt you. At least, I don't think he will. I think he was trying to protect me. Kat, get off. Move." I put my arms around Kat's neck and pulled him toward me. Bart escaped from under the weight of the huge cat.

"Find Dad. Something happened." We tried to keep our voices low. If we'd lost Scarlotti as we moved in the storm, we didn't want to advertise our position. The supposition was he could hear us over the roar of the storm. The unknown always seemed the worst, and not knowing what kind of sophisticated equipment Scarlotti had, or what he had planned was maddening. Total darkness, the intense storm, and the attacks magnified fear and frustration.

We crawled around in the dark, feeling for my father, for arms, legs, any sign of my parents who had been so close minutes before. Why had Dad cried out? What happened to him? To them?

They were gone. Simply disappeared . . . I was going to say off the face of the earth.

"Bart—a deep hole?"

"Possible. With Scaddono, anything's possible. Be careful. Stay on your hands and knees. Feel before you move."

"I need a light. What time is it? Shouldn't this night be over soon? Listen! The wind's dying down, or is it my imagination?"

"No, I think you're right. Jack, can you hear me?" Bart's call was not loud. More like a stage whisper. "Can you reach him, Princess?"

I tried, concentrating again on sending a telepathic message. This time I got an answer.

"He's in deep water, can't keep his head up. Come back this way."

We crawled over razor-sharp palm fronds, branches, and fallen trees. How did he get so far away from us? He'd been right behind us. It must just seem further on my hands and knees. Then I found the hole—in fact, I almost fell into it.

"Dad?"

"Allison! Help, quick," Dad called out softly.

Bart and I both reached out in the darkness toward the sound of splashing. I touched a hand, grabbed it, and pulled it toward me. It didn't respond to my touch.

"I've got Mom, Bart. Help me."

"Take her, Allison," Dad said, gurgling as he went under water. "Get Margaret out. Be careful."

Bart and I gently drew my mother from the water, put her on the ground, then pulled Dad out. He immediately gathered Mom in his arms.

"Dad . . ." I didn't know what to say. What do you say to someone who won't let go of the dead?

Dad interrupted me, speaking quietly. "I walked into one of Scarlotti's traps. Fortunately the storm had filled it with water. The bottom was probably lined with knives or sharpened sticks, but there was so much water we never touched them. Nearly drowned though.

Had a hard time keeping Margaret's head and my own above water."

"Dad . . ." I reached for him in the dark, hoping to console him, to help him understand she was gone. I heard a low moan and touched Mom. She moved. She was alive!

I gasped.

"Shhh, Bunny," Dad whispered. "Come closer."

I maneuvered around so Dad could whisper in my ear, pulling Bart in close beside me.

"Your cry, when you thought she was dead, was what we needed Scarlotti to hear. The arrow pierced her breast and went into the fleshy part of her arm. I broke off the shaft, but the arrowhead is still there. She hit her head on a rock when she fell backwards, knocked her out. Sorry I had to let you think she was dead, but he needed to think she was. That big gust of wind must have affected his aim, thank goodness."

I whispered the good news to Bart. Kat intruded on our conversation, dropping his big head in my lap.

"Kat, do you have a den nearby, someplace warm and dry? I'm cold and wet and miserable." I scratched behind his ears with one hand, holding Mom's hand with my other. I didn't want to let go of this most precious life. I felt a weak squeeze back. It was the most wonderful feeling I've ever had.

The wind stopped suddenly, almost as if someone turned off a giant wind machine. Angry black clouds lightened to stormy gray as inky blackness softened into dusky predawn.

Suddenly Kat got up, moved away, then stopped and turned, waiting for us to follow.

"Come on. I think this supercat understood me again."

Dad gently picked up Mom. With one arm dangling loosely at her side, she looked so lifeless I had to touch her to make sure she was still breathing.

Kat headed into the thickest part of the jungle where the tangle of trees and vines seemed impenetrable, forcing us to crawl in some places to get under the dense twist of branches that coiled around each other.

Dad got on his knees and Bart carefully draped Mom over Dad's back. She couldn't use her arm to crawl and we couldn't take a chance on Scarlotti seeing her move on her own. We had no way of knowing if he was still watching us with the night scope, planning his next victim, or if we'd lost him.

The ground sloped steeply upward. We were on the mountain itself, not just the high ground around it, and finally emerged from the braided vines and underbrush to the rocks. Kat waited patiently at the bottom of a craggy, moss-covered rock, then leaped gracefully to the top just above Bart's head. He turned as if to say, "Come on, this way."

I started up, slipped on the moss, and tried again. Bart boosted me to the top from behind and followed quickly, then we reached down to help Dad get Mom up. We managed, but I could tell it hurt her. Silent tears washed streaks down her mud-splashed face. I ached for her, and wished I could make her pain my own.

Kat turned and walked along a small ledge just wide enough to hold him, then disappeared. I followed, hugging the slippery rock, and discovered a small opening barely big enough for Kat to squeeze through.

"Let me go first," Bart whispered.

"No. If Kat's there, it's safe for me. He may not like you coming in first."

I crawled into the black hole in front of me, not knowing what to expect. My claustrophobic tendencies evaporated with the anticipation of shelter from the storm.

The entry to the cave sloped steeply upward and curved, like a tube slide at a water park. How would Dad ever get Mom through this? Where would it end? My cut and bruised knees couldn't endure much more, nor could my blistered hands. Then the tunnel widened into a black void.

"Kat, where are you?" I reached out, feeling the floor of the cave in a circle around me, not wanting to disappear into a hole in the floor. There were no holes. Bart followed on my heels and we explored the walls of the cave, determining we were in a small cavern roughly eight feet across, about seven feet wide, and six feet high. Bart couldn't stand up straight.

I found Kat and scratched his smelly, soggy head while Bart went back to help Dad get Mom up to Kat's sanctuary. When she was unable to crawl, they laid her on Bart's jacket and he dragged her through the tunnel, backing his way up the incline.

"How's Mom?" Her silence worried me.

"I think she passed out from the pain, but her pulse seems steady . . ." his voice faltered.

Bart felt for me in the dark, pulled me onto his lap and wrapped me in his arms to warm me. I couldn't stop shaking. What I wouldn't give for another session in that magical bathtub of Scarlotti's, to be clean and warm and feel the healing essence of herbs, the soothing jets of water massage my tired, aching, abused body. And I'd love to have more of the old man's potions that drew the pain right out of my wounds. Mom needed his medicine even more than I did. Shame stabbed me, dissolving self-pity. Mom's situation was far worse than mine.

We huddled close together while Dad and Bart discussed strategy. Kat shifted his huge head so the scratching behind his ears could continue. My arms were too tired to keep rubbing his ears, but I was shivering so severely, simply resting one trembling hand on his head gave Kat the impression he was being rubbed.

"I can't hear the storm. Is it because we're in here away from it?" I asked.

"No. Either it's blown over or we're in the eye of a hurricane. We'll know shortly," Dad said.

"We're above the high water mark, aren't we? I don't want to be trapped in a cave in case of a *tsunami* or something."

"*Tsunamis* are caused by . . ." Bart started softly.

"Earthquakes," I finished. "I know, but everything else has happened. Why not that, too?"

We lapsed into temporary silence. I wondered what else could possibly happen to disrupt my honeymoon. I'd almost forgotten I was on a honeymoon.

Kat suddenly growled. A low rumble started in his throat and worked its way back through his massive frame. He moved to the entrance of the cave, still growling. None of us stirred.

The growl intensified into a snarl as Kat disappeared down the curved tubular entrance.

"It's okay, Kat. It's just me. Come here, boy."

Scarlotti! He'd found us!

Kat's growl didn't stop as I'd expected when he discovered his master was the intruder.

"Kat, it's okay. I'm looking for Allison. Where is she? Where's Allison, Kat?"

Kat replied with a snort and a snarl.

"Move your carcass over, Kat. This hole isn't big enough for the two of us, and I want in."

Kat's growl intensified to a roar. Could he actually be protecting us, blocking Scarlotti from the entrance to the cave? *Oh, please, dear God, let it be so.* Scarlotti would have lights to see and methods with which to dispose of us. I shuddered. To dispose of my family. Then it would be my turn. But my demise would not be sudden. I wondered if his diabolical mind had already hatched some horrible fate for me, or if that was still in the planning stages.

"Kat, move." Scarlotti stopped demanding and began pleading, cajoling. "I'm wet and cold. The storm's about to hit. Please let me in."

But Kat held his ground. There simply was not enough room for anyone to squeeze by, even the slender Scarlotti, and if the lion refused to budge, the entrance was blocked until Kat decided to yield. Over and over I prayed he'd stand firm and continue blocking the entrance, keeping Scarlotti from my beleaguered family.

"Kat, what's the matter with you? Get out of my way!" Scarlotti's voice filled with fury at not being obeyed.

Suddenly a shot echoed through the cave, blasting our eardrums. Kat's roar, nearly as loud, reverberated up the entry and filled the cave. Then there was silence . . . an eerie, expectant silence. No sound from any quarter. No Kat. No Scarlotti. No storm.

Chapter Twenty-Five

The silence was frightening. Had Scarlotti shot Kat? Why wasn't he coming for us then? I started for the entrance, but Bart held me back.

"You could meet him on the way in. Wait," he whispered, wrapping his arms securely around me so I couldn't slip away. I couldn't stand the suspense. Why didn't come Kat back? Why had he stopped growling? Where was Scarlotti?

"Bart, I've got to know what happened."

"Then you wait here and I'll go." He released me and crawled away so quietly I didn't hear him leave. Icy tingles ran up my arms. I shivered, forcing myself to stay put.

Minutes stretched on endlessly while I waited for Bart's return, then suddenly he reappeared as quietly as he had gone.

"I'm afraid they're both dead. I think Scarlotti must have shot Kat, then Kat jumped on him, knocking him to the rocks below. Kat's on top of Scarlotti. Looks like a lot of blood on the rocks around them, but everything's so wet I couldn't be sure, and it's not light enough to see things clearly."

Suddenly the storm hit again with violent intensity. The howling of the wind rose in a mighty crescendo, whistling and roaring around the rocks. The whole mountain trembled under the fury of the hurricane. We huddled close together in the cave, grateful to be sheltered from the tempest.

I could feel Dad gently rocking Mom in his arms, hear him quietly whispering encouragement, telling her how much he loved her, needed her, begging her not die. When there was no response, his body shook with silent sobs.

"Jack, do you believe in God?" Bart asked quietly. "If Margaret . . ." his voice quivered, stopped, then resumed almost in a whisper, ". . . doesn't make it, you can still be with her forever. God doesn't intend for us to nurture these relationships all our lives, only to wipe them out at death. When you're ready, let me tell you about it."

The gentle rocking didn't stop, but Dad was quiet, his body no longer wracked with sobs. No one spoke. Eventually I stopped trembling and the relentless pounding of the storm became a monotonous lullaby that lulled me to sleep.

I woke as I connected with the cold, hard floor of the cave. Bart was gently lowering my head from his lap.

"Sorry, Princess. Didn't mean to wake you. Storm's over. We're going to check the damage and see what happened to Scarlotti and Kat."

"I'm going, too."

"I'd rather you stayed with your mother," Dad suggested.

"I just want to peek out of the cave and see what the storm did."

"Don't go too far and leave me behind," Mom said in a very small voice.

"How do you feel?" I asked, ashamed I hadn't thought of her first.

"I've felt better. Hurry back." Her voice was so weak it frightened me.

I followed Bart and Dad down the entry tube, trying to be as stoic about my wounds as Mom was about hers. They stood on the ledge looking down at Kat's torn and bloody carcass. Scarlotti was nowhere to be seen, though scraps and pieces of torn black fabric clung to branches and brambles everywhere. Bart climbed down to examine Kat's motionless body.

"Can you tell what happened?"

"Something's torn him to shreds. Scarlotti's clothes, bits and pieces, at least, are here."

"The peccary!"

Bart stopped short of a graphic description, but it was apparent even from here that something savage had ravaged Kat's huge body. Had it also torn Scarlotti's apart and dragged it away? "Poor Kat. He died defending us." Sorrow at the loss of the magnificent beast washed over me, but I couldn't mourn Scarlotti's demise.

"Dad, you've got to find the old man. He might be injured somewhere . . . or worse. But be careful. Watch out for the peccary."

"Stay with your mother while we do a quick check of the island. We need to contact somebody to come after us and get your mother to a hospital as soon as possible."

I got halfway up the entry to the cave and met Mom coming down. She couldn't crawl, so she scooted as best she could on her back. I helped her get comfortable on the ledge so she could watch as Dad and Bart made their way cautiously down the hill and around the island.

Her wound was bleeding freely again from the activity of leaving the cave. I tore two long strips from my sarong, and wadding one up as a compression, wound the other tightly over it, circling her arm and torso to stop the bleeding. Her face was pallid, making her brown eyes look like two large dark hollows with shadowy half moons underneath.

I sat close so she could rest her head on my shoulder as we leaned against the rocks. Occasionally the sun peeked out from behind dark clouds, warming us momentarily. How good it felt. Our clothes were almost dry from the drenching the storm had given us, but we were filthy from crawling through the muddy jungle. I longed for a hot bath, then remembered the metal shield that had enclosed Scarlotti's house.

Was the house still there? If it had withstood the tempest, could we get in? If we got in, was there a telephone? Mom was unusually quiet. Not a good sign. She needed a doctor immediately, but that didn't seem likely to happen any time soon.

Suddenly the hair stood up on the back of my neck. Bart and Dad had just walked out of sight on the beach below, but someone was on the rocks above us, climbing down to where we were sitting. The men Scarlotti was bringing to search for me! Could this be some of them? Had they waited until our men were too far away to help, then come after the two women left behind?

I scrambled back into the cave for the gun Bart had taken from Lt. Ishigo's body. Bart and Dad would never have left their weapons. Why did I?

The climber descended quietly, but it was easy to follow his descent from falling pebbles and shoes scraping on rocks for footing. I hugged the rock, facing the place I figured he'd end up. First came the sandals, brown, well-worn, and scuffed, then baggy brown trousers, then finally the whole man came into view. The old medicine man. I breathed a tremendous sign of relief.

"Am I glad to see you! Please come quickly and help my mother. She's bleeding badly."

Moving to Mom's side, the old man peered over the ledge at the body below, the scene from which I had carefully kept my eyes averted.

"What happened?"

"Scarlotti tracked us in the storm, killed the four policemen with us, and shot my mother with an arrow. Kat appeared out of nowhere and led us to this cave. When Scarlotti trailed us here and tried to come in, Kat blocked the entry and wouldn't move. I don't know whether Scarlotti meant to shoot Kat or just scare him, but there was a shot, and a terrible roar. Bart saw Scarlotti on the rocks with Kat, but when the storm was over, Scarlotti's body was gone and Kat's was mutilated. Could the peccary have done that? And dragged off Scarlotti?"

"An ignoble end for a noble beast, but a fitting end for a cruel man." He ignored my question. "I was surprised Kat became so devoted to you. Love does strange things. Kat felt your love and responded."

"He saved my life—twice." A sense of sadness overwhelmed me.

Through the entire time he was checking her, Mom offered no more than a wan smile. She didn't even have the strength to speak. Thank heaven the old man had come.

Thank heaven. You haven't done that yet. I leaned my head against the rock and said a silent prayer of gratitude for our deliverance from the storm, from Scarlotti, and now for the timely appearance of one I had the utmost confidence could help my mother.

Forgive me, Father, for doubting. Forgive me, please, for my lack of faith.

"Get your men back here quickly. I'll stay with your mother. We need to move her to the house where I can get her cleaned up and treat her wounds. They're not good."

I looked down at the rocks and the stretch of jungle and beach I'd have to traverse. My body ached thinking about it.

"Bart! Dad!" I called as loud as I could. Then I sent a telepathic message: *Come back. The old man is here.*

He smiled, a knowing twinkle in his eye. "I guess that's the quicker way."

"I don't even know your name."

"People call me Old Kahuna."

When I looked at him in disbelief, he nodded. "You understand *Kahuna* to be a hot-shot surfer. In Hawaiian, *Kahuna* means priest, medicine man, or witch doctor. I've been called all three."

I'd call him a miracle worker, I thought.

Within minutes Bart and Dad returned and as gently as possible carried Mom down the mountain to the house. Old Kahuna activated the switches that turned off the electricity on the fence, opened the gate, and raised the steel shield that had protected the house from the onslaught of the storm.

Mom was barely conscious by the time Dad got her to the bedroom. Kahuna prepared a medicinal bath while Dad started removing Mom's muddy clothes.

Following Old Kahuna's instructions, Bart located the phone to send for a medi-vac helicopter and notify the authorities of the deaths of the four policemen. He led me to the room Kahuna had shown him, a concealed room I hadn't found, full of monitors and speakers and switches. Scarlotti could, indeed, sit at this console and watch whatever was going on in every room in his house and throughout the grounds.

I was amazed that anything worked after the storm's destruction, but Scarlotti's generators had never missed a beat in the hurricane. Bart conducted a search of the control room while I hurried back to Mom's side.

From the pouch he had slung across his shoulder, Kahuna withdrew several kinds of herbs, sprinkling some in the bath and mixing others in a glass of hot water.

"She must drink this to compensate for the loss of blood she's had." He thrust a glass of vile-looking liquid into my hand. I coaxed it down her while Dad held Mom tenderly, the worried look on his face mirroring my own.

"Go clean yourself so I can look at your wounds," Kahuna directed, indicating the room I'd occupied during my imprisonment on the island. "I've added some herbs to your bath to begin the healing. Relax and soak. It'll be good for you."

I started to object, but Dad sent me off with a wave of his hand.

"I have Kahuna to help me take care of Margaret's needs right now. You go take care of yourself."

Stripping off the ragged, muddy sarong, I found the infamous pearl still hanging around my neck. It had been the cause of all our misfortune since our arrival on the islands. Granted, it was the most beautiful pearl I'd ever seen, but nothing was worth the terrible price it had cost since it had been stolen . . . so many lives lost . . . so much anguish for my family.

I was so dirty I needed a bath before my bath. I shed the top layer of mud in the shower, then immersed in the marvelous, herb-scented water. I remembered the last time I'd been here, Kat draped gracefully on the side of the tub, one giant paw dangling in the water. I looked into the garden, almost expecting to see him ambling up the steps. Something moved in the shadows. Or was it just shadows moving with the wind that was finally blowing itself out?

As I leaned back, Beethoven's "Moonlight Sonata" surrounded me from hidden speakers. It jerked me upright and sent cold chills all through me, even in the hot bath.

Relax. The music always comes on when you lean against the back of the tub, remember. Scarlotti is dead. You're safe now. Closing my eyes, I tried to relax weary, aching muscles, tried to terminate the worry for Mom, tried to think beautiful, relaxing, healing thoughts.

My reverie was abruptly interrupted by Bart's cheerful voice. "I swear, Princess, you could sleep anywhere!"

"I'm not asleep. Just resting my eyes—and every other part of my weary body. This tub is wonderful. Put your hand here and feel the water jets. It's just like a therapeutic massage. That, and Kahuna's mysterious additions to the water, relieves all aches and pains. If I'm going to keep living this strenuous lifestyle you've plunged me into, I'm going to need one of these for sure."

"You mean you'd rather have one of these than a hot shower and personal back-scrubber?" Bart's voice was filled with disbelief, but his eyes were full of mischief.

"How about both?" It was wonderful to be free from the terrible threat of Scarlotti, to be back with Bart enjoying relaxing banter, and feel his love and concern for me. Now if Mom would rally to Kahuna's ministrations.

"Would you mind finding me something to wear from the closet in there?"

"I have a better idea," Bart offered with a lecherous grin.

"I don't even want to hear it," I laughed.

"You might like it even better than this," he countered as he scrubbed my back enthusiastically before leaving to find some clothes while I rinsed the last of the shampoo from my hair.

The old man shook his head as we entered the bedroom where Mom lay, white and still. "I've done all I can. She's lost too much blood. She needs more immediately."

"The helicopter's on its way, Jack," Bart said quietly, "but it could be more than an hour before it gets here."

"Don't you have any more miracles in your magic bag of medicines?" I asked hopefully, clinging to Mom's small, cold hand. A wave of black despair swept over me. My mother was dying and there was nothing we could do for her.

Old Kahuna shook his head. "The miracle you need is not in my bag, nor in my power to give."

"And I don't have it yet," Bart muttered in anguish, "but . . ." His words trailed off as he dropped to his knees beside Mom's bed.

Michael's three-year-old voice flowed through my mind, "Daddy, does Amber need a blessing?" The picture of four people bowed low over a tiny infant's still body was clearly etched in my memory. I slipped to my knees beside him. Prayer was all we had. It would have to do.

My father sat on the other side of the bed, softly stroking the limp hand he held, his glazed eyes never leaving Mom's ashen face.

Bart bowed his head and began softly, "O God, the Eternal Father, Thou knowest all things. Thou knowest and lovest this, thy daughter, who lies without sufficient lifeblood to sustain her. We have no way to supply that. Thou art all powerful. I beg Thee to keep her stable until she can receive that which she needs."

Bart paused, overcome, not able to continue. My tears flowed freely at the heartfelt intensity of his fervent prayer and my own prayers and faith joined with his.

There wasn't a sound in the room. No one stirred, or even seemed to breathe. Then a sweet spirit of peace enveloped me. I knew Bart's prayer had been answered.

I reached across the bed to Dad, who didn't appear to have heard a word, who seemed not to have understood the miracle that had just taken place.

"Dad, she's going to be all right." I squeezed his hand. He turned to me, his steel gray eyes filled with a depth of sadness I couldn't believe. It was almost as if he didn't see me, wasn't aware of anything except the nearly lifeless form he loved so consummately lying before him.

"Dad, did you hear me?" I shook his hand gently. "She'll hang on until the helicopter gets here with her blood."

He finally focused on my face. Pain filled his voice. "She's dying. They'll never make it in time." He dropped his head and his shoulders shook with great silent sobs of grief. I went around the bed and took him by the shoulders.

"Dad, listen to me. Mom isn't going to die."

He clung to me. "I can't even imagine life without Margaret. I don't want to live without her." Anguish filled his voice and choked him. In blocking out everything but thoughts of how life would be without her, he suffered intensely.

I held my father close, wanting him to feel the comfort and peace I felt, needing to give him the sure knowledge I had that Mom would live, that she would recover.

"Dad, please listen. Bart asked for a miracle and God granted it. Mom *will* be all right."

He let go of me and shook his head. "There are no miracles, Bunny. The heavens are closed. God's too busy doing whatever He does to be concerned with the likes of us. We're not that important to matter."

The pain he felt at a loss he'd not yet experienced frightened me. I thought I knew how much my parents loved each other, but in my naivete and inexperience, I couldn't even guess at the depth of their feelings. My love for Bart was all-consuming, but it paled in comparison to the intense affection these two shared. They had something only a lifetime of loving and caring could give. My father was inconsolable as he felt that bond coming to an untimely end.

"Dad, miracles do happen. I've experienced at least a half dozen in the last few days. How do you think I could have survived all I've gone through? God heard my prayers and worked miracles on my behalf. That's the only reason I'm here."

My words finally penetrated his grief, but his reaction astounded me. Instead of acknowledging my belief, he tried to explain it away in a voice tinged with anger.

"No, Allison. You survived because this remarkable woman taught you self-reliance. You survived because you learned so well all that Margaret spent her life giving you, teaching you, instilling in you. God didn't have anything to do with it, nor did miracles. Except maybe the miracle that she was herself."

"You're wrong, sir," Bart said firmly as he stood and walked around the bed to put his arm around my shoulders. "For a brilliant man, that was a rather stupid observation."

Dad jerked his head up and stared at Bart.

"Sorry, sir, that was to get your attention so you'd hear this."

Bart knelt beside the bed and touched Mom's pale cheek. He looked into Dad's puzzled face.

"If we have enough faith in Jesus Christ, we can ask for those righteous desires of our hearts and He'll grant them, because He loves us so much. Look at Margaret. God just granted a miracle. Jack, she'll be all right."

Dad's face revealed nothing—no understanding, no emotion of any kind. He was still in a fog, unable to absorb what we were trying to tell him.

Kahuna shuffled slowly toward Dad until he stood directly in front of him, his morning-glory-blue eyes alight with zeal that contrasted starkly with Dad's cold gray stare.

He pointed a walnut-colored finger at my father. "You were the only one in this room who did not feel the miracle. Even your wife who was not conscious felt the effects of that prayer of faith. Your eyes looked only for death, so you didn't see life flow back into her body. Look at her with believing eyes. Feel her. Life is no longer ebbing away. Don't stop this miracle with your unbelief."

Kahuna turned and walked from the room, his flowing white hair giving him the appearance of some ancient prophet.

Chapter Twenty-Six

Bart leaped to his feet when we heard the helicopter and rushed to the beach to guide the medics in. I looked up at my father, sitting numbly on the side of the bed, grasping Mom's motionless hand as though if he let go, she'd slip away from this life. He did not believe. *Please, Father, help his unbelief. Comfort him as you comforted me.*

I got stiffly to my feet and put my arms around him. "Dad, the helicopter's here."

Bart ushered the medics in and they attempted to set up the line to transfuse liquids, struggling to find a vein. Minutes stretched agonizingly on before they got a line going, and eventually had Mom stabilized. They transferred her to a lightweight gurney and slid her into the helicopter. Dad clung tightly to Mom's hand throughout the procedure, boarding the chopper with her.

"Will you come with us?" I asked Old Kahuna.

"No. I'll stay. When the police finish their investigation of Scarlotti's death, I'll bury Kat, and Scarlotti, if there's anything left of him."

"Then what?"

"I'll notify his mother and see what she wants to do about the island. Possibly stay and take care of it for her."

He handed me a small jar of ointment. "Rub this on your cuts and scratches, especially the ones on your feet. It'll help them heal faster. Put some on your mother's wound. Here are some healing herbs for your bath. Goodbye."

"*Mahalo,* Old Kahuna. A thousand times." I kissed his brown cheek gratefully, aware I owed my life to this little old man.

Kahuna turned to Bart and took his extended hand. "Take good care of her. She has good *mana.* She's a special *wahine.*"

"Thank you, Kahuna. I know how special she is. It looks like my life's work will be trying to keep her in one piece since she seems to have an affinity for finding trouble."

Before I could reply, Bart hustled me onto the helicopter and we took off for the hospital in Oahu.

"What do you mean, I have an affinity for finding trouble? I never had any of these problems until you came back into my life!"

"Sorry, Princess, can't hear a thing you're saying!" he shouted with a grin.

I contentedly leaned against Bart with his arm firmly around my shoulder as we watched the medics care for Mom. The dazed look on Dad's face worried me. In fact, I was far more worried about him than about Mom right now. I'd had assurance that she'd be okay. I'd had none about him, and mental attitudes were often more difficult to treat than physical ailments.

As the chopper droned over the still turbulent waves below us, my thoughts turned to Scarlotti and Kahuna. Strange, I'd never thought of Scarlotti having a mother. Where did she live? Kahuna said Scarlotti was an only son. Did she have daughters? She'd lost both husband and son in a matter of days. Was she alone, or did she have someone to help her through this devastating time? Was that a role Kahuna might play? Did she know of the evil nature of her men, or was she unaware of the unhappiness and death they'd caused so many, and loved them simply for what they were to her?

Mom's recovery once they got her into the hospital was nothing short of miraculous. Dad was something else. He never left Mom's side to shower or shave, and hardly ate a bite of the food offered to him. The doctors and nurses couldn't pry him away, and he ignored them when they ordered him out. Even the police couldn't get the necessary information from him for their reports. Bart had to supply what they needed.

I didn't try to break through his shell after my first rebuffed attempt. That could wait until Mom was released from the hospital and he could see she was out of danger. Then I'd try again.

Late that night we left Mom sleeping peacefully, and called Skip in Kahuka from a deserted waiting room in the hospital above Pearl Harbor.

"Where are you two? We thought you'd dropped off the face of the earth!"

"It's a long story we'll share on a slow night at your little hospital," Bart said. "Are Megan and Tapata still impersonating us?"

"No. After two days, their tail disappeared. Deserted them. When it became apparent they were no longer being followed, they came on home."

"Thanks, Skip. As soon as we get all the loose ends tied up here, we'll be over to settle up with Meg and Pat and pick up our car. Tell them thanks until we can do it ourselves."

Bart made a quick call to his parents, Jim and Alma, at the estate in California to tell them all was well and we'd probably be home in a couple of days.

"A couple of days! What about our honeymoon?" I demanded when he hung up.

"I thought you were tired of our honeymoon and ready to get back to something a little more normal," Bart said sheepishly, plopping on the sofa beside me in the waiting room.

"You're right about one thing. I am tired of this—*this* being the non-honeymoon we've endured for the past several days. What, in your mind, was something a little more normal?"

"We haven't had time to talk about where we're going to live or any of the little details that go into setting up housekeeping. I just thought since your time in Hawaii has been less than wonderful, you'd like to get to another location as soon as possible."

"Ask me what I'd like to do," I said, snuggling next to him.

"Sorry, Princess. What would you like to do for the remainder of your honeymoon?"

"First of all, it's *our* honeymoon, or was until Nate and Scarlotti interrupted it, and second, we didn't have one. If you're anxious to get back to something else, we'll go home, wherever we decide that's going to be. But if you're basing this decision on what you think I want, then I guess you need to know what that is."

Bart groaned. "I blew that. Tell me what you want to do." He slipped his arm around my shoulder and pulled me close against him. "I'm all ears and totally penitent."

I hesitated. If I told him, would he give up what he wanted just because I desired something else? Did he really want to forego our honeymoon? Was he tired of it—of me—already?

"Being married is hard, isn't it?" I said quietly, repenting of my indignation of a minute ago.

A look of alarm crossed Bart's face. "In what way?" he asked quickly.

"Bringing together two totally different personalities, with two basically differing agendas, and trying to mold them into one whole, united in purpose and design, without destroying the individuality of each. Do I tell you what I want to do, hoping that's really what you want, too, or do I quietly go along with what you suggest because I think you want that most of all?"

Bart's laugh was filled with relief. "You gave me a scare, Princess. Yes. Marriage is hard, but I can't imagine spending my life without you, just like your dad couldn't without your mom. This kind of reward justifies any difficulty."

He touched my cheek gently, tracing my eyebrow with his finger, down the side of my face, across my lips. His blue eyes gazed into mine, starting a warmth that spread through me like wildfire on Southern California hills. He tilted my chin up and kissed me softly, fanning the flames like a hot wind. I clung to him, hungry for these kisses I'd missed for so long.

Bart nibbled sensuously at my ear. "What is it you'd like to do?" he whispered, kissing my neck.

"Right now, or for the next few days?" I asked breathlessly.

"I think I have a pretty good idea of the now part," he teased.

"Too bad we can't just lock the door," I said ruefully.

"I think, my passionate Princess, we'd better exit stage left as quickly as possible or we may bring shame upon our parents for our disreputable behavior in public."

Bart stood and pulled me to my feet, stopped for one more kiss, and guided me to the door.

"You didn't let me tell you what I wanted to do," I objected as we wasted little time finding our way to the exit.

"Yes, I did, and yes, you did," Bart laughed. "First stop is our room at the Turtle Bay Hilton. We'll have our honeymoon. That is what you want, isn't it?"

I blushed and nodded.

"If we rent a car, you'll have to drive. If we splurge on a taxi . . ." I got no further.

Bart waved at a waiting taxi.

"I like the way you think," he grinned.

"Turtle Bay Hilton and don't take the scenic route," he instructed the driver, who didn't bother to turn around. Then he settled back and pulled me into his arms. "If we splurge on a taxi, I can do this all the way across the island." I knew I was going to enjoy every minute of the drive as he proceeded to light those wildfires again.

Everything but the passion I felt for Bart and the joy at being safely in his arms was blocked out, until the taxi driver cleared his throat for the second or third time, and I realized we were stopped in front of the hotel.

I glanced up expecting to see the smiling face of the driver making fun of us. My blood went cold at the sight of a long black ponytail.

"Turtle Bay Hilton," was all he said, but it was enough to send chills through me. Would I forever see and hear Scarlotti wherever I went? How long would it take me to put his memory behind me? Scarlotti was dead. The taxi driver was probably embarrassed for us. That's why he didn't turn around.

Bart, flustered he hadn't noticed we'd arrived at our destination, turned slightly red as he paid the man. I was mortified and jumped from the taxi when the doorman opened the door, still shaken from the reminder of Scarlotti. The fresh ocean breeze couldn't cool my flaming cheeks as I waited for Bart to catch up and get our room key from the front desk.

We hurried through the lobby, caught an empty elevator to the sixth floor, and raced hand in hand down the hall to the honeymoon suite, laughing all the way.

"I'm sure much more has gone on in his back seat, but I'm also sure no one has been more embarrassed than I was a minute ago when I realized the taxi had already stopped."

"You're even more beautiful when you blush, Princess," Bart laughed, rolling on the bed with me in his arms.

"Actually, I hate to take the romance out of the amorous ride we've just had, but I think the red on my cheeks is as much whisker burn as embarrassment."

"Then we'll have to do something about that right now. Did I or did I not have a razor when we were here before?"

"We've spread things all over until I'm not sure what we have. Except I'm quite sure the shower is still here, and that's very good news."

Bart called room service and they delivered a razor, shaving cream, and cologne while I took inventory of what was left of my clothes and belongings.

At dusk we called the hospital to check on Mom and though she still sounded a little weak, she said she was well enough to be discharged tomorrow afternoon. She and Dad would come to Turtle Bay when she was released so she could spend a couple of days in bed and get better rest than in a hospital. Bart called the desk and reserved a room for them.

I lay back on the pillow and ran my fingers gently over the scars that crisscrossed Bart's muscular back. He turned to me and held up my arms, then uncovered my legs and feet, examining my scrapes, scratches, cuts, and bruises.

"You look almost as bad as I do. Want to tell me about it?"

I related in detail everything that had happened. He kissed my palms, then my arms, never taking his eyes from my face during the narration. As I finished, he raised my foot to his lips.

"What are you doing?" I laughed, pulling my foot away.

His periwinkle blue eyes twinkled. "Kissing away the hurt, and the memory, as best I know how." He pulled me into his arms in a bear hug that forced the breath from me.

"If that doesn't work, I'll squeeze it out, and if that doesn't do the job, I guess I'll just have to spend the rest of eternity making love to you so you can't think about anything but me."

We lay silently in each other's arms for a long time, relishing the closeness. I didn't want to break the spell, but there was this nagging little doubt in the back of my mind that wouldn't go away.

"I hate to bring this up, but I've got to know. Scarlotti is dead, isn't he? I can't help but think of Dad. Everyone told me Dad was dead, but there was no body. And it was all a ruse. We didn't see Scarlotti's body. What if . . . ?"

Bart leaned up on one elbow and looked down at me, his forehead wrinkled in serious contemplation. One finger wound around an errant wisp of my hair, then stroked it back into place.

"First of all, he had to have been seriously hurt, if not killed outright, in the fall to the rocks. Then it looked like Kat landed on top of him. That would have been enough to finish him if he'd survived the fall. Kat's body was ripped to shreds by the peccary. . . ."

"But it was all there, wasn't it? Nothing was missing."

"No, nothing was missing. All the parts were there. But I'm sure Kahuna will find something left of Scarlotti so we can bury your fears with him."

"Will you check with Kahuna? Will you have the police search the island? Wouldn't we have heard the wild animals tearing them apart? I don't remember hearing anything, except the storm. I know I sound paranoid, but somehow I can't believe the nightmare is over."

"Then I guess I'll have to see what I can do to make you believe and to forget the nightmare." His lips rekindled the fires, driving the nightmare into the dark recesses of my mind.

When Mom and Dad arrived late the next afternoon, Dad seemed in worse shape than Mom, weak as she was. Bart suggested we take a drive as soon as Margaret felt up to it.

"I think Jack needs this more than Margaret needs rest. We'll see how she feels tomorrow. It's only a short drive, and won't take long at all."

When Mom felt ready for a ride the next afternoon, we loaded her, over her objections, into a wheelchair borrowed from the hotel and into their rented car. Bart took the wheel and we exited Turtle Bay between bushes of bright blossoms, turning left on Kamehameha Highway, past the hospital and the Old Sugar Mill at Kahuku, to Laie.

Turning right off the highway, we faced a beautiful white building set back on the hillside, surrounded by tall palm trees. The grounds were immaculate, with shaped greenery outlining a columned pathway to the huge double doors of the temple on the hill. Fountains sparkled behind the wrought-iron fence, and American and Hawaiian flags flapped happily in the breeze.

"This is the Hawaii Temple of The Church of Jesus Christ of Latter-day Saints," Bart said as he parked the car. He turned to my parents. "I'd like you to see a couple of short films in the visitors' center. They'll explain much better than I can what you need to know right now. There's a way out of the agony you're experiencing, Jack."

He got the wheelchair from the trunk, and while Dad helped Mom into it, Bart came around and opened my door, offering his hand to help me. A wonderful feeling of peace and serenity surrounded me as I stepped onto the grounds.

Answering the question in my eyes, he said simply, "Now you'll see what Emile taught me."

Bart was right. All the questions we'd asked ourselves those many years ago were answered wholly and completely. Where we came from, why we're here on earth, and where we're going when we leave here.

"I'd like to talk to Allison alone for a few minutes. If you have any questions, the guides can answer them. We'll be out by the fountain." Bart took my hand and led me silently outside. We sat on the stone bench, which was warm from the island sun. He studied my hand, brought it to his lips, kissed each fingertip, then looked at me, searching for some clue as to what I was feeling.

"You know what this reminds me of?" I asked, remembering the stone bench at the Santa Barbara Courthouse where Bart had proposed in exactly the same way.

"Yes," he smiled. "I was thinking about that. And I'm doing the same thing again—asking you to marry me—except this time not just till death do us part, but for eternity."

"I want forever, too. But . . ."

"Princess, every time I think of losing you, for any reason, at any time, it's almost more than I can bear. Knowing that even death couldn't separate us is more comforting than I can possibly tell you." He let go and sat back to look at me.

"My heart and my mind tell me this is right," I said quietly. "I want what Michael and his family have. I want for us what those families had in the films. But I need to know so much more."

"I assure you, you'll know every jot and tittle," Bart smiled, his blue eyes cloudy with happy tears. "That's what our appointment with Bishop O'Hare is all about when we get back to Santa Barbara."

I hadn't heard Mom and Dad come up behind us. I jumped when Dad put his hand on my shoulder and his other on Bart's.

"Thanks, Bart. You were right." Dad paused, his voice soft and tender. "I couldn't bear how close I'd come to losing Margaret, wondering how I could possibly live without her. I'm not sure this is the answer, but it's closer than anything I've come across."

"Would you like to sit in with us and see if we can find the rest of the answers you need?"

Dad hesitated. "Give me some time to think about that."

"One more question, Jack." Bart stood and looked Dad in the eye.

"Yes?"

"Did you ever get on your knees and thank God for that miracle you didn't see?"

Dad's gray eyes were laser-like as they looked at Bart, penetrating, probing.

"You never give an inch, do you?" Dad asked.

"No, sir. Not in this area, at least."

Dad put his arm around Mom and looked down into her big dark eyes.

"I haven't yet, but I will."

"Speaking of giving, will you please return this to King Bhumibol?" I handed Dad the precious pearl ring. "I don't want the responsibility of caring for it, the memories it invokes, or the trouble that follows it. Did anyone ever mention a curse that went with it?"

Mom laughed. "I don't think the ring is cursed. I think you just attract adventure. Bart, you'll have to be on your toes from now on."

Bart feigned a groan. "What have I gotten myself into?"

About the Author

Lynn Gardner describes herself as "someone who can tell a good story." In building the plot and characters of her first novel, *Emeralds and Espionage,* she did extensive research on the countries described in the novel, and carefully gathered information on the FBI and various aspects of the military. Much of her military information came from personal experience: her husband retired as a colonel in the United States Air Force after nearly twenty-five years of service.

A writer's workshop at BYU-Hawaii provided the opportunity for research on the setting for her second novel, *Pearls and Peril.*

Lynn and her husband, Glenn, make their home in Quartz Hill, California, where Lynn is director of the stake family history center. They are the parents of four children. Among her many interests, Lynn lists reading, golf, traveling, beachcombing, writing, family history, and spoiling her four granddaughters and grandson.